I0762045

THE HEIR

TWISTED KINGDOMS BOOK 3

FROST KAY

Copyright

The Heir

First Edition

Cover by Story Wrappers

Formatting by Jaye Prat

Copy Editing by Madeline Dyer

Proofreading by Holmes Edits & Kate Anderson

Also By Frost Kay

THE AERMIAN FEUDS
(Dark Fantasy Romance)

Rebel's Blade

Crown's Shield

Siren's Lure

Enemy's Queen

King's Warrior

Warlord's Shadow

Spy's Mask

Court's Fool

DOMINION OF ASH
(Post Apocalyptic Fantasy Romance)

The Stain

The Tainted

The Exiled

The Fallout

The Chosen

MIXOLOGISTS & PIRATES
(Sci-fi Romance)

Amber Vial

Emerald Bane

Scarlet Venom

Cyan Toxin

Onyx Elixir

Indigo Alloy

ALIENS & ALCHEMISTS
(Sci-fi Romance)

Pirates, Princes, and Payback

Alphas, Airships, and Assassins

TWISTED KINGDOMS
(Fairytale Retelling)

The Hunt

The Rook

The Heir

The Beast

HEIMSERYA

THE WILDS
KOPAL
AZUL
BETRAZ
HEIMSERYA
HEIMSERYA
MERJERI
TALAGA
FIERGONE
Dotae
Shueshun
THE FIRE ISLES
N
Fiergone's waters
Taseri
THE HINTERLANDS

History of the Kingdoms

Once upon a time… Elves, Shapeshifters, Giants, Dragons, Humans and Merfolk were all at peace—all equals. Their lands and kingdoms were prosperous, and their enemies didn't dare attack for their armies were formidable. Generations passed and the people began to forget what was most important—love, courage, loyalty.

That was their downfall—for in self-indulgent ignorance they allowed darkness to creep into the land like a thief in the night. It started out slowly.

The Merfolk let vanity take root deep in their hearts, the Dragons became greedy from the skies, the Giants grew bloodthirsty, the Humans covetous, the Shapeshifters prideful, and the Elves allowed apathy to squeeze compassion from their hearts.

It was said that the earth rumbled and cracked, shaking the core of the world. When the tremors ceased, the Jagged Bone Mountain range surrounded the Elvish kingdom, cutting the elves off from every other living creature.

The Dragons abandoned their own kingdom and made their home in the Jagged Bones, threatening all who approached their lairs—making it impossible to pass through the mountains—though the Giants tried. As if the mountains of the Jagged Bones craved blood and hatred, many lives were claimed in the senseless violence there.

Upon witnessing such death, the Merfolk retreated to their watery homes, content to bask in the beauty of the sea and their own splendor, only occasionally consorting with pirates when it amused them.

Years passed and the myths faded from the world's mind.

The Elvish kingdom became the Wilds, the Giants sequestered themselves in their own kingdom of Kopal. The Fire Isle Kingdoms were forged by mercenaries—the offspring of pirates, Sirens, and Merfolk.

For a time, the Shapeshifters of Talaga held an uneasy peace with the Humans of Heimserya. The two kingdoms needed each other to survive, that all changed with the birth of a new plant and a royal son.

An extraordinary flower—the Mimikia—was discovered in Talaga. When distilled, it was a powerful drug capable of healing any wound. It was practically magical. The applications were limitless and its worth immeasurable. In their pride, the Shapeshifters boasted of their discovery, of their brilliance.

Word reached the Humans of this new source of wealth. They coveted this new miracle plant and the temptation proved to be too much for the newly crowned king who sought to enrich his kingdom. With his greed dawned a new era of bloodshed, prejudice, addiction, and depravity.

Welcome to the Twisted Kingdoms.

Chapter One

Thorn

"Ten pieces."

"Four."

"Ten pieces," Thorn said, narrowing her eyes.

"Four."

"Ten—"

"You know as well as I do, you won't get a better deal anywhere else in this town, Thorn," Jones insisted. He was the blacksmith for the town of Rubelle, and he crossed his muscled, hairy arms across his chest, which was uncovered to the air despite the biting chill of the wind and the snow beneath his feet. "Four is my final offer."

Jones was constantly a pain in her butt, but a small part of Thorn loved to haggle with the gruff man. She glanced down the sloping lane, her gaze skipping over the stone roofs of the solemn houses that lined each side of the road like rigid soldiers. Despite the outward appearance of the settlement, it was one of the best towns, in her opinion. The people as a whole were hardy, fierce, and straight to the point. She liked Rubelle even though it was covered in heaps of snow nine months of the year. It was the closest organized settlement to the Dread Mountains, where she did most of her scavenging. Thorn preferred to sell the items she found to her town rather than taking them elsewhere. Although, desperate times called for desperate measures. Treasures weren't easy to come by, these days.

Thorn rolled her neck and eyed Jones. He was playing hard to get. He *always* bought what she found…eventually. The items she sourced from the dangerous passageways through the Dread Mountains were of the highest quality. They were often lost from merchant wagons—usually those traveling from Kopal, the kingdom of giants, to the capital of Heimserya—when they hit a storm or when bandits and mercenaries struck and looted. She'd seen some pretty heinous things as a treasure hunter. People would do just about anything for money.

Don't pretend you're not as bad as them.

Her jaw clenched, and she brushed the dark thought away. Survival wasn't easy as a single woman. Choices had to be made. Usually ones that left a scar.

"Are you really going to be stubborn?" she asked softly.

"Times are hard, missy."

That was the damn truth, but he was out of line. One time, she had brought Jones a handsome broadsword. Another time, it was a rare pearl necklace strung together with white gold. This time, she had a burnished silver candlestick worth more than what she was asking for it, and they both knew it. Thorn narrowed her eyes at the big man. He glared right back.

"Bold of you to assume I would only try and sell it here," she told the blacksmith, waving the candlestick in front of him. The silver glinted tantalizingly in the flickering light of his workshop. "I was giving you first dibs, that's all. So, if you can't see fit to pay what the damn thing is worth, then I'll be on my way."

Thorn managed to take all of three steps toward the exit before the large man let out a huge, resigned sigh.

"Wait, girl, wait!" Jones called out after her, and a smile curled Thorn's lips.

The blacksmith was predictable, and that's what she loved about him. He always bought what she sold. She knew the precious metals she provided him would be melted down to make a wickedly sharp sword or two, which Jones would be able to sell for ten times what he paid her as she only asked for the amount to cover the raw materials. Civil war was on the horizon, and weapons were highly sought after.

Her fingers clenched the huge candlestick, coolness seeping through her gloves. Everyone—the lowest rung of soldiers, townspeople, and the richer folk—was kitted out in the bare minimum of armor and weapons. But the highborn were willing to spend half their fortune on uselessly beautiful, intricate swords and rapiers and spears. Not that they would do any of the fighting. But the noblemen always wanted to look the part, even if the points of their swords never pierced souls. It was pure vanity.

Vanity you profit on. Better you than someone else.

Thorn turned back to him, the heat of the forge washing over her face.

Jones let out another sigh. "You will bankrupt me, Thorn," he complained, though he fished through the hidden pocket of his leather apron and handed over the promised ten pieces, and nothing less.

She barked out a laugh. "I hardly think that's true. The impending war has been good for you, Jones. Your business is doing rather well."

"You talk as if we haven't been at war for generations now. What I wouldn't give to have fewer coins in my pocket but safer roads around the Dread Mountains."

That sobered her. "The mountains will never be safe, even if there was no war."

Thorn eyed the older man and the scars that wrapped around his thick throat. Jones's early life had not been easy. Being Talagan, a shapeshifter, was a brutal life in Heimserya, especially for a young boy. Luckily for him, he had found haven in Rubelle after he'd fled a Talagan death farm. Rubelle offered a hodgepodge of cultures and races. Acceptance was their motto. As long as you treated others with dignity and respect, that's what you received in return.

Jones rolled his eyes. "Optimism, Thorn. You could do with some. If the capital spent less money and fewer resources on pointless skirmishes with our neighbors, then they could send some of those fancy purple-haired Hounds up here to deal with the bandits."

"Careful, Jones, that reeks of treason." Anyone who spoke against the Crown found themselves dead.

The older man's expression soured like he'd eaten a bad pickle. "Although, I bet even if there was peace, we'd never get one of them to *deign* to help us."

"Oh, I wouldn't be so sure about that," Thorn replied, thinking of the female Hound she had met a few days ago.

Their conversation had been brief, and the woman had been in disguise, but it hadn't fooled Thorn. She made her living by hiding in the shadows and dressing in disguise so Thorn could search for treasure without trouble from other hunters. Experience had taught Thorn to see past the surface to what lay beneath. Even in disguise, there was something about the female Hound that spoke of honesty, and if Thorn were to believe any of the rumors, Tempest was a good person. Well, as good a person could be while also being an assassin and engaged to King Destin. Thorn hid her shiver. She'd only been to the capital a handful of times. Once, she'd glimpsed the king while he moved through the market—or, more like, *prowled.* There was something feral and dangerous about the man. The king was known for his dominating ways. The question was: why was his betrothed traipsing through the Forbidden Wood toward the Dread Mountains? And where had she disappeared to?

Questions for another time.

Jones clicked his tongue, pulling her from her musings, and took a step closer. She pocketed her money and held out the silver candlestick. He took the treasure from Thorn carefully and glanced toward the open entrance of the forge, his shrewd eyes scouring the lane. One could never be too careful; while the townspeople were mostly honest, it didn't mean the travelers passing through were. She glanced over her shoulder and pulled her cloak tighter around her body. Another storm was brewing. The bitter wind cut right to the bone.

She turned back as Jones moved farther into the forge, tucking his new acquisition away from prying eyes. Thorn frowned when she noticed his limp was more pronounced. The scars weren't the only thing his old masters had given him. They'd broken his leg in two places to keep him from running away all those years ago. That didn't keep Jones from trying. He got away, but his gait was the cost.

"You're staring," he mumbled, his broad back still to her.

Thorn grimaced. "How bad are you hurting?"

"My leg aches something fierce." He spun to face her, leaning a hip against his workbench. "This storm will be bad. My leg never lies." Jones tilted his head to the side. "Are you staying the night, Thorn?"

Her stomach dropped. Winter's bite, not this again. She shook her head, which slightly unfurled the deep crimson scarf wrapped around her neck. The blacksmith's eyes strayed to the left side of her face, to the pale scars that she knew ran down the side of her neck and shoulder.

Thorn made no effort to hide them from him; Jones had witnessed the mess of her skin on several occasions. Her scars were the result of a fire that burned much of the left side of her torso when she was younger. Most folk recoiled from the sight, but not Jones. It was one of the many reasons Thorn enjoyed trading with the man. He was real and honest. If he hadn't been nearly twenty years her senior and married, she'd have snapped him up.

You would seduce him even at his age if he wasn't married.

But those were just fantasies. Marriage was not for the likes of her.

"You know, Thorn," he began in a tone that suggested she absolutely would not like what he was about to say. "I really could do with someone as tough and tenacious as you in the family. My oldest son is still looking for a wife. If you were to marry, then—"

Not this again.

Thorn burst into laughter and clutched her stomach. "Y-you can't be serious, Jones?" she cried, beyond amused. "Me? *Married?* And to that man-whore you call a son? You know I love you, but I'm sorry. I don't see myself as the neglected wife of a man who's slept with every woman in the town—and most of the ones who pass through, too."

If it had been anyone else, they would have been insulted by her candor. Not Jones. The older man was used to it, and he also knew Thorn *did* speak the truth about his eldest son. There were several little black-haired, blue-eyed children running around already. Thorn knew Jones did his best to support the children that were left in their family's care, now that their mothers had moved on.

"Do you need help with the little ones?" Thorn asked. "You know I don't mind helping out."

Jones ran a large hand over his sweaty face. "I'm sure my wife would appreciate the assistance. I just wish things were a little different. Someone needs to tame that son of mine."

"I'm not the woman for it," she said firmly, but she softened her words with a crooked smile. "Someone would be dead by the end of the week if we were wed. Matrimonial war is never good for a family."

"Nobody will pin you down, will they, missy?" he murmured.

"Doubtful." Thorn darted forward to give the big man a quick hug before stepping back to rewrap her scarf around her neck so it covered her mouth and chin. "Think of all the loot you'd miss out on if I was forced to be a proper wife."

"That's why marrying into the family is so perfect."

She grinned behind the scarf and pulled the cowl of her cloak over her white hair, then moved toward the open exit. He was like a dog with a bone. Old Jones would never let it go. "Is there anything you need?" she called.

"A wife for my spirited son," Jones grumped.

She huffed out a laugh, then glanced over her shoulder to wink at Jones. "I don't think such a woman is out there, but I'll keep a look out. Good evening."

Jones waved, and Thorn was still chuckling to herself about the blacksmith's suggestion when she reached the edge of Rubelle. The singular road that cut through the center of town disappeared to the south in the dark woods. She paused near the baker's shop and eyed a group of soldiers on horseback who were approaching, the horses trudging through the fresh snow. Thorn stood silently beneath the nearest porch and waited patiently for the soldiers to move along. It was better to stay out of their way and not draw attention to herself.

She watched them from the corner of her eye as they slowed. Damn. They weren't just passing through. What were they doing there anyway? There was nothing of value this far north.

First the female Hound, and now soldiers.

They certainly were not there for bandits, based on the armor and weapons they were carrying. The soldiers nudged their mounts toward the inn just across the way that conveniently sat next to the brothel. Their poor horses looked exhausted, foaming at their bits and in desperate need of rest. Poor creatures.

Looking around, Thorn noticed the residents of Rubelle peering out at the soldiers from behind curtains, doors, and street corners. The place was largely a shifter town, and everyone knew what King Destin's opinion was of them. It was smart to keep hidden until they had an idea what the king's men wanted. In her gut, Thorn knew that the soldiers spelled trouble.

The men slid from their mounts and one glanced in her

direction, catching her eye. Thorn silently cursed. What bad luck.

"And who do we have here?" he called. "What a lovely creature to welcome us."

She bristled and tilted her chin up to stare down the smirking soldier across the road. He gave her a smile that was probably meant to be friendly but came off as more of a leer. So, he was *that* type. The kind of man who thought he was charming, but deep down was a poison to the soul.

"No comment?" he goaded. The bastard cocked his head to the side, as if to further regard Thorn when she didn't answer him. His smile turned sharp. "Oh, I do like the timid ones," he drawled, elbowing the soldier next to him to point her out to him. The new soldier's lips twisted into a feral grin when he took in Thorn's cloaked, slight appearance.

Were any of the king's soldiers decent men? Perhaps they may have been, once upon a time, but their position of authority over the masses had clearly twisted them into arrogant, entitled blackguards.

Thorn smiled grimly behind her scarf and fluttered her lashes at the men. They didn't know who they were dealing with. She wasn't some helpless maiden to be ravished and tossed away like rubbish. Her fingers loosened the scarf covering her face and neck. She pushed back her hood until both men could see the twisting network of scars that marred the left side of her jaw and throat. They were ugly, and she hated them most of the time, but they also provided protection on more than one occasion.

The soldiers' smiles turned to grimaces, and disgust plastered across their expressions. They dismissed her and turned toward the inn, before making their way inside. She released a small sigh, her breath freezing in a white puff. For a moment, she reveled in how satisfying it was to manipulate men, but that feeling soured almost immediately as her gaze moved toward the brothel—her home. These soldiers would no doubt end up there and torment one of her sisters tonight. Thorn glared at her boots. This was the part she loathed. While she wasn't part of the sisterhood of night walkers, they'd raised her. Thorn had been told over and over how women held power because of their sexuality, but it seemed to her that they were constantly being used and taken advantage of. Being born a woman was the bane of her existence.

More snow fell as she rewrapped the scarf around her neck and face, then lifted the hood of her cloak over her hair. Her fingers and toes were half frozen already. Thorn ghosted past the soldiers' abandoned horses and ran her hand along the back of the huge black beast at the end of the line, then walked down the small alley between the inn and the brothel, until she reached the brothel's rear entrance. She kicked the bottom step, knocked the snow from her boots, and then opened the door.

The smell of rose perfume, pine tea, and stew permeated the air. Thorn yanked her cloak off and shook it outside.

"Close the door, lass!" Grey bellowed.

Thorn hung her cloak on the wall and closed the door, her boots leaving small damp puddles on the floor.

She held up her hand in apology to Grey, the cook, and gravitated toward the giant fire. Thorn stripped her gloves off and stuffed them into the pockets of her heavy skirt.

"Sorry, Grey," she called softly. "I'll mop up when I'm done warming up."

The short, older man bustled to her side and clasped her right hand between his own calloused hands. "What have you been up to, lass? You're frozen through!"

"The soldiers wanted to have a little chat."

Grey's wiry brows slashed together, creating a wicked-looking caterpillar that she swore could have walked off his scowl.

He tutted. "I'm sure you taught them some manners."

"Something like that," Thorn muttered. She dropped a kiss onto his grizzled cheek and gently pulled her hand from his. "I'm really tired. I think I'll head to bed early tonight. Do you have any bread and cheese I could take with me?"

Grey harrumphed and scurried to a pan of steaming, warm rolls. He nimbly grabbed one, sat it on top of a bowl half-full of steaming lamb stew, and plopped a chuck of butter on top of the bread. The cook stormed back to her side and thrust the bowl into her hands.

"A person needs a warm meal on such a night as this. Eat," he commanded. "You're too skinny as it is."

Her fingers curled around the bowl. "Thank you."

Grey waved her away. "Now get on with ya. I have much

to do, and I don't want intruders in my kitchen."

Thorn mock-saluted him and retreated from the kitchen. She moved down the hallway and paused when she caught sight of a soldier entering the establishment already. Her stomach twisted, and an uncomfortable shiver ran down her spine. Quickly, she took the servants' stairs up to her room and darted inside, making sure to lock the door behind her. She leaned against the door. Her fingers trembled the smallest bit. Foreboding crept up her spine. Something was wrong. Terribly wrong.

Chapter Two

Tempest

"I thought I was supposed to look *good* in my wedding dress?" Tempest muttered.

"Whatever do you mean, Lady Tempest? You look breathtaking!" the seamstress crowed.

The wedding dress itself was not awful to look at. Tempest shifted uncomfortably, staring at her reflection in the ceiling-to-floor mirror. The long, lacy sleeves were tasteful, and the low, sweeping back would have excited her if she was marrying someone she actually loved. The bell-like skirt however was a different story. There was one too many petticoats for her liking. She could barely walk in the blasted thing. Her fingers drifted over the featherlike milky silk. In truth, it was a beautiful dress—just not the dress for Tempest.

She lifted her gaze and met her own mercurial gray

eyes in the mirror. Who was she? Over the past few months, she'd played so many characters that it was hard to decipher who the real Tempest was anymore. She glanced at the seamstress who knelt beside her, working on the hem of the skirt. None of this was right.

A pang of sorrow struck her in the chest. Not for the first time—and certainly not for the last—Tempest wished her mother was here to help figure everything out. She should've been the one working on the wedding dress, not some stranger. Life was confusing as it was, then add a mad king to the mix and things got dicey. Daughters should always have their mothers with them to help them before their wedding.

Would you have really wanted her here for this farce though? Your choice would have broken her heart.

Tempest sucked in a sharp breath at the thought, and the seamstress cast a wary look in her direction before continuing her work. Tempest once again smoothed her shaking hands along the silk. Her mother had always been a great romantic, and the sham of a wedding would have broken her heart.

You're not completely alone.

That was technically true. She had the support of the Hounds and the Dark Court. Even with the love and affection of her uncles—Brine, and Briggs—she still was isolated. They were men. Neither of them were in the position of marrying their enemy and possibly bearing children for a monster. Her shoulders drooped, and she stared at the floor. Maybe it was best that no one close to her really understood the gravity of her mixed feelings. No one could see her shame and misery.

You made your decision. No going back.

The die had been cast the moment she declined Brine's offer of escape from Dotae in order to stand her ground by the side of the king. Her life had always been difficult, but she'd managed to carve out her way, to make a family despite the adversity. Tempest would do it again. The kingdom needed a queen, and, as loathe as she was to step into that role, someone had to do it. It might as well be her. At least she was difficult to kill.

"It'll be a miracle if I get this finished by the wedding," the seamstress muttered.

Tempest grunted in a very unladylike manner, which earned her a look of disapproval from the seamstress. The rushed betrothal had surprised her. With the kingdom on the brink of war, it would have made sense to postpone the ceremony. Instead, the king had moved it forward. It surprised her, and Tempest hated surprises. What was his motivation behind such a decision? How was he planning on using her?

A brisk knock rattled her door before it swung open, revealing the petite form of the princess in the mirror's reflection. Ansette's gaze swept the room, apparently missing nothing, her chin at a haughty tilt. Her attention settled on Tempest and then on the seamstress kneeling in a half-bow on the floor.

"Leave us," the princess commanded. "You can return in a half hour."

Tempest watched silently as the seamstress pushed to her feet and bustled out of the room, closing the door behind her. Temp gazed at Ansette's reflection. The girl's indifferent personality seemed to melt away as she moved farther into the room. She paused next to Tempest. Her lips pursed as she stared down at the heavy bell of the skirt.

"It's quite impressive."

"If one wants to look like she has the desire to be trussed up like a piece of meat, yes," she muttered.

Ansette snickered and fingered the material. "The fabric is quite fine. My father's spared no expense, I see."

Tempest kept her revulsion from her face and managed to paste on a pleasant smile.

The princess had been gracious and helpful to Tempest after her initial outburst against her brother's death—*murder*—and Tempest's betrothal. For one so young, it was clear Ansette understood that Tempest was not in this for any kind of personal gain—not that Tempest could imagine *anyone* gaining something from marrying such a king.

Money, prestige, a title...

Well, not anything that *really* mattered.

The princess shocked her by placing a gentle hand on her arm.

"You know I'm here for you," she said softly, her face completely serious. "Just so you know, you have my support. I believe you have the kingdom's best interests at heart."

Pretty lines from a royal. Could Tempest trust her? She scrutinized Ansette. The girl was a confusing mix of innocence and experience. She seemed nothing but sincere, but she'd been raised by Destin.

The princess continued: "And I know your reasons for marrying my father have nothing to do with love and affection." A pause. "Though, I must admit that I am just a little bit happy that *you* are marrying him and not anyone else. I hope we can be friends."

Something warm entered Ansette's eyes as she smiled up at Tempest. Yearning. That's what it was. Swallowing hard, Tempest nodded with a small genuine smile of her own. Over the years, she'd yearned for female companionship. Juniper was her only female friend, so she didn't have much experience with other girls. It was a tempting offer to take, but at what cost? Could she trust the princess? Her mind said no. She couldn't trust anyone, especially not the king's daughter.

Don't allow your bitterness to blind you to a potential ally and friend.

It was a fine line she walked, balancing between her head and heart. Tempest's instincts said that the girl meant no harm, but this did nothing to make her feel better. Her focus needed to stay on the mission. Tempest's purpose was not to befriend the girl any more than it was to become merely the queen. She couldn't help but like Ansette. Even though Temp admired the princess—really, truly cared for her—close friendship with the princess would be dangerous for both of them.

The king had a way of killing anyone who gained his attention.

"I appreciate your friendship, my lady," Tempest murmured at last.

Ansette watched her. "You guard yourself."

It was a statement, but it seemed like there was a question hidden among the words.

"Raised among the Hounds, one is trained to guard themselves in all ways. Old habits die hard, I suppose."

"Those are good habits to have. I wouldn't let them die so soon," the princess remarked.

"Oh?" Tempest asked, eyeing her.

The princess cocked her head, and Tempest blinked once. In that moment, all she could see was Pyre. It was there one moment and gone the next. She shook her head to dispel the image.

"Court is a dangerous place, you'll find," the girl commented. "Your skills as a soldier and spy will serve you well as queen. Most say one thing and act another. Hypocrisy is a lasting trend that I'm doubtful will ever disappear."

That sobered Tempest further. She once again looked in the mirror, staring at the imposter gazing evenly back at her. Maybe once, she'd been completely innocent, but no longer. When the Jester had called her a hypocrite, he was right. She had been so busy painting him as a villain, she'd missed the change in herself. In some respects, Tempest was just as guilty as Pyre. *Some*, but not all.

You are not as far gone as that degenerate. You will

recognize your mistakes and learn from them.

So why did that feel like a lie?

Ansette sighed and squeezed Tempest's hand once. "I'll leave you to your fitting. If you need me, feel free to reach out."

"Thank you," Temp said genuinely with a small smile.

The girl gave her another smile and left quietly.

The princess was barely out the door before Tempest's expression slipped from her face. Her skin heated, and the dress seemed to scratch her skin painfully. She hastily tugged at the buttons, not caring when she yanked a few free, and wiggled out of the monstrosity. Her chest moved up and down as panic tried to swallow her. She kicked the dress for good measure and placed her hands on her hips as she calmed down. She never wanted to wear it again.

For a few moments, she watched the puddle of white lace, silk, and crinoline lie dejectedly on the floor like a wilted flower. The seamstress would be back soon, no doubt, and no one's hard work deserved to be treated like that, even if it was ugly. She groaned as she picked up the heavy dress and laid it gently across her bed. The last thing she needed was for the dress to become stained or creased by her own hand.

Chills erupted across her skin, reminding Tempest how naked she now was—and how vulnerable. She moved to the wardrobe and pulled her Hound uniform out and put it back on, feeling far more like herself. She sighed and rolled her neck before adorning her weapons. Putting on her uniform felt like coming home.

Tempest glanced at the bed and then to the door to her left. If she was quick, she could avoid the seamstress. The dress was too fitted already. She strode toward the door and grasped the handle as someone knocked on the door. She barely managed to keep from jumping. Had the seamstress made it back already? She glanced over her shoulder at the bed, and more specifically the pair of windows that bracketed the headboard. If she made a run for it, maybe she could scale the castle wall?

Stop being ridiculous and open the damn door.

Stifling a groan, she turned the handle and opened the door.

Nobody was there.

She pulled a blade from the sheath at her hip and carefully stepped forward into the hallway, prepared for attack. A servant rounded the corner at the corridor, disappearing from sight—the soft sound of footsteps swiftly retreating down the stone steps were the only proof a person had been there in the first place.

A spy? No, they wouldn't knock.

Carefully, she canvased the area for anything out of the ordinary.

Her shoulders sagged as she noticed a note written on thick, yellowed parchment sitting on the floor, waiting innocuously for her to read it. While hunting for rogues among the shadows, she missed the apparent summons. Maxim would have smacked her on the back of the head for being so obtuse.

She swooped down and plucked the letter from the

ground and check the seal for tampering. Nothing. Tempest broke the seal and opened the letter, her eyes eating up the words on the page.

A call to action.

She smiled grimly, and a tingle of excitement filled her at the prospect of finally being put to use. Future queen, she might be, but Temp was a Hound, first and foremost.

It was time to fight.

Chapter Three

Tempest

The whistle of an arrow passed Tempest's ear, narrowly missing her head.

Winter's bite, that had been a close one.

She ducked behind a nearby building and caught her breath, her heart hammering in her chest. This was not what she'd expected when she'd received the summons. Assisting the Hounds with squashing a Talagan uprising—the very people she wished to protect from King Destin—was not what she'd call fun. Although, the dark part of her did enjoy a good battle. It got the blood up. Her vision seemed to tunnel, and time slowed down.

Tempest peeked around the corner of the building before jerking back as an arrow sank into the wood where her head had been. The occupants of the province of Merjeri were fierce opponents, but if she had as much wealth to lose as they did, she might be more bloodthirsty, too.

Wiping the sweat from her eyes, she glanced at the flames one building over, and her lips thinned. Destruction never seemed to bring about the results that others thought they would. What had started as a skirmish between Lord Merjeri and his workers had now escalated into an all-out battle. The workers had set fire to the lord's fields and grain silos. But the flames had spread, as they always did, and now reached a nearby farming village.

A village full of the very workers who'd set the blaze. The fighting needed to stop.

A rebel rounded the corner, waving a pitchfork. Tempest butted him on the forehead with the pommel of her sword, and his eyes rolled up, his makeshift weapon tumbling uselessly from his hand as he crashed to the ground, unconscious. The fewer lives she had to take the better. The workers rebelling were desperate and scared. Lord Merjeri was known to be cruel and dishonest. In her mind, he'd driven the people to act. At least the fighting was lessening. Most of the rebels had abandoned their weapons in favor of buckets of water from the nearest well. That meant the Hounds could spend more time containing the flames and saving those in real danger.

She snuck along the side of the building and crept around the back. There were always those stubborn few who didn't want to be reasonable. She darted around the corner and sprinted toward an archer who faced her. He fumbled with his bow as she crashed into him, his head slamming against the wall of the building. He groaned, and his feet went out from beneath him. Tempest yanked the bow from his loose fingers as he blinked up at her, clearly dazed.

"You gonna kill me?" he mumbled. "On my own property?"

Tempest squatted down and grabbed his chin, so he looked her in the eyes. "No," she said softly. "Defending one's home and livelihood isn't wrong, but waging war and causing devastation is not the answer." She released him and stood. "Let your head clear, and then join everyone else in containing the fire."

She left him and approached the next house, banging on the front door.

"Fire!" she bellowed. "Evacuate your family now!" No sound. Tempest sighed. "I will come in there and drag you out if I have to. Think of your children."

A scuff sounded, and the door cracked open, revealing the wrinkled face of an old woman. She eyed Tempest from head to toe and inhaled deeply.

"I can smell the ash on the air," she said. "We'll leave. No need to drag us from our bed."

Tempest nodded and spent the next hour running to and from burning houses, stables, and fields in between skirmishes with the rebels, saving each and every soul she came upon. She passed Dima, who carried two screaming toddlers in his arms. He nodded to her. Even with all the pandemonium, she could hear Maxim yelling orders.

A whimper caught her attention, and she paused when

she spotted two round faces, peeking out from behind a barrel. Her eyes stung as she approached, the smoke burning her throat. She slowly rounded the barrel and bent low, to make herself seem less scary. Tempest smiled at the two children and held out her hands.

"Little ones, let's go."

They all but wrapped themselves around her, and she staggered as they moved toward safety. The people had congregated in the large cobblestone square that remained untouched by the fire. Everyone uninjured was working the well, bringing up buckets of water for anyone assisting in putting out the blaze.

"Temp!" Maxim called.

Tempest relinquished the children to an older woman and moved in his direction. Dima stood by Maxim's side, and both of their faces were streaked with soot. She smirked at Dima. Her uncle normally had an immaculate appearance. If it wasn't for the situation, she might have laughed at his disheveled hair and filthy skin.

She stood in front of them, aware of the sharp pain in her lungs that said she needed to slow down and take a breath. "What is it?"

Dima indicated the large home that was burning to the west with his thumb. "There's a child in here," he said. "The parents are beside themselves with worry. Entrances have collapsed and we're too large get through."

Tempest frowned, her gut churning as she began moving toward the home. She'd already checked the house prior, and she'd thought there was no one inside. "Didn't we search in there already? I couldn't find any—"

"The mother said her daughter likes playing in the servant's quarters at the back of the building. It's possible she's in one of the service—"

"Enough said."

Primal fear washed over her. She knew what it was like to be trapped in a burning building. Temp wouldn't leave a child to suffer what she had. She wrapped her scarf around her face and sprinted around the building to the damaged, back entrance, soldiering forward into the hot, smoky entrance vestibule, squinting as her eyes watered.

"Is anyone here?" she yelled.

For a moment, she thought she was dreaming. A man stumbled down the burning stairway streaked with sweat and ash, a child in his arms. There was no way he'd fit through the collapsed doorway.

"Give me the child!" she yelled over the roar of the flames. "Both entrances have collapsed. I can get her out through the back, but you'll need to break one of the windows."

He drew close, and Tempest missed a step as she recognized him. Even through the ash and dirt, she spotted a swath of white hair. Bloody white.

Mal, also known as Pyre.

The vile man said nothing. He didn't even look at her when he handed over the child and rushed past them. Tempest held the little girl close and hustled back the way she'd come.

Heat seared her arm as she lost her balance and brushed against the burning wall. She gritted her teeth and crouched low. The building groaned ominously when she reached the back entrance. They had just barely exited when the house suddenly gave way, the splintering wooden beams collapsing in on themselves.

Tempest pressed the child into the ground, using her body to shield the girl from the heat that exploded outward and then receded. Tempest scrambled away, dragging the child with her as she searched through the plume of smoke and ash. Where was Pyre? Had he made it out?

The little one began hacking so hard her body shook in Temp's arms. They couldn't stay here. She moved west and stumbled into the square. A man cried out as he caught sight of them and rushed forward, relief on his face.

"P-p-pa-papa!" the little girl croaked, wiggling out of Tempest's arms and jumping into her father's embrace.

"Thank you," the man cried, tears running down his dirty face. "Thank you so much."

"It's nothing," Temp rasped out. She pulled the fabric from her nose and mouth and bent over, coughing. Bloody hell, it hurt.

"You all right, Temp?" Maxim's voice reached her ears.

Dima squatted down, his hands running over her limbs, searching for injuries. She could barely breathe, and they all knew it. Too much smoke. She glanced toward what was left of the burning home. Where was Pyre?

She wiped her burning eyes and blinked as tears ran

down her cheeks. Surely, he'd gotten out... Pyre had to have gotten out, right? He was the fastest person she'd ever met. Her heart clenched. She didn't want to feel worried about him, but she did.

"I think I might need to sit down," she admitted. Her legs were shaking, it was impossible to catch her breath, and she couldn't stomach the idea of the kitsune not making it. Her body was thick with the noxious fumes. She needed a gallon of water, at the very least, to dilute the toxins she'd breathed in.

Dima and Maxim each grabbed one of her arms and directed her toward the unburned village hall that had been turned into a medic area. She spotted Aleks's familiar face, and her lip curled. That man... He disgusted her.

Dima took one look at her face, moved her away from her disowned uncle, and sat on the steps that lead up to the building.

"Take a moment and recover," Dima said in his no-nonsense tone. "Though make sure you do go to Aleks if you need to. Though he's busy with particularly bad burn victims, so perhaps wait a few minutes."

Tempest could only nod numbly as her uncles left her to it before they went to check in with Aleks. She hated the feeling of uselessness that overcame her when she stopped moving. Chaos embodied the square as crying families were reunited. It should have made her happy, but all she could think about was what had been lost. How many lives had been extinguished? How many homes destroyed? Crops ruined?

She tapped her right foot on the stair as impatient energy filled her. She fidgeted with her hair, though it felt disgusting. The blaze had died down, but the fields still burned, the sickly-sweet smell of mimkia hung in the air. Her lips thinned. There would be hell to pay for the loss of the precious crop. The Crown would crack down hard upon those who'd led the rebellion, as well as their supporters. Her gaze moved back to the people filling the square. They all would suffer.

You will have to do something.

Tiredly, Temp dropped her head into her hands and tried to steady her breathing. She coughed again and spat on the ground, her mouth tasting like ash. Time passed slowly as she rested. When her eyelids began to droop, she forced herself to stand. If she sat for much longer, fatigue would surely claim her, and she'd be asleep before she knew it.

Padding up the stairs, Tempest edged around wounded workers and moved deeper into the town hall that had been made into a makeshift infirmary. A large screen had been set up to form a surgery room. She paused behind a column near the back of the surgery area and frowned. When had Madrid arrived? Her uncles spoke in low tones.

She brushed the thought away as the patient on the cot nearest to her moaned. Aleks bustled over to the badly burned villager and carefully applied salve to the man's skin. Not a single inch of the man's skin had escaped the lick of the flames. Temp held a hand over her nose and breathed shallowly. Even from here, she could smell the charred flesh. A vivid memory of her mother in their burning home flashed through her mind. Her stomach rolled, and she dry-heaved once before getting ahold of herself. She eyed the man in sadness. Aleks was doing his best, but the man wouldn't survive.

She moved away from the healer and crept through the dark toward Maxim, Dima, and Madrid.

"...can't believe she's truly working with the shifters," Dima was muttering.

Tempest concentrated hard to hear what he was saying, and a small frown creased her brow.

"Did you see the man that came out of the building? He couldn't keep his eyes off our girl. He knew her. My guess is that he was a member of the Dark Court."

Her heart stopped. *Pyre.*

"You don't think he was—"

"There's no time for speculation on this," Madrid said firmly. "And it does not matter how Tempest came to work with the shifters, only that we have them on our side."

Tempest flinched.

"The prejudice she held against shifters ran deep, though," Maxim pointed out. "She believed they killed her mother. She had every reason to continue hating them."

"I told you we should have told her," Dima growled.

"She was too young," Maxim argued.

"And now?" Dima demanded. "Secrets do no one any good."

"Enough," Madrid cut in. "Protecting the girl from the truth was a sacrifice we all made."

Tempest froze as she caught sight of Madrid's expression. The man was unshakable, and, yet, he was ashen in a way that had nothing to do with the literal ash clinging to his skin. For the first time in her life, she saw sorrow in his eyes. Unspeakable pain.

"I should not have said that," Dima apologized. "There's no point in bringing up past wounds. Better to move ahead. At this point, the news would only harm our girl."

Temp swallowed down her questions and backtracked, feeling like she couldn't breathe—and it had nothing to do with the smoke. She limped out of the building and rounded the side before she did anything rash. Her whole life, she'd been led to believe shifters had killed her mother. She squeezed her eyes shut and leaned her palm against the stone wall of the town hall. The shifter from her memories wasn't made up. He had been there for the fire. He'd killed her mother; she knew it in her bones. Why then had Maxim made it seem like that wasn't the case? Who would have wanted to hurt her mum? She was a village girl, nothing more. She had no connections.

Temp bowed her head, her loose hair falling around her face. She stared at its periwinkle color and blinked slowly. She'd been so focused on her mother's death, she'd never really given much thought about her sire's actions.

It was never about your mum, but your father.

She gasped at the revelation. She'd been so focused on finding the killer, she never really looked into his motives. Her uncles had told her the man had been a lowlife drifter just passing through. But what if it was something more?

A commotion by the well house broke through her thoughts. She pushed away from the building and began descending the stairs from the town hall as a stately man riding a black horse followed by soldiers moved into the square. Tempest eyed the newcomers, noting the Merjeri crest on the soldiers' uniforms. Her attention moved to Lord Merjeri as he wheeled his warhorse around, almost trampling a small child in the process.

Tempest decidedly hated him.

"Arrest the rebels!" Lord Merjeri called from atop his black horse.

Tempest rushed through the villagers as Merjeri's men began rounding up the frightened, soot-stained shifters. Understandably, some of them were fighting back. A battle was on the cusp of breaking out. Her lungs screamed as she bolted through the writhing fray, her target the haughty lord. Even from a distance, she could tell by the way he looked at the people, he thought he was better than everyone else.

An old man stumbled forward and dropped to his knees near the lord. "Please have mercy!" he cried.

"Get out of my way, old man," Lord Merjeri growled, brandishing a wicked-looking club.

"Please, my lord! We took no part in the burnings!"

Tempest sped up as Merjeri lifted his club. She burst through the people and skidded in front of the old man, wielding her sword. Her arms trembled, but she held steady. Just barely.

"What do you think you're doing?" she demanded.

"Get out of the way, wench," he sneered.

She didn't budge. "I asked you what you think you are doing. Answer me."

Merjeri's lip curled back, and he lifted his club once again as if he planned to strike her. Tempest gave him a dark smile.

Just try it, you bastard. I'll gut you.

She braced as he swung.

Maxim jostled her, and Tempest glared as he managed to grab the lord's arm, halting the blow. Where in the bloody hell had Maxim come from?

Your uncle doesn't deserve your rage.

Tempest shifted her anger toward the lord shouting at Maxim and took one step forward—but a hand on her shoulder stopped her from attacking the lord.

"Stay calm," Dima whispered into her ear. "Do not ruin our victory here today. Let Maxim deal with him."

"I want to rip his arms off," she snarled quietly.

"As do we all," Dima said softly. "Calm yourself. All will be well."

"I do not think there is a need for such violence," Maxim said magnanimously to Merjeri. "We already rounded up the shifters responsible for the actual attack. The men and women you see before you are innocent. Let us see to their rehoming, my lord."

Lord Merjeri cursed and stabbed a finger at Maxim, with a quick glare at Tempest, before he turned his ire back on her uncle. "Your *woman* should know her place," he seethed, his voice full of hatred.

How original. Another woman-hater.

"May I remind you, my lord," Dima said, stepping up to flank Tempest on her right, "that you are speaking to your future queen."

Merjeri snapped his sullen mouth shut. Shock and disbelief, as plain as day, filled his face, followed swiftly by anger and distaste.

The feeling is mutual.

His dark eyes held mutiny, but he stiffly bowed his head. "My apologies, my lady. I did not recognize you in your state. One does not expect to encounter the king's betrothed among the rabble."

"Accepted, my lord," she said sweetly. "Imagine my surprise when one of the king's lords almost clubbed me over the head for helping his people. A strange world, is it not?"

Dima elbowed her in the ribs, but she didn't tear her eyes from Lord Merjeri. He was classically handsome—sharp jawline, haughty nose, full lips—but it was the hatred in his gaze and the blackness in his soul that made him ugly.

Merjeri smiled thinly. "Indeed, my lady."

Not even queen yet, and she'd already made a powerful enemy. It was clear in the way he scanned her from head to toe that he held contempt for any woman who rose above what he perceived to be a woman's station.

Tempest smiled sweetly before completely dismissing the lord and turning to the old man kneeling behind her. She took his gnarled hands in her own, and helped him to stand.

"Go and find your family," she said softly.

The old man kissed her dirty knuckles. "Thank you, my lady. Bless you."

Tempest felt the icy gaze of Merjeri on her, but she paid him no mind. There was no going back. She'd sided with the people. Now, she had to handle the fallout.

Chapter Four

Pyre

Pyre watched the ensuing drama from beneath the brim of his hat, hidden from the masses in the voluminous swaths of a dark cloak he'd stolen from a burning house. Tempest glared at the lord who stared down at her with murder in his eyes. As Merjeri's arm lifted the club, Pyre bared his teeth and surged forward without much conscious thought other than to protect what was *his.*

But Maxim burst from the crowd and caught the club, just as another Hound took up position behind Temp. Pyre paused, his fingers clenching around the hilts of the daggers he held in both hands. His bestial half raged to set loose on the lord who dared lift a hand against Tempest. The other half knew perfectly well that she could handle herself and that she had the support of her uncles.

Reluctantly, Pyre swung back into the shadows, forcing

himself to continue watching instead of interfering.

"Tut, tut," Chesh's voice purred from his left. "That puss is going to get you in trouble."

He flicked an irritated look the impish cat's way, and ignored his mercurial friend's twinkling gaze. Chesh couldn't help himself. He always liked to stir the pot.

"Go and do something useful," Pyre muttered.

The cat smiled and then sauntered away.

Pyre turned his attention back to the exchange, and a sliver of satisfaction moved through him when the haughty lord paled at Maxim's introduction. While Pyre hated the idea of Tempest being betrothed to the king, he was thankful for the protection it afforded her in this case.

Merjeri's expression morphed once again into something completely false. He smiled, but it was thin and cutting, his dark gaze holding only hostility. Pyre's hackles rose when the bloody man scanned Tempest from head to toe. He had no right to look at her like that.

You can't kill him. Calm down.

Pyre released a short breath while he seethed in silence. Tempest could handle herself. How many times had she told him that? He had to stop treating her like a damsel in distress. She'd proven herself to be a force to be reckoned with. It was still difficult to set aside his instincts when he saw someone trying to harm her—his *mate*—and it set his blood boiling. He palmed the blade in his right hand. It would be so easy to take Merjeri out now. The lord had been a thorn in Pyre's side for long enough. His gaze darted back to Tempest. She was completely against such displays of violence without a cause. And while the murderous lord had retribution coming, now was not the time. Merjeri still had too many moving pieces on the board. If he died now, Pyre wouldn't be able to root out all his accomplices.

He bit back a laugh as Tempest effectually dismissed the lord and helped the old man from the ground. Merjeri looked like he was ready to blow a gasket at the dismissal. They'd have to watch him. She'd made a powerful enemy.

Pyre observed her uncles, who were also watching the lord. At least, he'd not been the only one to notice it.

With one last baleful glance Tempest's way, Merjeri gathered his soldiers and retreated into the night like the rubbish they were. Pyre leaned against the unscathed building behind him, the night chill seeping through his cloak, and observed as the Hounds began helping the now-homeless people down the road toward temporary accommodations. Brine caught his eye from across the square and nodded. It was time to go. They'd done all they could here. He'd have Nyx arrange supplies for the people.

Pyre glanced toward Tempest as she scanned the people who were still lingering in the village square. He knew the moment she spotted Brine: her whole face blanked. He had to hand it to her, she really missed nothing. He dipped his hat at her and then walked away from the wall, swiftly turning the nearest corner to hide in a darkened alley. Skirting around abandoned barrels and ice patches, Pyre moved deeper into the darkness. He pushed through linen hanging from a nearby line and waited.

Soft footsteps reached his ears before Tempest lifted the hanging laundry, and paused, eyeing him, her fingers curling around the sheet as if she couldn't decide if she wanted to take one more step or retreat.

"You just going to stand there all night?" he drawled. He took a shallow breath and almost cursed. Even through the acrid scent of smoke and ash, her scent teased the air. His gut tightened, and his mouth watered. Even filthy, she was the best thing he'd ever inhaled.

"Are you mad?" she hissed, glancing behind her once before completely stepping through the laundry line. The linen flapped closed behind her, leaving them in a cocoon all of their own. "Do you understand how dangerous it is for you to be here? If someone identified you, the Hounds would have no choice but to—"

His heart stuttered as he picked up on something within her scent. Worry. She was actually worried for him. "Worried about me, love? I'm flattered." He regretted the sarcasm lacing his words immediately. He needed to do better. Sharp words never won anyone over.

Tempest flinched but then bristled. "I'm worried for our cause. Your presence jeopardizes everything. It's foolish for you to be here. You need to leave before you're discovered."

He hummed, his senses assessing her for injuries. He couldn't smell any blood, but from the raspy quality of her voice, he knew she'd taken in too much ash. "You need to use some medicinal smoke to open up your airways."

She blinked at him before looking away, her lips pursed. "I'll be fine. Plus, my health is not your concern."

But he wanted it to be. Her life meant more to him than it should. Even filthy and ragged, she was still the most glorious thing he'd ever beheld. Pyre found himself taking one step forward. All he wanted to do was kiss her frown away. Hell, just hold her for a moment and breathe her scent in.

She's marrying the king.

That thought alone sobered him. He'd never been one to go after another man's woman.

But she's mine.

Pyre swallowed hard and buried his feelings. They wouldn't do either of them any good. Tempest had made her decision, and it would benefit the rebellion. Having someone with a position of influence right beside King Destin was a huge win for the Dark Court and the Talagan people. And if the king just so happened to die... Well, then all Pyre had to do was be patient.

He will still touch what is yours.

That wasn't a thought Pyre could afford to dwell on. If he did, he'd do something stupid like kidnap Tempest and tie her to his bed until she agreed to be only his.

He wiped a hand down his gritty face. This was not what he should be thinking about. She was a bloody distraction he couldn't afford.

"Why are you here, Jester?" she demanded, breaking the silence.

The use of his title cut through his emotions and helped

him to focus. "I'm sure you've heard whispers of Lord Merjeri's goings-on?"

"I have," she said lowly, her nose wrinkling. "A charming man to be sure."

"Indeed," Pyre said with false sweetness. "The lord is particularly harsh on his slaves and workers." He leaned against the stone wall and tilted his head upward, eyeing the smoke and soot that blanketed the sky. "Recently, a rebel group has cropped up here that truly believes shifters are supposed to rule and that the human race should be subservient to them—their slaves."

"How original," she muttered.

"Extremists, of course," Pyre continued. "We do not endorse them. That's why my men and I are here. We can't allow this to continue. The violence has to stop."

Temp snorted. "So, it's okay for you to cause violence and bloodshed, but not if someone else does? Sounds a bit hypocritical, if you ask me."

That was harsh, but not completely untrue. He ignored her comment. They could argue over morals another time. "Radical dissentions like this will keep the Talagan people weak," he said. "I don't desire to see anyone hurt, but I won't stand by and allow senseless violence to happen when I can prevent it."

She opened her lips to reply and wheezed. Quickly, she held a hand to her mouth and coughed, then hacked again and again and again, each one progressively harder and harsher than the one before.

Concern overtook him, and he closed the distance

between them. He rubbed a hand against her back in soothing motions as she tried to catch her breath.

"You're okay," he crooned, running a hand down her sooty braid—the periwinklecolor looked gray.

Tempest shrugged away from his touch, and Pyre clenched his fingers into a fist and pulled away. Rejection and anger churned in his gut.

"Just wanted to help," he bit out.

"Didn't ask for it," she wheezed.

"Because the high and mighty Lady Hound needs no help," he retorted. Why did she have to be so difficult?

"Not from you. All I want from you is the support of the Dark Court."

She glanced up at him and squinted. He schooled his expression when she softened just the smallest bit.

"I really am fine," she croaked. "Are you telling me that I just saved a bunch of murderers and arsonists, then?" She braced her hands on her knees and slowly straightened.

She licked her chapped lips; the bottom one was more swollen. He wanted to bite it. He blinked and tried to pay attention to her next words.

"Because we didn't kill many of the shifters. We—"

"No, you did the right thing," he assured her. "Most of the people here are completely innocent or had no choice but to go along with the whims of the extremists for fear of their own life. Limiting casualties was the correct thing to do." He sighed heavily, pinching his nose and twitching his fox ears beneath his hat. He was desperate to free them of the wide-brimmed thing. It was itchier than the devil. "We need to talk, Tempest."

"We are talking right now."

Pyre chuckled darkly. "You know what I mean. There are some things we need to discuss before anything moves forward."

"Now is not the time." She coughed. "And my throat hurts too much."

"I don't want you to talk. I want you to listen," he said, and she glared at him, but he continued. "I did not have the Crown prince killed."

She stilled, her gaze locked on his. "Don't you lie to me. I know what I saw."

"Do you?" he asked softly.

"They were *Talagans*, Pyre."

"I'm not responsible for every shifter who does something wrong."

"You sure act like you are," she retorted.

"They were hired mercenaries," he added. "Chesh traced their origins back to Dotae." His ears picked up Chesh's languid strides moving down the alley, and he noticed Tempest straighten. "But we can pick up this conversation later. Your men will be looking for you. I'll send for you soon."

She rolled her eyes, an act that was both endearing and irritating beyond belief to witness. "I'm under too much scrutiny to be scampering off to you, Pyre," she bit out. "You need to come to *me* or send someone in your stead if you wish to continue this conversation. It is dangerous enough for me to be speaking to you here."

She was not wrong, but the wedding was in just a few weeks. They had little time to put everything in place.

"Fine," he relented. "I shall come to you."

"Do you think that's wise?" she mumbled.

"There are some things you have to do yourself. Happy?"

The barest of nods was all the reply she gave him before she strode toward the laundry. She lifted the sheet and startled. Pyre saw Chesh tip the brim of his hat up and wiggle his brows at her.

"How good to see you," the cat murmured.

Pyre clenched his jaw as Chesh bent and rubbed his cheek against Tempest's temple.

"Ew," she complained, pushing the cat away. "Your beard is scratchy."

Chesh gasped and ran a hand along his bristly jaw. "I've been assured the ladies adore it."

"I'm not one of your ladies." Tempest took two steps, as if to leave, but then she halted, her spine straightening. "I'm sorry, Pyre."

Pyre frowned. That was not what he was expecting. "For?"

She sighed and stiffly glanced over her shoulder. "I've been too judgmental of you. I'll try to be more open-minded—but make no mistake. I'll be double-checking your story about the mercenaries."

She disappeared behind the swaying linen before he could respond. What had brought about that change of heart? She'd basically condemned him to be the lowest of the low the last time she'd seen him. Tempest was a prideful creature, and for her to apologize meant something.

Chesh grinned. "Didn't think you had it in you."

"What?" Pyre asked.

"The prowess to lure your female back to you."

He narrowed his eyes and growled. "Next time, keep your filthy paws off her."

Chesh winked. "We'll see."

Chapter Five

Tempest

There was no amount of soap or perfume that could fully eliminate the stench of smoke from Tempest's nose. She was certain her skin still smelled of it, too, despite the brand-new gown she was now dressed in for her betrothal ceremony to King Destin.

The celebration was in full swing. Lords, ladies, and aristocrats surrounded her. She took a sip of her wine and nodded vaguely when a woman she hardly knew tried to draw her into the conversation. Tempest scanned the room, noting the Hounds littered amongst the aristocracy. Madrid managed to catch her eye, and he gave her a small smile of encouragement—well, calling it a smile was generous. It was barely a curling of the corners of his lips. She lifted her goblet and went back to watching the merriment around her. The memory of her uncles' conversation was still at the forefront of her mind.

It made sense that her uncles knew more about her mother's death than they had originally let on. Trust was already thin between them and her these days, and this was the icing on the top of the cake. Tempest set aside her anger and tried to look at the situation logically. They must have had a very good reason to keep her in the dark. They loved her.

She took another sip of her drink and smiled at the balding man next to her who kept gesturing wildly, while her mind tried to unravel what her uncles had been speaking about. What were the facts? A shifter had hurt her mum and abandoned Temp in a burning home. The Hounds had retrieved her from the mountain village, and she'd become a ward of the Crown. 'Owned' was a more fitting word. Every child of the Madrid line belonged to the king.

Her gaze moved toward the new Crown prince, Maven, who had women and men fawning about him. He reminded her of his father. They had the same oily presence. Destin wasn't to be trifled with. Anyone who struck at him was hit back twice as hard. Maybe she'd been looking at this wrongly the whole time. Her mum should have been part of the king's court, and, yet, she was a lass from the mountains. Tempest should have grown up in the city, and, yet, she'd never seen another person other than her mum until she was five years old.

Your mum could have run away with you.

She brushed aside that idea. While she couldn't

remember her father's face, she remembered periwinkle hair. The Hound that had fathered Tempest had known about her birth and kept them secluded in the mountains.

They were protecting you.

Her hands shook as she turned away from the Crown prince and stared up at the dais where the king's throne stood, proud and majestic. One of the Hounds had dared to steal from the king. Whichever one of her uncles was her sire hadn't wanted this life for her. She took a heavy gulp of her wine, feeling slightly hollow. Her parents had wanted freedom for her, and she'd ended up in the devil's lair anyway. What would her mother say if she could see Tempest now? And her father?

She examined the room, her gaze touching on each Hound old enough to be her father. She'd always wondered who it might be, but it hadn't bothered her since she was raised by so many uncles. It was like having a whole battalion of fathers. But now... This changed things. Did her sire rage against how it all turned out? She was marrying the king, after all, and that king was a despot. Her life was veritably in the king's hands.

She couldn't imagine her father had ever wanted that for her.

All she wanted to do was question her uncles to unravel the mystery of her birth, but before that...she had a job to do. Countless lives depended on her playing the part of King Destin's queen, and despite the forces that put her in the deranged king's path, she would damned well play this right. Once her position was secure, she'd ferret out the truth.

She chuckled at a lame joke the old man recited, and scanned the room again out of habit. Many flicked looks her way—some in greed, some in malice, some in pity, and others in jealousy. The king still hadn't made an appearance, even though it was his betrothal celebration. He was usually late, but this was taking things a bit far, even by his own standards; most people had been waiting over an hour for his arrival. Some men and women had already managed to get too deep in their cups before their king had even arrived.

And they said the upper echelon had more class. Well, these people were drunk before their sovereign had even arrived. Not that it bothered *her* too much. The less she saw of the king, the better. It was difficult to feign interest in a man she loathed and had no respect for.

All in good time.

She liked to imagine that, in time, a good and fair ruler would ascend the throne whom she *could* respect, and that then the highborn would learn some manners.

A pig cannot be anything other than a pig.

She smirked and batted her lashes at the man across from her before glancing toward Maven who was watching his companions like a land shark. The former Crown prince hadn't been a good man, but he'd been better than the sadist his younger brother was. A twinge of grief filled her heart at the thought of the Crown prince's death. It felt like years ago, but it was in fact a scant two weeks prior. Blain hadn't deserved to die, no matter how useless he was.

The heir caught her attention, excused himself from his company, and crept across the marble floor toward her. It bothered her. Maven didn't prowl like his father. A lion, she could anticipate. He was too unassuming; even as he wound around the upper class, the prince seemed almost invisible to the eye. The highborn men barely paid him any mind, despite the fact he was their future king. It was a skill Tempest was more familiar witnessing from the members of the Dark Court. It made the prince feel dishonest. Scheming.

Untrustworthy.

He moved and acted like a viper. It was only a matter of time before he struck at her.

She locked away her dislike of him and arranged a placid smile on her face when the prince finally arrived at her side. The older countess fluttered her fan, and smiled at the prince.

"Your Royal Highness," Tempest said, curtsying slightly. The aristocrats around her followed suit. "A pleasure." *A lie.*

He smiled. "The pleasure is all mine." *Another lie.*

"Any update on what is holding your father up?" she asked lightly. "The wine will soon be gone at this rate." The women tittered, hiding their smiles behind fans covered in too many ribbons and lace.

The prince shrugged, the impassive look on his face never slipping. "My father does as he pleases. You and I both know this." A slimy smirk played across his lips that

Tempest did not like at all. "I must say, Lady Tempest, I do look forward to calling you *Mother* in the days to come."

Tempest resisted a shiver. The comment was made in a jesting manner, but he said it as if he meant it, sincerity ringing in every word.

"You're a good boy," the countess praised, her reedy voice syrupy sweet.

"I try, my lady. I am the lucky one to gain such a mother," he all but crooned. No animosity colored the prince's voice, nor any derision or sarcasm. It was spoken as if it was an entirely genuine sentiment. That's why he was dangerous. He spun lies like sugar. He may even believe his own lies.

You need to tread carefully.

"I am so very honored to be welcomed into your family," Tempest murmured, the words tasting sour.

The familiar scent of jasmine wafted in Tempest's direction right before the princess arrived to her left, sweeping into the conversation with grace.

"I've been surrounded by men my whole life. What a treasure Lady Tempest is to have in our home. Now, I will have someone to discuss the latest fashions with!"

"Princess Ansette," Tempest said with a genuine smile. The girl knew the perfect time to intercept. "How are you this evening?"

"Oh, you know, enjoying the lovely celebration." Ansette wrapped her hand in the crook of Tempest's elbow. "If you'll excuse us, we must see to the other guests." She waved a finger at her brother. "We can't keep our Lady Hound to ourselves."

Tempest sighed as the princess steered her away from the new Crown prince. Still, she swore she could feel his gaze between her shoulder blades. "Thank you."

"Not a problem. Just trying to keep the guests entertained until my father deigns to make an appearance," she said, laughing softly.

Ansette drifted through the room like a leaf in the wind, introducing Tempest to one highborn after another. After the seventh, Tempest began to see a pattern in the people she was being introduced to. They worked with the biggest merchants in the country or held political power along the borders of Heimserya with their neighboring nations—particularly those with which they were not friendly.

They all seemed to hold the princess in high regard. Interesting. Tempest glanced at the girl from the corner of her eye. Ansette was forming alliances that her father was not necessarily privy to. Many saw a spoiled fourteen-year-old girl, but she was so much more than anyone gave her credit for. And Ansette clearly liked it that way...

Just what are you up to, Princess?

Ansette had many masks, apparently. She spoke about topics from trade to embroidery and everything in between. Not only that, but she remembered something personal about each person they spoke to. Tempest did her best to engage in the conversations, but the longer this went on, the more she felt like she didn't belong.

You belong wherever you want to.

Dima's words came back to her. She'd struggled as a young girl when training in espionage. He'd helped her to think like her targets and to become whoever she desired. That's all this was. She needed to stop thinking that she was separate from their world. If she was to appeal to them in the days to come, she needed to take a page from Ansette's book. So, Tempest laughed and joked and made witty comments until the aristocrats laughed and joked alongside her, until they weren't looking at her like she was an outsider. It was a small victory, but a victory all the same.

The king entered the room, and the sea of people bowed. He caught Tempest's gaze and smiled, holding his hand out to her from across the room. A blatant command.

"If you'll excuse me," Tempest murmured politely.

Her heart beat in sync with the clack of her heels as she crossed the marble floor. She wasn't one for being summoned, but one never refused the king.

"Hello, my darling," he whispered as he took her hand and led her up the stairs to the dais.

"My lord," she said softly as he released her and took his throne. She sat demurely at his side. A banquet of food was laid before them on the table.

"You look beautiful," he murmured, signaling to the rest of the room that they should be seated and begin eating. His eyes roved over Tempest's frame, but she resisted the urge to shiver in disgust.

"You look handsome as always, Your Grace," she replied.

A pleased smile crossed his face, then he picked up a goblet of wine and began the meal.

Not much was said throughout dinner which was a boon in her eyes. She exchanged pleasantries with the king as they made their way through the seven courses presented in front of them.

"Aren't you going to ask where I was?" the king asked.

Tempest blinked and stared into his golden eyes. What did he want her to say? "It's not my place to ask," she answered carefully.

"Come, now. Aren't you the least bit curious?" he teased.

"Curious, sure, but a Hound isn't privy to information that's unnecessary. If it's necessary, you'll tell me, I'm sure."

He chuckled and reached for her left hand. He kissed the back of her fingers. "Conversing with you is always stimulating. What an interesting woman you are."

She shrugged, not knowing what to say to that.

"There have been more attacks," he murmured.

"Where?" she asked.

"Along the Dread Mountains and in Betraz. It's seemingly random, but I've had the infantry in the areas mobilized."

"Betraz?" She took a slow sip of her wine. What were they doing near the giants' border?

"Yes. If the mongrels make trouble between Kopal and Heimserya, I won't be pleased. Luckily, an ambassador of Kopal should be arriving soon. In fact..." the king trailed off, his gaze scouring the room. "I half expected him to be causing a ruckus among our guests."

"Intriguing," she said, her mind still focused on the attacks. Were they of the Jester's designs or of the extremists? "Am I needed there?"

Destin glanced back at her with a smile and kissed her knuckles. "No, my dear. You're exactly where I need you."

She almost gagged. Where she needed to be was far, far away.

Madrid materialized, seemingly out of nowhere, and leaned in to whisper in the king's left ear, his gaze meeting hers before settling over her shoulder as if Tempest was not there at all. Destin released her hand, and Tempest focused on her creamy dessert, her ears straining to hear what Madrid was saying.

Blast it. She couldn't hear a bloody thing.

Madrid's words were barely a whisper, and Destin's expression was blank. The king betrayed nothing when he waved Madrid away. Then he stood up, and Tempest braced for the betrothal toast.

"Ladies and gentlemen," the king said, sweeping his arms in a grand gesture until the room was silent and all eyes were on him. "It is my greatest pleasure to have you all here to celebrate my betrothal to Lady Tempest. Many of you had hoped—nay, had pushed—for me to remarry, so I hope my choice of bride satisfies that desire."

Cheers and whistles filled the air.

She kept her smile in place.

"Tempest has brought me many things," Destin

continued. "Joy, excitement, companionship. But she has brought me far more than such personal feelings." He paused for dramatic effect. "She's delivered triumph after triumph for our country against the enemy. I have made no secret that she is responsible for bringing the heart of the Jester to me. Then, she fought valiantly by my son's side when he was ambushed. Though she could not save him..." the king trailed off as if choked up.

Tempest's smile didn't waver despite her sorrow and the disgust she felt for the king. He was a liar. *He* was partly responsible for his son's death. It was vile.

"She made certain as many rebels as possible who were responsible for Blain's death were slaughtered. So, it gives me great pleasure to tell you—tell *her*"—Destin turned his gaze to Tempest, a fierce grin on his face, and her stomach dropped—"that we have abducted several members of the rebellion who were found sneaking into the city. They will be executed in three days' time as payment for the death of my firstborn son. Though nothing will bring him back, I feel their deaths are appropriate retribution for his slaughter. Let this be a warning to the rebellion that we do not stay our hands. We will wreak vengeance upon them until they are completely snuffed out."

Destin's speech was met with rapturous, fervent applause, which she had to work hard to emulate. Tempest's mind spun. Who had he captured? She'd dealt with those who'd attacked the former Crown prince. Sure, the Dark Court had been present and were guilty, but it was the king who'd had the information leaked about where his son would be. The king held responsibility for killing his own flesh and blood.

The king turned to her and held his hand out. She had no choice but to take it and stand. He brushed his calloused thumb across the top of her hand and crooned in her ear, "Won't you join me in my chambers for some fire whiskey after this, my Lady Hound?"

Refuse.

Every fiber of her being wanted to say no, but the die had been cast. She took a step closer to him, the metal of the blade at her thigh and the heavy weight of the poisoned pins in her hair giving her strength and courage.

"It would be my pleasure."

Chapter Six

King Destin

He could spend ages watching the Lady Hound. Destin observed her over the rim of his glass of fire whiskey, a small smile on his face as Tempest—his queen-to-be—warmed herself by the fire. There was an alertness to her posture, evident even with her back turned to him, that gave away the fact that Tempest was no soft lady but was, indeed, a formidable warrior. Even the delicate, sweeping dress with its embroidered bodice and jeweled neckline could not hide this fact. Tempest was dressed as a lady, yes, but she was most definitely *not* one. She was something feral...

A lioness.

Amusement simmered in his chest as she slightly turned, so he was awarded with her profile. Her gaze may have been on the fire, but her attention was most certainly focused on him. The king had always liked that about

Tempest. She was a born and bred predator, just like him...which made the hunt even more fun. His heart rate increased in anticipation when she took a deep breath, her breasts straining against the top of her dress. Sweet poison, the temptation to lure her into his bed was almost impossible to resist, but that would ruin all the fun. Destin had been seducing women for long enough to know that the hunt was the best part. He had to extend it for as long as he could, so the victory would be all the sweeter.

He stretched and stood from his chair, his fur robe trailing behind him. The king approached Tempest and soaked in the heat from the roaring fire. He hid his smile behind his glass when she turned to face him. Always wary... It would be an immense pleasure bringing her to heel.

She met his gaze head-on, as she always did, and his body heated. She never hid from him, nor cowered. Tempest was wise enough to fear him and yet...she still held her ground, apparently not intimidated one bit. He reached out slowly and brushed his thumb along her collarbone, noting the small change in her placid expression and the hitch in her breath. His lips hooked to the side in a crooked smile. The little Hound wasn't completely unaffected by him.

Destin dropped his hand.

"I must be honest, my Lady," he said. "I'm surprised you accepted my invitation to have a drink." He arched a brow as he eyed her empty hands. "Though, I must note that you don't actually *have* a drink."

"You never offered, my lord."

He smiled and gestured to the fire whiskey. "What is mine is yours, darling. What would you like?"

She shifted, putting more space between their bodies. She smiled ruefully at him and shook her head, a loose periwinkle curl falling against her pale cheek. "I assure you that I had enough wine earlier. If I add that to the mix, I'm sure I would be very ill come morning."

"Ill?"

Tempest frowned. "I suppose I'm not to speak about such things, or so I'm told."

"Your candor is welcome," he murmured.

She scrutinized him like she was trying to decipher if he meant his words or not. "If you wish." Tempest rubbed the back of her head. "If I'm honest, my head aches something fierce from all these bloody pins, and I can barely breathe in this dress. I swear a sadist must have invented the corset. It is a torture device to be sure."

Destin chuckled. "I'll make sure to mention that to the dungeon master."

"Just make one of the prisoners wear one of these for an hour, and they'll give you any information you need."

He shook his head and took another sip of whiskey as they both lapsed into silence. "It was a long day, wasn't it?"

"Yes. I'm so tired, I feel like I could sleep on my feet." She gestured at his whiskey. "Another reason why I'm abstaining from spirits. I'm sure the alcohol would knock me out where I stand." She paused and then glanced up at him from beneath her lashes. "And I don't think either one of us wants that."

The king blinked slowly and cocked his head. Many

women had looked at him with hot eyes and come-hither smiles in his lifetime. He knew she was an innocent, but the heated look she threw his way could have made the most seasoned courtesan proud. What was his betrothed playing at? Whatever it was, he was willing to wager she wasn't prepared for the outcome.

Destin set his glass on the mantel and took one gliding step forward. He brushed a hand down Tempest's left arm and clasped her fingers between his own, satisfying himself by bringing her hand up to his lips and kissing the back of it. She was a puzzle of opposites. The back of her hand was soft while her fingertips were calloused.

He flicked a glance upward as he turned her hand over and kissed the inside of her wrist, making sure to drag his tongue along her pulse point. A shiver worked through Tempest's body that caused her hand to tremble ever-so-slightly between his. He grinned against her skin as her expression melted into one of apprehension. Pleasure ran up his spine as he met her gaze once more and sucked lightly on her wrist. Anticipation filled him as he pushed up her sleeve, revealing more creamy skin. Just how far was she willing to go in this game she'd started?

Destin lifted his head to place a kiss just beneath her elbow when Tempest skillfully twisted her arm and deftly moved out of his grasp. He watched her from beneath the fringe of his hair and straightened. She was slippery. One moment in his arms, the next warming herself next to the fire like nothing had passed between them. That could be problematic in the future. He would need to acquire more rope and manacles. His last rope had been disposed of, alongside his mistress.

Tempest caught his stare and gave him a small smile, color high in her cheeks as she held her hands out to the flames. Her embarrassment was a surprise. He hadn't expected a blushing virgin, but he was enjoying it. Although he knew she was innocent, he had expected her to be more open and honest about her interest in such matters as to what went on behind closed doors at night. She clearly wasn't naïve as to what happened between men and women. Hell, she'd grown up in the barracks. Perhaps what made her so worldly was almost what made her innocent. The Hounds no doubt had protected her from any advances. As they should.

He smirked.

Women had one purpose and one purpose only: to create heirs. They were never supposed to be promiscuous...or, at least, not unmarried women. And though he enjoyed the company of loose married women, reveling in their skill in the bedroom, once the pleasure dissipated, his loathing for them returned. It was in a man's right to take whom he'd like to bed, but women were the vessels for the next generation. By tainting themselves with lovers, they polluted the highborn bloodlines, which was unforgivable. Which is why the moment he tired of them, they were disposed of. A female creature driven by lust was the devil in disguise and deserved to be destroyed.

What kind of woman was Tempest? Would his queen be honorable, or would he kill her?

Only time would tell.

Destin contented himself with the soft silence that settled between them once again. He plucked his whiskey from the mantel. Slowly, he took a long sip, his attention moving between the flames and his soon-to-be queen.

She rubbed the back of her skull and then pulled a long pin from her coiffure. Shining periwinkle curls tumbled down her back, and she sighed. The king froze, his arousal rising as she shook out her hair. A soft moan escaped her lips. Tempest was playing with the devil, and she didn't even know it.

His betrothed stiffened and abruptly faced him, looking like she'd just taken a tumble in his bed. She stepped into his space and pushed onto her tiptoes, placing a feather-light kiss on his cheek.

"I am very tired, Your Grace," she whispered breathily. "Perhaps next time, we do not wait until the end of a banquet to converse with each other in private. Good night."

He reined in his rampant desire and watched silently as she pulled open his door and left. Despite what he had decided earlier, he was tempted to run out after her and drag her back to bed by her glorious hair if he must.

Destin ran a hand over his face and chuckled to himself. Either she was the world's best actress, or she really was genuine.

If it was the latter, it was a shame he'd have to ruin her.

Chapter Seven

Tempest

Somehow, Tempest always found herself fleeing from the king's chambers. Goosebumps still stood along her arms fifteen minutes later, and she scowled and rubbed at them. She was a bloody Hound for heaven sakes. Why was she running from that scoundrel? It wasn't as if she couldn't handle him.

He scares you.

She wrenched her door open and stormed inside her rooms. Two maids squeaked in surprise at her arrival. Tempest paused and eyed them as they gazed back with wide eyes. Licking her lips, she smiled softly and held her hands out placatingly. She didn't need to scare the poor staff any more than she already had. Plus, most of the castle suspected Tempest had gone with the king; no need to stir up gossip about how ruffled she was.

"I can handle it from here," Tempest said gently.

"We haven't finished turning down your bed and your dress, my lady," the maid closest to the fire murmured with a little curtsey.

"I've been undressing myself the entirety of my life. I can manage one more night. Thank you for your help, but you're dismissed."

Both maids bobbed curtsies and scampered from the room.

Tempest's smile fell, and she stared at the closed door for far too long, rubbing her bottom lip. She cringed and rushed toward the wash basin sitting on an orange side table to the left of her bed. The skirts of her dress tangled around her legs. She yanked them out of the way. Hastily, she poured some water into her mouth, swished, and spat into the basin before using clean water from the pitcher to scrub her lips and face. Even though the king hadn't kissed her lips, she still swore she could taste his whiskey in her mouth. The stuff was that potent. She snatched a mint leaf from a dainty saucer and popped it into her mouth. The sharp, pungent flavor drowned out the fire whiskey.

What had she been thinking tonight? It was one thing to tolerate Destin's advances but another thing to encourage them. She cringed at the memory of him sucking on her wrist. Tempest yanked up the long lace sleeve of her dress and cursed. A mouth-sized red and purple bruise was already forming. He'd given her a love bite.

Disgusted, she tugged the sleeve down over the

evidence and prowled toward the fire, shivering. The memory of his touch made her feel cold and empty.

At least, he believed you enjoyed it.

Holding her hands out to the fire, she huffed. Tempest had never been able to blush on command, but her cheeks always pinkened when she was angry. The king had no clue how close he was to being stabbed in the throat.

He'd probably like that.

Another shiver wracked her body, and she wrapped her arms around her waist. He hadn't bothered to hide his thoughts tonight. The king's expression had been far too heated, and his eyes had darted toward his bed one too many times. It hadn't escaped her, either, that he had circular hooks on all four posters of his bed—presumably to tie all his mistresses down.

All his *dead* mistresses.

"Don't dwell on such things," she muttered.

Abandoning the fire, she moved to the large mirror to the left of the hearth. There was no way she'd be able to get out of the tight dress without using her reflection. Tempest turned her back to the mirror and reached her hands to the laces in the back, craning her neck to make sure she didn't knot the ribbons. She slowed as she noticed how pale her complexion had grown. Just a few minutes in the king's presence, and he'd reduced her to a quivering ninny.

"You're no shrinking violet," she whispered to her reflection. "You're better than this."

Tempest managed to unlace the gown without cutting

the laces and tossed it onto the nearest brocade chair near the fire. Pondering the king's depravity wouldn't help her. In fact, there were much more important goings-on that deserved her attention.

The Crown had rebels in their dungeons. The question was who were they? Just some poor Talagan scapegoats? Or were they from the Dark Court? Either way, she needed to know what was going on.

Her skin pebbled as she moved away from the fire and into the wardrobe. She pulled on a pair of simple trousers and a cotton shirt, grabbed her boots, and then moved back to the fire, sitting on the floor to put her boots on. It was time to make a plan. It wasn't a question of discovering the rebels—Tempest already had their location—but she could hardly walk down to the prison and sleuth around, let alone free anyone who needed to escape.

Or could she*?*

Learning the guard rotations was one of the first things she'd done after being moved from the Hounds' barracks to the palace. She squinted at the clock on her nightstand. Only half an hour until the guards changed rotation. That was hardly enough time to get to the dungeons, but Destin had announced that they were to be executed in three days' time.

Her stomach twisted uncomfortably. Trusting anything that came out of the king's mouth was a risk. She couldn't rely on his word. Destin could change his mind and have them killed the next day. She had to move now.

With a deep, shuddering breath, Tempest finished lacing her leather boots, braided her hair back, and slipped a midnight-black cloak over her shoulders. Her fingers dug into the pockets, double-checking her weapons. Satisfaction curled through her when she felt the hilt of a small dagger and the little leather pouch that contained her lock-picking tools. Her gaze darted to the sword leaning against the trunk that rested at the foot of her bed, but she thought better of it. Tonight required stealth, not power. And, besides, if she was caught fighting, it would only put her in hot water. If anyone managed to catch her, she had to rely on her lying skills.

On silent feet, Tempest ghosted out of her room, down the corridor, and then down several flights of stairs, making sure to keep to the shadows when anyone passed by. It was ridiculous how easy it was to slip through the palace unnoticed. No one noticed her as she glided down the servants' corridors. Music echoed through the hallways from the betrothal ceremony that still raged on. She rolled her eyes. The courtiers never needed an excuse to drink themselves into stupors and make asses of themselves. Her mind turned back to the king. Had he returned to the celebration or stayed in his room? The last thing she needed was to run into him.

The music faded to a dull roar as she descended deeper into the belly of the castle. She slowed as she neared the dungeon. Tempest peeked around the corner, and her heart thumped when she caught sight of the large, wooden door to the prison cells. No guards. She'd arrived at the perfect time.

Tempest wasted no time rushing around the corner and got to work with her lock-picking tools. Within seconds, the mechanism in the lock clicked, and she eased the door open, wincing when it creaked loudly on its hinges. It was either laziness or brilliance on the guards' part to leave it so no one could sneak out without making some sort of ruckus; she was guessing laziness.

Tempest tucked away her tools in her little pouch and edged inside the dungeon, making sure to close the door behind her. Carefully, she snuck down the dark staircase to the prison below. Everything had gone so smoothly. Her uncles would have been impressed by her abilities. She slowed near the bottom.

You have five minutes, maybe less. Find the rebels and then get out.

The dungeon was one long, solitary corridor lined with cells on either side, with a shadowy alcove between each space to separate them. She made sure her hood was pulled low over her face as she stalked across the dusty stone floor, making sure to peer into each and every cell for a face she might recognize. Many prisoners were asleep. Others called nonsensical things to her, but the ones who stared blankly at her like their soul had long since departed the world left her chilled.

Whispers followed in her wake, and she resisted the urge to hide. There wasn't time for such a thing. A huge man approached the bars of his cell and licked his lips.

"Come closer," he whispered.

She ignored him and continued on, even though her skin was crawling. There was no way he could discern she was a woman. Perhaps he was just trying to intimidate her or take advantage of the situation. Her pulse ratcheted up as each excruciating second passed. How the bloody hell would she know which ones were the rebels?

Tempest rushed forward and glanced to her left, then almost missed a step.

Brine.

Oh, God.

Forgetting to be cautious, she lunged for the bars of his cell and wasted no time getting to work on the lock. She had to get him out *now.*

"Time to go," she murmured, her fingers steady despite her fear.

Brine's wolf-like eyes glowed in the darkness as he pushed away from the back wall, his chains slithering across the floor. She'd be able to break the locks on the manacles easily, but it would still eat up valuable time.

He paused on the other side of the bars and curled his fingers around hers. "No," he growled, urging her to stop.

"It's already done," she hissed, pulling another lock-pick from her cloak, pressing it into his hands. "Get started on your cuffs. We don't have much time."

Brine shook his head. "I am exactly where I need to be. Do not get me out."

Tempest paused and met his stare, not believing what she was hearing. "They will behead you in a matter of days," she snapped quietly, tripping over her words in her urgency. "There is no guarantee that I'll have a better opportunity than this to get you out. And the king might change his mind and kill you *tomorrow* for all I know. So, I—"

"*You* must get out of here," he cut in, voice far gentler than Tempest was used to. He squeezed her hands. "It is far too dangerous for you to be here." He quirked a smile. "Do not worry about me. I know what I am doing. This isn't my first time in a royal prison, pup."

"That isn't funny."

"It wasn't supposed to be."

"Then—"

An ungodly yowling filled the air from the end of the prison, freezing both Tempest and Brine to the spot. The man responsible for the noise screeched and screamed all manner of incomprehensible things and rattled the bars of his cage until the inevitable sound of guards' heavy footsteps tramped down the stairs.

"Go," Brine urged, holding the lock-pick out to her. "I'll see you soon."

She stared at his outstretched hand and snarled at him. "Keep it. I'll not leave you without some sort of weapon." There's no way she would leave him without helping in some way.

Tempest retreated into the closest alcove, hoping against hope that the shadows in the dungeon and her black cloak would obscure her from the eyes of the guards long enough for her to escape. A dark smile drifted across her face when the guards thundered past her, their armor clattering as they moved deeper into the dungeon. People only saw what they wanted to see. They were too focused on the screaming prisoner to even consider there was an enemy lurking in the shadows.

Fools.

All the better for her.

Taking advantage of the clamor, she crept out of her alcove and ran through the dungeon as quickly as she dared. She slowed when approaching the stairs. There had been two guards who had come to investigate. That should have been all that were on duty, but one could never be sure. Tempest almost rolled her eyes as she reached the top. The guards had left the door open. Someone needed to train their men better.

Get out. Their laziness is your good fortune.

She held her breath as she slunk away from the prison doors, keeping an eye out for anyone who might be lurking about.

Tempest exhaled one huge breath when she had put three levels between herself and the dungeon. The corridor to her rooms came into view, and her heart began to slow. That had been too close. If the guards had been even the least bit competent, she would have been discovered.

She let herself into her room, closed the door, and leant her back against it. What the wicked hell was going on? Why was Brine in the prison, and why did he want to be there? Sweet poison, she hated being out of the loop. The Jester would be hearing about this. Her gaze strayed to the bed as fatigue washed over her.

He'd hear from her in the morning. Maybe he'd have a reasonable explanation.

She snorted.

Highly doubtful.

Chapter Eight

Tempest

Sleep evaded her.

She glared at the moonlight shining through her southern window, her mind reeling with unanswered questions and possible conspiracies. Was this how Pyre planned to send a man in to meet her? It seemed a bit extreme, but the Jester was known to be unhinged. She punched the pillow, trying to get comfortable. If Brine wasn't there for her, why was he here? And why was he in the dungeon? Brine was one of the stealthiest people Tempest knew. What was the ploy?

She needed to talk to him properly.

There was no way she could reach him until at least the next change in the guards, which wouldn't be until well after dawn now. There was no choice but to let things remain as they were for now.

Go to sleep.

Temp huffed and kicked at the long nightgown she'd been given. It was undoubtedly the softest thing she'd ever worn, but it tangled around her legs every time she went to bed. It was so annoying. If someone attacked, it would be a hazard to try to escape. It would be better to just sleep naked. Her lips twitched at that. Her maids would be shocked.

Her arms wrapped around the down pillow as she flipped onto her other side so she could stare at the flames dancing in the hearth. Her eyelids began to flutter, and, at some point between worrying about Brine and plotting her next move, she sank into an unsettled, reluctant slumber.

Dark dungeons and bloodthirsty lions greeted her.

Tempest gasped and rolled out of bed, blade in her hand.

She scanned the room, her heart threatening to pound right out of her chest. Was it the nightmare that had awoken her or something else? Her vision was gritty, limbs heavy, and the moon was still out. Not more than a few minutes or hours must have passed. What time was it anyway?

She straightened, her toes curling inward at the chill of the floor. She rubbed at her left temple as her brain fought against her grogginess to function properly.

A piercing scream cut through the night.

That wasn't something she'd imagined.

Bang. Bang. Bang.

Despite herself, Tempest jumped at the pounding on her door. It was as if someone was trying to break down the door. She lifted the hem of her nightgown and tied it into a knot, exposing part of her calves, ankles, and feet. Silently, she retrieved her sword from the foot of the bed, pulled it from the scabbard, then approached the door.

"My lady!" a man bellowed from the other side.

She yanked open the door, her teeth bared, ready for a fight. The soldier blinked at her, his gaze moving from her sword to her hair and then down to her bare feet.

"What is going on?" she barked, pulling his attention back to her face.

"You need to evacuate."

"What..." she broke off as an almighty yell echoed down the hallway, followed by harsh commands.

King Destin.

Without waiting for the soldier to explain the situation further, Tempest pushed past him and sprinted down the corridor, her bare feet slapping against the cold floor. She skidded around the corner into the wing and froze to the spot, not daring to breathe.

King Destin knelt on the floor, clutching a small body to his chest with shaking hands. Blood spattered the floor around him. A brown braid trailed over his arm and pooled on the carpet.

Ansette.

"No..." Tempest uttered, not daring to believe what was before her eyes. "No, not—"

"My daughter is fine, by a stroke of luck I will forever be

thankful for," Destin said. He lifted his head and glanced over his daughter's body.

Tempest took several slow steps forward and edged around the king, then knelt near the princess's slippered feet. The king loosened his hold on his daughter just enough for Ansette to sit up. Her eyes were wide and white, her face tear-stained, her opulent lilac dress a macabre mess of blood and dirt. What the bloody hell had happened? Not to mention that Ansette should have been in bed at this time. Why was the princess still galivanting around?

"What happened here?" Tempest asked gently, placing her hand on the girl's leg. "Where are you hurt?"

"I'm not."

"I'm glad to hear that," Tempest murmured. She glanced at the blood soaking the blue carpets. "Whose blood is this?"

Destin trembled, and he glared at the floor. That was an interesting reaction. She'd thought him a man with no heart. He hadn't even wept for his oldest son, and, yet, he seemed genuinely shaken and upset about the princess. More upset and in shock than angry, even, which was more genuine emotion than Tempest had ever seen from the king.

It doesn't change anything.

He was still a mass murderer who'd allowed one of his children to be murdered. His favoritism for his daughter wouldn't sway her view of the man.

"S-s-some..." Ansette stuttered, her bottom lip

wobbling. "Someone tried to—"

"Someone tried to murder my precious daughter," Destin muttered, his shock contorting into rage. "Had my rebel of a daughter not decided to sneak back to the party downstairs, they would have succeeded."

"Rebel?" Tempest ventured, flinching at Destin's choice of words.

"I—I did not mean to act so improper," Ansette cried, rubbing her tears into her father's chest. "But I just wanted to stay at the party. It was going on so late, I didn't want to go to bed, I—"

"Then who was hurt?" Tempest asked, pointing at the blood on the floor. "The would-be assassin?" Her gut told her that this was not the case.

Destin sighed. "Ansette knew I would not be happy if she returned to the party so late. She changed into another gown, so she would not be recognized, and had her handmaid sleep in her bed, so if anybody checked in on her, they would believe it was Ansette asleep there. It is the handmaid's blood you see on the floor, Tempest. The handmaid was murdered."

Sword in hand, Tempest stood and moved cautiously into the princess's room. The huge four-poster bed was a mess of feathers and torn silk curtains, bathed in crimson. She'd seen battle, even some carnage, but nothing like this. Everything was red. It was a literal bloodbath. Her stomach rebelled at the stench of iron in the air, and she gagged before holding a hand to her mouth when she spotted what remained of the handmaid.

It had not been a clean and simple assassination. Whoever had committed the crime, reveled in the pain and destruction.

Thank the stars that Ansette had not been in bed.

No one deserved such a death. The poor handmaid.

"Someone needs to notify the girl's family," Tempest muttered, feeling a bit numb herself.

"It's already done," Madrid's voice said softly from the shadows.

Tempest's blinked hard when he materialized at her right side. In the madness, she'd completely missed his presence. That was sloppy.

"Any idea who did this?" That should have been her first question.

"No."

"No one saw anything?"

Madrid glanced toward the grim soldier staring blankly at the room. "No one saw anything. The guards outside the room were drugged, and the blood now in the corridor was from the traffic in and out of this room. It's been suggested that the assassin fled through the window."

Tempest blinked at the open window. Scaling the palace would have been nearly impossible without being discovered.

Madrid watched her. "We are dealing with no ordinary assassin."

No ordinary assassin… Did he mean he thought they were dealing with someone who was Talagan? "A shapeshifter?"

"A bird is easily unnoticed."

The king stepped into the room and stood at her left side.

"You believe the rebellion did this?"

"I have their men," Destin said. "*Of course* it was them. They were taking their revenge." He was vicious in his certainty.

While it was possible it was someone with the ability to shapeshift, Tempest doubted this was the work of the Dark Court. Even Pyre, in all his cruelty as the Jester, would never lay a hand on the princess. Ansette was innocent. She was good. She was not like her father at all.

"Triple the guards on this floor," Destin ordered Madrid. "We will not have a repeat of this attempt on either my daughter's life *or* that of my future queen. Do you understand?"

"Understood, my lord," Madrid murmured with a bow. "I will make sure my men protect what you hold dear."

Destin wrapped a hand around Tempest's forearm and led her from Ansette's bedroom. Madrid soon followed, barking orders at the soldiers. The men retreated down the corridor to their stations as Madrid had commanded. Something told Tempest that this was a pointless endeavor. Whoever tried to murder Ansette had made their point; they would not come back to finish the job *or* to attack Tempest. Whatever their goal, they'd given up the element of surprise. Even though they hadn't killed the princess, they'd struck fear into the heart of the palace.

The question Tempest had to work out was why the

princess had been the target in the first place. Ansette was a smart girl, but by all accounts, she held no favor with the king, nor any power. Why not strike at the newly announced heir?

The king released Tempest and retrieved his daughter from the stone wall, and escorted her down the hallway with Tempest on one side and Madrid on the other. He halted in front of Tempest's rooms and let himself in. She blinked and followed him in as he set his daughter in the pink brocade chair near the low fire. Tempest swept past them and added a few logs to the fire, staying quiet as they lit, creating a warm blaze.

A troop of maids entered the room, first curtseying to their sovereign before converging on the shivering Ansette. Destin caught Tempest's eye and held his hand out to her. She sheathed her sword and laid it on the end of her bed before taking his hand. The king led her from the room and closed the door behind them. Madrid stood at attention as the king dropped her hand.

"Find who did this," Destin demanded.

"It will be done," Madrid answered solemnly.

The king focused his full attention on Tempest. "I leave my daughter to your care for the night. I can trust you to do this, my lady?"

"Of course, my lord." She'd never said more honest words to him. Tempest wouldn't let anything happen to the princess. "I'll guard her with my life. Your family is my family." The last bit wasn't true, but it was exactly what he needed to hear.

Destin nodded, his blazing, golden gaze softening just a touch. He brushed a kiss over her forehead. "I will not forget this."

What was supposed to sound comforting sounded more like a threat. Tempest read between the lines. If she kept the princess safe, he'd be in her debt. If Ansette came to any harm, there'd be no place Tempest could hide from his wrath.

He pulled away and prowled toward the banister, his purple robe trailing behind him. "And prepare to wake at dawn," he growled. "The rebel scum shall meet their ends as the sun rises."

"Dawn?" she managed to ask evenly.

"They do not deserve to remain breathing," Destin spat, spinning to face her. "If they have no qualms about murdering an innocent girl, they deserve no mercy. They die at dawn."

He strode away, his arms snapping at his sides as he yelled at the soldiers he passed. She watched his imposing figure disappear around the corner, and her shoulders sagged. It was mere hours until the sun rose.

"Best go to bed, Tempest," Madrid murmured, his gaze roving the area for danger.

"As if I will gain any sleep," she muttered.

He glanced at her, her bared legs, and then the myriad of soldiers inhabiting the corridor. "You're unclothed."

She snorted. "I've run naked through the barracks before. My ankles will hardly offend anyone with what is going on. I'm sure none of them have even noticed."

"They've noticed. Did Maxim teach you nothing of men?"

"It's skin. Nothing else."

"You are the king's betrothed and one of his trusted ones. You must act accordingly."

That sobered her. Her gaze strayed back to the closed door. The princess was now in her care. Tempest nodded to Madrid and entered her room. The maids had changed Ansette into a nightgown from Tempest's wardrobe. The girl looked awfully small with her knees hugged to her chest.

Striding over to her small collection of spirits, Tempest poured some whiskey into a cup and maneuvered through the servants who were crooning at the princess. Tempest held the glass out to the princess.

"Drink it," she commanded softly.

Ansette took it gingerly from her hand.

"Do it quickly so it doesn't taste as bad."

The princess tossed back the alcohol and grimaced before handing back the cup.

"It's time for bed."

The girl stood and woodenly moved to the bed. Tempest pulled back the covers and tucked Ansette in before rounding the mattress and crawling in on the other side. She stared at the maids.

"If you intend to stay, make your pallets on the floor and keep silent. The princess needs rest."

Tempest wiggled her body backward until her spine pressed against the headboard. The servants quickly made their beds on the floor and fell silent.

"You're not going to bed?" Ansette whispered to her.

Tempest glanced down at the girl and shook her head. "I'll stay awake to keep watch."

The princess's eyes filled with tears, and she held her hand out. "Thank you."

She eyed Ansette's hand before taking it in her own. The girl squeezed it once before closing her eyes, tears silently tracking down her round, pale cheeks. She never let go. Tempest stared at their clasped hands for a long time. This was not what she'd expected when she'd accepted the king's offer. This was dangerous territory. Unbiddenly, she began to hum her mum's lullaby. The princess's breath eventually slowed and evened out. Even then, Tempest never released the girl's hand.

She gazed out the window.

Dawn would arrive too soon.

And so would Brine's death.

Chapter Nine

Tempest

Tempest's eyes burned as she disentangled herself from the sleeping princess. She'd finally given up and laid down in the bed when her back began to protest sitting in the same position for so long. Two of the maids roused when she sat up, but Tempest waved them back down. Someone might as well get some sleep. She swung her legs over the side of the bed and rubbed her tired eyes, then her hand crept beneath her pillow to retrieve her trusty dagger. There was no way she could lie in bed any longer. She blinked slowly when her fingers came in contact with a piece of parchment. Carefully, she pulled the note from beneath her pillow and tucked it up her sleeve. There was only one person brazen enough to sneak into her room and leave a note.

The Jester.

How had he snuck in? She scanned the room. There was no way he would have risked entering her chambers after the assassination attempt. He must have left it prior. Sloppy. She hadn't even noticed. Tempest glanced over her shoulder at Ansette. What if it had been a poisonous snake or scorpion put into the bed and not a harmless note? Some Hound she was. Her mind turned back to Pyre. Had he left this note or had it been one of his cronies?

What if the Dark Court is responsible for the attempt on the princess's life?

Time to find out.

The rumpled edge of her nightgown fell to her feet as she crept from the bed, skirting around the maids sleeping on the floor. Tempest moved on silent feet into the bathroom and closed the door. Each of her breaths seemed overly loud in the marble room. She pulled the letter from her linen sleeve and unfurled the thick piece of parchment.

Meet me where the bread is made.

How delightfully vague.

She frowned, the cogs in her head working hard to make sense of the Jester's words. A bakery, clearly, but which one? The city hosted hundreds of bakeries.

You've only spent time at one.

Hopefully, he meant the one that served the barracks. If he meant any other one, he should have been more damned specific. She strode to the privy, ripped up the note, and dropped it in before relieving herself. Quickly, she scrubbed her hands, face, and teeth then exited the bathroom and entered her wardrobe.

Tempest settled on a tight-fitting pair of leather trousers and a white blouse along with the same dark cloak from the night before and a pair of thigh-high lace-up boots. With her hair braided back and tucked into the cloak, Tempest looked every inch the nondescript city-dweller. Perfect for blending in.

Dawn was still several hours away. That should be enough time to sneak out and back in before the execution.

She smiled reassuringly at one of the maids who lay awake on their pallet, watching her, before slipping from her room. Soldiers lined the hallway, silent sentinels. Madrid cocked his head in question.

"The princess has had a rough night. I'm going to fetch her something tasty and warm from the bakery. It always calms me when I've had a rough day," she murmured, holding Madrid's gaze.

A young guard smiled at her from down the corridor. "That's very nice of you, my lady."

An older guard next to the boy thumped him on the back of the head. "Do not speak to your betters unless they speak to you," the older man growled.

Madrid arched an eyebrow, his silent communication clear: he didn't believe her story.

Not that it mattered. He was on her side. At least, for now.

She drifted down the hallway and took the servants' stairway. By the time she'd reached the central wing of the palace, the entire place was crawling with guards, who were all incredibly anxious and on-edge. She made sure to keep her hair covered. It would not do well for her to draw undue attention to herself. Surely, rumors were running rampant among those in court about the prior night. The king's betrothed leaving the palace in the early hours of the morning would surely be construed as suspicious to some.

Her gut churned as she checked the sky once more. Dawn would arrive soon, and with Brine and others in the dungeon, she prayed that Pyre had a plan to get his men out.

Her steps slowed when she reached the stairs that led into the grand entrance hall. It would be tricky escaping without being questioned. The entire staff was being questioned by the guards. If she was caught in those passageways, it would seem even more suspicious. Tempest fidgeted and plastered a look of concern on her face when soft footsteps approached almost out of nowhere. She spun to face the new arrival, lies and excuses hovering on her tongue.

Dima blinked at her and placed a hand on her shoulder, his gaze full of questions. "Where are you going?"

"As you know, the princess had a rough night. I thought she might need some comfort this morning. I am going to see the baker about something that might tempt her."

"I see," Dima murmured. "Are you speaking about the kitsune baker?"

She eyed her uncle. Madrid had sent along help.

Or a spy.

"I am."

"Perfect. I have wanted to visit him myself. Follow me," he said, before striding down the nearest servant corridor.

Tempest kept her head down and kept close to Dima. They passed several soldiers interrogating individuals, but no one paid them any mind as they exited through a small kitchen to a narrow hallway. Her uncle yanked open a rough wooden door and gestured for her to go through first. She stepped out into a dark courtyard. Tempest spied sacks of grain leaning against the walls. So, this was where they kept the grain for the castle.

Dima closed the door. "So, a baker, then?" he asked, unlocking the nearest gate and pushing through.

She followed, trying to map out where they were—the west side of the castle, near the barracks, if she had to hazard a guess. Her uncle locked the gate and headed toward the Hound barracks without being prompted. Temp huffed out a breath as she struggled to keep up with Dima's huge strides, although thankful for his speed. There wasn't much time.

"I can only assume that Madrid sent—"

"Yes. He sent me as protection."

That wasn't what she was going to ask. "Protection? I am perfectly able to protect myself."

"True, but you wouldn't have escaped the palace without notice today. This is a dangerous game we're playing. Never let pride stop you from accepting help."

She nodded. "Thank you."

"I'll always help you, lass."

They swept through the quiet upper-class circle of Dotae until they reached the bakery that supplied the barracks. A bell chirped merrily as they opened the door and stepped inside, the scent of yeast, cinnamon, and toasted nuts teasing the air. The baker lifted his head and pointed upward to the attic before returning to sliding out several freshly baked, delicious-smelling loaves of bread from a wood-fired oven.

"I shall remain out here," Dima muttered.

He really wasn't there to spy after all.

Tempest nodded and mouthed a silent *thanks*, then she stalked upstairs. The carved door to the attic was open just a touch. Tempest slowly pushed it open and stepped into the cramped room. Pyre sat on the windowsill, his gaze pinned to the darkness outside. One ear flicked her way before twitching back into place. She closed the door softly and eyed the silent man.

"You summoned me, so here I am," Tempest said flatly.

He glanced at her from the corner of his eye, his lips curling into a small smirk. "Who knew you could be so obedient?"

"Enough," she demanded. "We don't have time to quibble. I need answers. What the bloody hell is Brine doing in the dungeon?"

"Gathering information," he replied, not looking at her. "We were getting ready to release Destin's political prisoners from the dungeon. The king pushing forward this execution has...interfered with those plans."

"*Interfered*?" Tempest hissed, stepping away from the door. "He's doing a bit more than interfering, Pyre! Brine is going to die! Along with anyone else you've placed in that prison."

"It's not ideal—"

"Not ideal?" she whispered. "Would you really let them die?"

He tossed a baleful look her way. "Of course not! Do you think me so cold-blooded?"

Tempest snapped her mouth shut. She was not going to answer that question.

"You do, don't you? You believe I would let my own men die."

"You had the former prince murdered in cold blood."

His upper lip curled, revealing two long canines. "That's not true. The king had his son killed."

"Your men were there," she said harshly and then waved her hand in the space between them. "I'm not here to argue with you. What is your plan?"

"We're going to get them out now," he said, once again staring out the window.

"And how will we manage that?"

"I'll take care of it, *my lady*. You just play your part as the dutiful future queen. Bring no suspicion upon yourself. The king is wily and has many years of experience. He will discover your secrets if you're not careful. I cannot protect you inside the castle."

"I don't need your protection."

"Because you don't need help from anyone?" He

chuckled. "Just stay out of this, Temp."

As much as she wanted to fight against him, she knew he was right. Damn him. Working on the front lines on this particular rescue attempt would jeopardize everything she'd been working for. Even meeting with the kitsune was dangerous enough. Every time they did something like this, the chance of Tempest being caught increased tenfold.

"We cannot meet like this again," she whispered.

He nodded and swallowed. She followed the motion and noticed he was wearing his favorite forest-green cloak, fastened around his neck with a delicate gold chain made up of interlocking leaves. He looked far more like the man she'd first met than he did the Jester or Mal. He looked like...*her* Pyre.

She paused, realizing she'd taken several steps toward him.

Don't be stupid. He's dangerous.

He turned his attention from the horizon back to her face. Dark smudges marred the skin beneath his eyes. He looked tired—more tired than she felt, which was a feat in and of itself. Was it due to stress or had he been up at all hours of the night?

"Pyre," she said softly. "The king has ordered Madrid and me to discover who made the attempt on Princess Ansette's life. I need to know that—"

"It was not my people. We did not attack the girl."

She studied Pyre. He held her stare, his gaze never wavering.

"I believe you," she said finally. His shoulders seemed to sag a little bit at that. Or had she imagined it? "Ansette has been given into my care for the time being but if there are any leads you can give me that would help me catch the one responsible—"

"I will."

"I know I can't personally be involved with this, but if there's anything I can do to help..."

"You can help me by treading carefully," he said, very quietly. "You must be careful with this task he has given you. Destin is not in the habit of keeping around powerful women, Tempest. He is playing a game with you."

"I know that."

"Do you really?" His eyebrow rose in a silent challenge.

"Do you really think I am not always on my guard around him? That man is as dangerous as a southern viper and just as slippery."

"An apt description." He stood, bringing their bodies closer. Tempest tipped her chin up, so she could see his face. "Don't think for one second that he trusts you. Destin might have left Ansette's care in your hands, but it's a trap. It always is."

"I'm not naïve." The threat had been clear the prior night.

"He's trying to draw out those who oppose him by using his children. Don't let him snag you in one of his webs. There's only one way out: death."

Pyre's gaze scanned her face, his expression softening. He reached for her cheek, and Tempest's traitorous heart flipped. She took a small step back, and his fingers curled into a fist. He lowered his hand, all expression wiped from his face.

"Please be careful," he said, emotion leaking into his voice. "I'm serious, Temp. Listen to me this time. For once in your life, just...listen to me. Do not do anything rash today."

His desperate words slammed into her. Tempest felt like she could barely breathe. There was real emotion in Pyre's words—and on his face. She hadn't dealt with this side of the kitsune in a long time. She'd almost convinced herself that it didn't exist.

His ears twitched, and he inhaled deeply, something warm entering his molten eyes. Panic seized her. She couldn't deal with him like this. Handling the stony faced Mal or the care-free Jester was one thing, but the soft, caring side of the kitsune she had met in the forest? She had no defense against him.

Pyre took another step closer as she took one backward, keeping the same amount of space between their bodies. But then he glided forward, his steps predatory. Tempest halted, refusing to run. Letting him stalk her would only rouse his baser instincts. His hands cupped her face and tilted it up to him as her hands rested on his chest to keep him from getting closer. Pyre paused, his mouth an inch from hers, and the world around them began to fade. Tempest shuddered when his warm breath teased her lips. Her pulse raced through her veins.

"Temp, I want to kiss you," he whispered, his voice all

honey and sin. His hot amber eyes soaked in her expression. "Yes or no?"

Yes. *Yes.*

Her hands softened against his chest for one second before reality came crashing in. Despite her hatred for the king, she was no adulterer.

"We can't." The words hurt to say.

He lifted his head, iron stillness running through his body. "I want you. This isn't a game to me."

Her will wavered, and she almost swayed against him. It would be too easy to fall into his arms.

Neither one of them could afford that.

"I made promises. Please don't make me break my vows. Or my honor." It was a plea, but she didn't care.

Pyre shuddered, his eyes closing. He tore away from her and stalked toward the window. The look he shot Tempest was dark, dangerous, and hungry. "You want me. Your scent calls to *me*."

"What I want and what I should do are not the same." Her words felt hollow.

He glanced away. "I always forget that you're a better person than me."

Her heart ached as she took another step toward the attic door. If she didn't leave now, she'd do something stupid. "I'm not any better than you. We're no different."

A dry chuckle escaped him as he ran his hands over his head, disheveling his hair. "That's where you're wrong, love. I would lie, cheat, and steal to obtain what I want." His molten stare left nothing to the imagination of what he wanted. Her.

"Just save Brine and the rest of your men," she finally uttered. "Just...save them."

"I will try," he answered.

He pushed the window open, and leaped from the windowsill into the dark pre-dawn without a goodbye.

I will try.

His words chilled her to the bone.

The Jester had always been cocksure, arrogant, and certain. The was never a question of whether or not he could accomplish anything he set his mind to.

But the Jester was just a mirage.

Pyre was a man with faults and limitations like any man.

Brine could die.

Trust him to succeed.

There was nothing she could do now *but* trust him.

When had she become so useless?

Chapter Ten

Pyre

He'd made a mistake.

Pyre should have sent someone in his stead. But, like a fool, he'd arranged a meeting.

Scrubbing his hand over his face, he stared at the storm approaching as the sky began to lighten. The ship rocked beneath his feet as he pinched the bridge of his nose and tried to calm himself down. Each time he left her behind, his soul rebelled. If he wasn't careful, he'd cross a line that neither one of them could return from.

Would that be so bad?

He cursed and dropped his hands, glaring at the turbulent ocean waters. As soon as she'd stepped into the attic, all he'd wanted to do was kiss her and press her back against the faded paint of the bakery wall and lick his way down her throat.

It was dangerous and dumb.

"It's almost time," Chesh said softly.

Pyre scowled. He'd been so lost in his thoughts about his mate he'd not even heard the cat approach. He glanced to his left and eyed his friend. Chesh pulled at the collar along his throat, exposing several intricate tattoos.

"Good. If everything goes to plan, the men will be on your ship within a few hours," Pyre muttered.

The cat flicked an amused look his way. "And yet that's not what's on your mind. You stink of frustration. You should have just kept her locked away in your cabin until she capitulated and accepted you as her mate."

He glared at Chesh. "You would keep your mate as a prisoner?"

"There's no telling what I'd do if I came upon my mate."

"That's the damn truth." Pyre turned his attention back to the ocean, observing the occasional fin slice through the inky water. It seemed like he'd reeled himself back hundreds of times when it came to Tempest. He'd need to make a decision soon on how to proceed. If he didn't, his shifter side would make the decision for him. Neither Tempest—nor he, himself—would enjoy that. "Have you spoken to Damien?"

Chesh eyed him but allowed the subject change. "He's causing mischief as always, but he has the militia well in hand. Our men are ready. Did Brine get the information he needed?"

"He did. Let's hope it was worth the cost." Pyre nodded as the first snowflake fell from the sky. "If anything goes south, you'll have to sail in this weather."

The cat smiled lazily. "No need to be worried. I love a spot of adventure."

Chapter Eleven

Robyn

Helping the local people of Locksley was the highlight of Robyn's week.

It always started with a visit to the bakery with her elderly father to pick up hot bread rolls for the children at the local school. Many of them were orphans or from families with so many children that they could not hope to feed them all properly. While it killed her not to be able to donate food every day, she took pride in what her family was able to do. The fiefdom of Locksley may have been small, but they prided themselves on generosity.

Next, Robyn and her father moved to the town hall to speak with the elders, who, more often than not, complained about the war brewing just under the surface of their province Merjeri. It always soured her mood. Former Lord Merjeri had been a horrid man who'd deserved to be strung up for his crimes and yet had gotten away with everything. His son was even worse. His prejudice didn't extend to only the Talagan people, but also to the poor and those born female. Her stomach always churned when his lordship was brought up. He cared nothing for the people he governed, and had more blood on his hands than the Jester. Something needed to change. The villages in the province were proof of that, with their poverty and lack of working-age men and women within its walls. Too many of the residents were old and infirm or so young they were yet to possess any adult teeth—not that it kept the lord from working them to death.

After meeting with the elders, Robyn and her father would part ways for the afternoon; she'd head to help the few young maidens who *did* live in the village with washing and dyeing fabrics while her father visited the blacksmiths to see if he could help with the horses or any leatherwork. Back in his day, he'd been incredibly gifted with both and had been an asset to the army.

He was still an asset, despite what others may think.

She pinned a length of cotton to the line and pushed an errant hair from her face, her heart aching for her father. During the last rebellion, her father had permanently damaged his left leg and right shoulder. She'd been just a toddler at the time and didn't understand why he hadn't picked her up or chased her like other fathers did. Despite his injuries, he'd always been a major part of her life. Always setting aside his work when she or her brother wanted his attention.

Her breath caught, and she stifled a gasp as grief threatened to choke her. Robyn's eyes watered, and she stared at the basket of wet laundry, her hands on her hips. The death of her twin had left a gaping hole in her soul. Most days, she felt like half of a person without John. She had been the first born and John had arrived a few minutes after her. He hadn't grown like the other boys of the village and had a weak constitution. Her parents had kept him sheltered from the world—not out of shame, but to protect him. John had been a sweet idealist with a generous heart and gentle soul. It still seemed unfair that such a person was gone from the world.

Most days, she felt like she should have been the one to die.

Robyn wiped the back of her arm across her eyes. Now, she lived for both of them.

She reached for the next linen and frowned when the thunder of approaching horses reached her ears. Robyn straightened and glanced at the three young women working around her who all had their eyes trained on the soldiers approaching.

Please, let it not be Lord Merjeri and his men.

The soldiers had a foul reputation of accosting young women, and recently Merjeri had turned his attention toward Robyn. She shuddered as she thought of the courting gifts he'd sent, her eyes pinned to the approaching mass. Even if she had to disgrace herself, she'd make damned sure that he'd never get access to her or her dowry. Dotae only knew what he'd do with the wealth.

The tension between her shoulder blades disappeared as she spotted several purple-haired members flanking the group of soldiers. The King's Hounds. Maybe they were going to put a stop to Merjeri's corruption for once.

Robyn snorted and watched as the soldiers passed by, their hooves clacking against the stone cobbles of the village street. She peered down the lane as the soldiers leapt from their mounts and began systematically moving to each home, leaving either a scroll with the owner or nailing it to the door.

She dropped the linen back into the basket and nodded at the girls. "You stay here. Keep your head down and don't draw attention."

"Yes, my lady," the girls chorused.

Robyn edged along the madness as the townspeople began to make their way to the village square. She lifted her hood over her hair and melted into the crowd as a Hound jumped onto the edge of the well that sat in the middle of the square. The crowd murmured around her, and she spotted her father, his limp more pronounced as he shuffled toward her. He would definitely need a poultice tonight to help with the pain. Maybe some salts and incense from the apothecary for his bath as well.

Her father made it to her side, and she wrapped her right arm around his waist, supporting some of his weight.

"Sweet girl, I am all right."

He wasn't, but she wouldn't point it out. "Do you know

what this is about?"

"Something Merjeri has done, no doubt," he muttered.

Her left fingers curled into a fist. Locksley was always taxed the hardest for Lord Merjeri's mistakes. The bastard.

"Come forth and heed your king's decree!" the Hound called, his voice cutting through the murmurs.

"What is it now?" Robyn's father grumbled. "There is nothing here for them. Nothing for the king. What could he want from us?"

Robyn knew he was not talking about crops and livestock.

The Hound held out his hand to a messenger dressed in finery. The thin man stepped up onto the well's edge as the Hound jumped down. The pompous man unrolled the parchment in his hands. He peered over the top of the edge and then began in a nasal voice.

"War is upon us!"

She froze, her heart thundering as her father cursed.

"The king's army has already suffered heavy losses at the hands of the Talagan traitors. Therefore, we must turn to our ever-faithful, loving citizens to draft new soldiers for our kingdom."

And there it was.

Robyn gritted her teeth and glared at the messenger. They were taking people for the fight—people the village could not afford to spare. There were hardly any men left after the last uprising.

"Each family shall submit every man over the age of

fourteen to our cause. No family will be spared the sacrifice, low or highborn. But, rest assured, each and every one of you should be honored to do this. It is a privilege to fight for your country. The king is proud and grateful to call you his subjects."

But that means...

Her body flashed hot and then cold as she turned to her father whose face had become ashen. He was the only man in their family. The *only* one.

They meant for *him* to fight in this war.

It meant certain death.

"This is madness!" she cried before she could stop herself. Robyn released her hold on her father, storming forward. The village folk parted as she strode toward the impassive Hound and haughty messenger.

"And who are you?" the messenger sneered, his eyes raking her clothing.

Robyn pushed back her hood, held her head high, and didn't let herself waver as she felt the gaze of the soldiers on her. "I am Lady Marian of Locksley." Her formal name felt odd on her tongue. She waved around at the frightened members of the village. "Can you not see there are no men capable of fighting here? And winter is upon us—we need what few young men we possess to help with the last of the harvest. You cannot expect the elderly, or families who haven't the sons to spare, to take part in this war!"

"Ah, Lady Marian. Women do have such bleeding hearts," an annoyingly familiar voice laughed.

Her hackles raised as Lord Merjeri stepped from the crowd behind the well. He smiled at her, his expression patronizing. Her hand tingled, itching to slap his smug face.

"You know nothing of the honor of war, my lady," he crooned. "Every man in this village—young *and* old—wants to fight for their kingdom. Dying for one's king is a noble thing—"

"Death is not noble, my lord. Glory will not feed the people, will not fill our king's coffers—"

"Robyn, stop this," her father chastised quietly.

His fingers brushed against her right sleeve, and she swallowed down the treasonous words she'd been about to spout. It was a difficult thing, but out of sheer respect and trust in her father, she bowed her head and played the spineless, submissive woman Lord Merjeri expected her to be.

"Your men have three days to arrive at the war camp with your orders," the messenger called. He rolled up the scroll and waved a negligent hand at the crowd. "Be off with you."

Her father gently gripped her arm, and Robyn kept her eyes on the cobblestones, so no one saw the rage and mutiny that writhed inside her. She and her father made their way back to their mounts they'd left at the tavern stable that morning without a single word. Her mind spun during the ride through the fields back to Locksley Keep. What were they supposed to do? Her father could no more fight than she could turn into a shifter.

Snow began to fall as they entered the grounds of the keep. Jim, the old horse master, met them in the courtyard and took their horses. Maya, the housekeeper, opened the huge double doors. Maya's round cheeks were pink as they made it up the stairs and into Robyn's family home.

"There's a hot bath awaiting you, my lord," the housekeeper said to Robyn's father with a small curtsey.

Robyn yanked off her cloak and hung it, her back to her father. "What are we going to do?"

"We will discuss it later," he said firmly.

She swung around and snapped her mouth shut at how weary he looked. There would be time to speak later, once he'd warmed up. Shame started creeping up her spine as she gazed at her father. "Are you angry at me?"

He shuffled over to her and pressed a kiss to her brow. "I'm not angry at you, dearest."

Her shoulders slumped as he limped away and disappeared around the corner.

"You look mighty upset, miss. Is there anything I can do?" Maya asked, her brown eyes full of concern.

"Not yet." Robyn sighed, massaging the back of her neck. "Where is Mama?"

The housekeeper pursed her lips. "In bed. She has not left it all day. It has been a...bad day, Lady Robyn."

If Maya was admitting it was a bad day, then it must have been truly horrendous. Her mother was rarely lucid these days, and her manic days were the worst. Robyn reached out and clasped the housekeeper's shoulder. Maya had been her mum's companion before she'd married. They had spent nearly thirty years together.

"She'll be better when he visits her," Maya said softly.

Robyn nodded. Her father was the only one who could calm her mother when she flew into manic rages. He dutifully read to his wife every night and made sure she was treated with love and respect. It was plain as day to see it broke him a little more each day, but his love never wavered.

Robyn released Maya and drifted toward the stairs, fighting back a sob as she took each step. If her father went to war, how would her mother survive?

Locksley Keep was barely held together.

Chapter Twelve

Tempest

I will try.

Tempest tried to keep her nerves in check as she snuck back inside the castle, Pyre's warnings and wishes ringing loudly in her head. Dima accompanied her until they once again reached the grand hall. Not once had her uncle spoken since they'd left the bakery. He gave her a short nod and disappeared back the way they came.

She gazed after him for a moment before moving swiftly up the nearest set of servants' stairs. Two warm pastries wrapped in paper crinkled with her movements. Her legs burned as she sprinted up each level, her gaze constantly straying to the windows as the darkness turned from black to dark gray to a light blue far more rapidly than she was comfortable with. The rebels' execution would be held within the hour, which meant she had no time to waste in getting back to her chambers and getting dressed for it.

Her pace slowed as she neared the royal wing, and she pulled the pastries from her pocket, hoping they weren't too squished. She exhaled slowly and stepped from the servants' corridor. Her footsteps echoed on the marble and then her boots squeaked as the floor transitioned to a deep, dark, polished wood. Tempest glanced around in confusion. Where were all the guards?

Something wasn't right.

The hair along the nape of her neck stood, and goosebumps prickled along her forearms. She paused and glanced down the empty hallway that eventually led to her rooms and listened carefully. Nothing. It was too still.

Someone is following you.

Tempest feigned calmness and began walking once again as if she didn't have a care in the world. Her ears strained as she listened for any sign of pursuit. The scuff of a boot against stone was her only warning. She clutched the pastries with her left hand and grabbed the hilt of her sword as she spun to face the intruder.

No one was there.

The bastard was hiding.

"Show yourself," she demanded, settling into a fighting stance as she pulled her sword free from the scabbard.

"But I've been so enjoying our little game of hide and seek," crooned a familiar, haughty voice.

The curtains at the end of the hallway were swept away and out stepped the prince.

Winter's bite. Just what she needed.

Maven was thoroughly disheveled, his dark hair and clothing so rumpled, she had no doubt he'd thoroughly celebrated the night before in bed with a woman or two. *Like father, like son.*

Tempest schooled her expression. There was something about him that sent chills skittering down her spine. An emptiness in his eyes. No, that wasn't right. It was the darkly calculated way he looked at her, like he was thinking of a thousand different ways to hurt her, all while wearing a smile.

He tilted his chin upward and sniffed in distaste. "Men's trousers? I thought my father would have trained you better by now."

"I assure you, no man would be able to wear these trousers, my lord. They were made for a woman." She cocked a hip out, pulling his attention to the curve there. Maybe she could distract him enough that he would go away.

"I suppose they are flattering in a crass sort of way," he drawled. "Must be difficult to remove, though. A pity," he murmured.

Tempest slid her sword back into the scabbard at her hip and shrugged. "No more than a corset."

"Trousers, corsets, and sneaking about." Maven sighed. "We'll never make a lady of you. Speaking of which, where have you been? You weren't in your chambers."

"You were in my room?"

He waved a hand at her and sauntered a few steps

forward. “There is no place I cannot go in the palace. It is all mine. No one and nothing can keep me from what I want. Now, answer me. Where have you been?” Suspicion saturated his tone.

Maven had every right to be leery of her. She should have been asleep. It wasn’t even dawn yet, after all. She had no reason to be out so early.

“Where I am and what I’m doing is of no concern to you,” she replied, trying her best to project haughtiness right back at the prince. Then she added a bow for good measure. “Your Royal Highness, you say I was not in my room. Were you looking for me for something in particular?”

“I wanted to see what you thought of the attack on my sister’s life. So, where were you?” His eyes narrowed. “You may be betrothed to my father, but you’re not queen yet. I am your prince. You will answer me.”

She held out the pastries in her left hand. “After the night Princess Ansette had, I thought she might like something yummy.”

“The palace could have provided something twice as scrumptious,” he pointed out, taking another step in her direction.

“Probably, but there’s nothing better than a well-meant gift from a friend after experiencing something horrific.” Tempest held her ground and took a step toward the prince, determined not to let him frighten her. “And, as for my thoughts on the attack against your sister, more information is needed before I can truly make any sort of sense of the atrocity."

"What diplomatic words," Maven sneered. "Maybe a lady can be made out of you yet." He paused and tried to smooth out the wrinkles in his waistcoat. "Does my father know about your good deeds?"

That was a threat if she ever heard one. She kept all expression from her face. "Feel free to tell him." Tempest beamed at him. "I'm sure the king will appreciate my good deeds toward his *favorite* child." That may be too far, but she had to come away from this conversation triumphant. Bullies like the prince always got worse until someone stood up to them. "I'm sure your father would be curious about why you thought it prudent to wake his queen-to-be before the sun had risen to question her about the horrors of the night," she said, trying to get the upper hand. "To wake your *future queen* from her sleep and to enter her bedchamber—"

"But you were not asleep."

"Perhaps I could not sleep because I was so disturbed by what I saw," Tempest countered. "As I've said twice now, it's none of your—"

"I am the heir to the throne," Maven bit out testily, anger leaking onto his face. "It *is* my concern."

"The last time I checked, I answered to your father."

"You gutter-side slut." He stormed toward Tempest until he was barely a foot from her. The prince towered over, but she forced herself to remain unperturbed. He was trying to intimidate her, and she wouldn't stand for it. Prince or not, if he got one more inch closer, she'd teach him some manners, the king be damned. Hell, Destin would probably thank her.

"What fine manners you possess, my lord," she said calmly, her left hand curling around the pastries.

"You should be careful what you do and say, *Lady* Tempest," Maven whispered, his voice soft and menacing. "You might find yourself playing right into the hands of someone who means to ensnare you."

"I'm an assassin. It's my job to do the trapping."

His lips split into a wide, mocking smile. Though, in the space of a second, it disappeared as if it had never been there in the first place. Tempest held stock-still as he raised his hand and fingered a curl that had escaped her braid.

"You've been warned."

He released her hair and turned on his heel, leaving with such abruptness that she found herself rooted to the spot as he disappeared down the adjacent hallway. She sucked in a sharp breath and blinked slowly, her heart pounding.

Why had the prince been looking for her in the first place? They had little need for each other, other than to throw barbs back and forth. Why bring up his sister's attack? It was clear there was no love lost between the two siblings.

He entered your room.

Maven was hunting for something. He was suspicious of her, but she suspected he was leery of everyone. Was it because he'd found evidence of her treason? She brushed that thought away. If he had actual proof, he'd have cast her to the lions already.

He was in your room.

Had Madrid let him inside? What was the prince after? He'd never sought her chambers before.

Ansette.

Her suspicion of the prince grew stronger with every passing second. What if he had sanctioned the attack on his sister? Tempest hadn't missed the flash of anger that had crossed the prince's face when she'd said *favorite child.* Destin gained nothing from his daughter's death, but the prince...the prince had everything to lose if he lost the favor of the king. Ansette could very well be named the successor of the throne if Maven caused too many issues.

Troubled, she made her way back to her chambers, noting Madrid was now stationed down the hallway, speaking in a low tone to the captain of the guards. She slipped into her room and frowned at the lack of servants. Why was the princess left alone?

Ansette stood by the southern window, her thin arms wrapped around herself. The girl glanced Tempest's way, before staring out the window once again.

Tempest closed the door and padded toward the princess. She halted, her cloak fluttering around her feet. "You should not be near the window, my lady," she said softly.

The girl nodded. "I know, but I feel like I can breathe better when I can see the outside."

That was something Tempest understood. She held out

the wrapped pastries.

"What are these?" Ansette whispered.

"Whenever I had a particularly hard day, my uncles would bring me a pastry from a nearby bakery. It didn't make the problem go away, but the tiny gift always gave me some comfort."

The princess's eyes filled with tears, and she gingerly took one of the treats from Temp's outstretched hand before throwing herself into Tempest's arms. Tempest huffed as Ansette hugged her fiercely.

"Thank you," she cried.

Tempest gingerly wrapped her arms around the princess. "It was nothing, truly."

Ansette pulled back and wiped her eyes. "In our world, it is everything."

A knock sounded on the door, and Madrid popped his head inside. "You have half an hour before I am to retrieve you for the execution."

"Thank you," she murmured as he closed the door.

The princess unwrapped the almond pastry and took a big bite. "So good."

"I'm glad you think so," Tempest muttered, her mind racing. "Did you see your brother this morning?"

"He arrived early to check on me," the girl said around another mouthful of food. "It was a surprise, to be sure."

Tempest massaged her forehead with the palm of her hand, beyond frustrated. Just what was the prince up to? Was he simply trying to create chaos—taking matters into his own hands to pin another crime on the rebellion? Or was he vying for the Crown by attempting to take out any possible threats to his future, including his sister?

She shivered. The second option felt too possible to her for her to discount it. People had killed for much less.

She had enemies coming from all sides, and no way to defend herself from all of them at once.

Chapter Thirteen

King Destin

The guards said nothing as he entered Tempest's room.

He closed the door behind him and observed the quiet space. His Hound was quite meticulous in how she kept her rooms. A splash and a soft curse alerted the king as to where his betrothed was. In the bathroom. What fun it would be to surprise her, only they didn't have time for that type of frolicking. He contented himself by nosing about the room, checking drawers here and there. One could never be sure what kind of secrets a lady kept.

Destin drifted into her wardrobe. Untouched dresses lined the walls. He ran his fingers along the fine fabric and jeweled bodices. Many women would kill for such a treasure trove of high fashion, but not Tempest. She was loath to wear extravagant garments. Such a fickle creature she was. He paused next to the gown she'd worn for their betrothal ceremony and sniffed the fabric. The hair along his forearms stood on end as the scents of lavender, mint, and something wholly feminine filled his nose. What was it about her that he found so alluring? Over the years, he'd had the pleasure of some of the most astonishing beauties in the kingdom, and yet, while Tempest wasn't a particular beauty, there was something that kept him wanting more.

You like her mind.

For someone so young and unseasoned, she was the perfect puzzle. No doubt her unusual upbringing had something to do with it. Even the most bloodthirsty women he'd come across still didn't like the nitty and gritty of real violence. The Lady Hound, on the other hand… She didn't bat an eye at the gore of the prior night. That was the type of queen Heimserya needed for what was to come.

At least, it was until she proved herself to no longer be useful.

In the meantime, he'd revel in the challenges she gave him. He would rise to eagerly meet the occasion until the novelty of his new wife grew old.

The door to the bathroom squeaked, and the king moved to the opening of the wardrobe. He leaned against the molding and waited for his betrothed to emerge. Tempest had a few questions to answer. Someone had tried to murder his precious daughter—the only member of his family he held any modicum of affection for—and he needed to make sure he could trust her. She'd proven nothing but faithful so far, but one could never be too careful. It was those who looked innocent who were sometimes the most dangerous. His father had taught him that lesson.

His betrothed took one step from the bathroom, a silk dressing gown clinging to her wet skin in patches. He grinned as she halted, inhaled deeply, and then pushed the skirt of her robe away, revealing a dagger strapped to her creamy upper thigh.

How delightful she was.

"There's no need for that, darling," he crooned.

Her gaze snapped to him, and she released the skirt of the robe, hiding her body from him once more.

A pity.

"I let myself in," he drawled when she said nothing.

"I can see that."

He arched a brow, and, as if remembering herself, she dipped into a low curtsey.

"My apologies, my lord. I was not expecting you." Her attention darted to the clock on the nightstand. "Is it time already? I was told I had at least a quarter of an hour before you expected me."

"True." He eyed her unbound hair. "Consider me pleasantly surprise to find you in such a state. Although, as I've been told by many women, getting ready takes much time."

His Hound actually smiled at that. "I'm not sure how so much time is wasted, but I can assure you, I'll be presentable if you'll give me fifteen minutes."

That was a politely worded invitation for him to leave if he'd ever heard one. Destin pushed away from the door jamb and approached her slowly. There were things he needed to discuss with her before they left this room. If the conversation happened while she got dressed, so be it.

He ran the fingers of his left hand over the loose sleeve and across the shoulder of her robe, and gently traced part of her collarbone with his forefinger. Physical touch always seemed to rile her.

"Where have you been, my lady?" he asked softly, watching her expression closely.

"Bathing as of recently."

"And before?"

She gestured to a pair of damp boots near the fire. "I retrieved some breakfast for the princess."

He cocked his head, smoothing his hand down her arm again. "Does she not have servants for that type of thing?"

"She does, my lord."

"So why then were you spotted outside the castle?"

Tempest sighed. "I wanted to make her feel safe."

"A legion of guards and Hounds protecting her is not enough?"

Her gray eyes met his. "Do you have something that makes you feel grounded? Any time I had a horrid day, my uncles would always bring me a treat from a nearby bakery. It brought me comfort. I wished to do the same for Ansette." She oozed earnestness.

The tension in his shoulders drifted away, and he smiled. "That was very kind."

She shrugged, very unladylike, and shifted on her feet. "It was nothing. Anyone would have done it."

"Perhaps so, but not for the reasons you've expressed." Destin crooked a finger beneath her chin and tipped her head back. "Why dress as a commoner? My men reported that you were not in uniform."

"It's far easier to move about when dressed like a commoner. It's much better for me to travel under the guise of anonymity. Almost from birth, I've been trained to blend in. I cannot blend in when wearing jewels and ballgowns."

Destin cocked his head to the side as he considered Tempest's answer. She seemed honest, and he agreed with her reasoning, but he had never met a *truly* honest woman. They always had secret agendas.

"Would you lie to me, Temp?" he murmured. "About anything?"

"You are trying to trap me in a complicated answer," she retorted. Her eyes were clear and straightforward, her mouth a hard line.

"I wish to know the truth. Now, answer me."

"I would lie to protect your life. That was part of the oath I swore when I officially became a member of the Hounds. I would lie, cheat, and murder if it meant protecting the crown. It is my duty. If this is not an acceptable answer, then you may send me away. I will not protest."

Her shoulders pulled back as she stood to her full height, which was nothing compared to his. Destin grinned at the stubborn point of her chin and the way she braced herself as if he'd toss her out that very moment. It was the absolute last thing on his mind. Her answer had been charming. It was well-spoken, and true. Now, all that was left was to kiss away her attitude.

The king leaned down and pressed his lips to hers.

For the briefest of moment, she froze beneath him. Destin wrapped his other arm around her waist and pulled her body against his own as her mouth softened and obediently parted when the tip of his tongue flicked across her bottom lip. He smiled into the kiss. It was a heady feeling to make the Lady Hound lose some of her composure.

Heat surged though him. This was the farthest he had pushed his queen-to-be so far, but that excitement quickly dampened. Tempest obediently gave him what he asked for. There was no challenge or passion in her kiss. It was as if she was merely acting the part of his future wife, taking part in the act only as long as Destin wished for it to continue. Maybe most men wanted a moldable wife in bed, but the king wanted someone to fight—to subdue.

He pulled away and brushed his nose along hers. "Do you not like this?" he murmured.

She blinked at him, color high in her cheeks. "I know nothing of such things, sire. I only wish to please you."

"You will," he assured her, releasing her chin and pushing loose hair from her face. "Do not worry yourself. I delight in your innocence. I'll simply have to work out how to entice you once we are married. It will be a learning experience for us both." He looked forward to owning her body and breaking her in slowly. It was a challenge he'd meet with eagerness.

Tempest touched Destin's right hand with her own. "I am tired, Your Grace."

Going by the dark circles under her eyes, he could believe it.

"After what happened last night and the fact I've only just returned, I must admit you took me by surprise. I—"

A knock on the door interrupted her, and a young maid with white hair entered without waiting to be told she could do so. "I'm the third one who's been sent up to rouse you," she said as she placed a fresh set of clothes on the chair near the fire, her gaze downcast. "The king will not be happy when you are late!"

"Indeed, I will not," he rumbled.

The young maid squeaked and dropped into a deep curtsey. "Forgive me, Your Grace!"

He eyed the girl who hadn't dared look up from the floor. Her hair looked suspiciously like feathers. *A shapeshifter.*

"Do not let the staff badger you, my lady," he said to Tempest.

"I'll try to do better, my lord."

He ignored the servant and pressed a kissed to his betrothed's lips. "I shall see you at the execution, Tempest."

Destin shot one more disgusted look at the servant girl and then exited the rooms.

Time to move another piece on the board.

Let the executions begin.

Chapter Fourteen

Tempest

Tempest couldn't even look at Juniper. Her stomach was sick; she'd been avoiding her friend for months. What was she supposed to say to her? She blankly gazed to the door, still reeling from the king's impromptu visit as well as his interrogation and kiss. Had the prince gone to his father after all? Thoughts for another time. She needed to deal with Juniper.

With a thump, Juniper tossed a pile of linens onto Tempest's bed, then retrieved the fresh underclothes from the brocade chair and stormed across the room. She thrust them into Tempest's arms. Her huge owl-like eyes narrowed.

"Are you going to say anything to your former best friend?" she demanded. "Or are you just going to stand there in silence and pray that I disappear?"

"You are not my *former* best friend," Tempest said, though her voice was small and listless. What right did she have to call anybody a friend right now? It was too bloody dangerous to have any friends. Especially Talagan friends. She hadn't missed how the king had looked at Juniper before he left.

"Oh, so you're *not* too good for me, then? You're not above having shifters in your social circle? Because it damned well looks that way to—"

Tempest dropped the undergarments and threw her arms around her oldest friend before she could stop herself, burrowing her nose in the girl's snowy hair and willing herself not to cry.

Juniper stilled in her arms before finally returning the hug.

"Tempest?" she said, though her voice was muffled against Tempest's chest. "Just what is going on?"

"I'm not above having shifter friends." Tempest pulled back. "That's never been the case. I'm sorry about the way I've been acting. I really am. I never wanted to hurt you."

"Then..." June choked on her next words and grabbed Tempest's hands. "Why the king? What in Dotae's name are you doing marrying King Destin?"

That was a loaded question.

"He took an interest in me."

"You're better than that," Juniper retorted.

"I want to make things better," Tempest whispered. "For *everyone*. In order to help as many people as possible, I have to make some personal sacrifices...including giving my freedom to the king. As queen, I can help *all* of Heimserya—and the Talagans, too, if I play my cards right."

"He'll never allow it."

"I can't do *nothing.*" She paused to rub her face against Juniper's hair, a gesture of affection in Juniper's family nest. "How can I stand by and not help when I've seen the way you've been treated our whole life? What kind of friend does that make me if I have the ability to make a change for the best but I do nothing?"

Juniper pulled out of Tempest's embrace, vehemently shaking her head. "We're speaking of your life!"

"I'm speaking of thousands of lives."

Juniper eyed the door nervously before speaking in an undertone: "There are...rumors...of King Destin killing his women. There's too much truth to them for *all* the rumors to be false. You know this! Marrying the king at this point feels like a death wish!"

"They're just rumors."

But Tempest knew they weren't. Three of the king's mistresses had been found dead in the harbor. That was no coincidence. And, after spending time in the company of the king, she was inclined to believe every depraved rumor abounding about Destin.

Tempest held her hands out, palms up. She'd made her bed, now she had to lie in it.

Preferably with a nine-inch blade in her hand and one eye open.

"You know *better,*" Juniper said.

She forced a smile to her face. "I'm a Hound, or have you forgotten that, Juniper? I am not so easy to kill. Who bested a lion? I'll be able to handle one man."

"He's not a man, but a monster."

"Be careful with your words," Tempest chastised gently. "You never know when someone might be listening."

Both women fell silent.

"So, you're to be married..." Juniper started. "Bloody hell, that is weird to say. And it feels like it was only yesterday that you had your Trial. How is that possible?"

"I feel years older."

In a matter of months, her life had been thrown upside down. So much had changed. Alliances had been made—and betrayals, too. Enemies and friends. Nausea rolled over Tempest, and she inhaled sharply.

Please, please let Brine and his men be okay.

"Temp?" Juniper cried, clutching at Tempest's shoulder until she steadied herself. "What is wrong? Your face—oh, you're so pale. Are you sure you're okay? I will kill the king himself if he has—"

"I'm just tired," Tempest said through gritted teeth. It was painful keeping the truth from Juniper. It would be so easy to spill her secrets to her friend. But the risk wasn't worth it. She had to protect Juniper. "I need to get ready. The king expects me."

Though Pyre had insisted Tempest not interfere with his rescue attempt, she couldn't hide in her room while it went on either. And besides, it was out of character for her *not* to attend the execution as Destin's fierce and fearless future queen, who'd given him the heart of the Jester and helped him quash the rebellion.

She had to get herself together.

"More is wrong than you just being tired," Juniper insisted, as Tempest strode into the wardrobe and selected a sober black-and-gray dress.

"Life in the palace is...a lot."

She exited the wardrobe with the garment, and June held out a glass of water and took the elegant dress from her. "Drink up."

Tempest forced the cold liquid down with shaking hands and inwardly berated herself for being so transparent.

Juniper laid the dress on the bed and began to unlace the back. "It's all abuzz in the castle. Did somebody really try to murder the princess last night? Is that why you're so upset?"

She nodded. In truth, she had no space in her heart right now to worry about Ansette. The princess was out of danger as much as she could possibly be. "It was fortunate that the princess had not been in bed. Not so much for her maid."

Her friend gasped.

Tempest glanced at Juniper and regretted her calloused words at once. She set her glass down on the trunk at the foot of her bed and swept the owlet into her arms. "I'm so sorry."

"Jess," June stuttered. "Princess Ansette's handmaid.

She didn't return to her room this morning when her shift had ended. She's dead?"

A lump filled Tempest's throat, and she felt genuine tears burn the corners of her eyes. What was wrong with her today? Her emotions were all over the place.

Hold it together. There's no other choice.

"What happened?"

Lie.

"She was covering for the princess so Ansette could stay at the betrothal ceremony longer," Tempest explained, choosing her words very carefully. "It was a horrible accident. But she—Jess didn't feel a thing. Her death was quick, and she was sound asleep when it happened."

"Her poor family."

She nodded, the memory of Ansette's room rising to the forefront of her mind. It was a sight she'd never be able to wipe from her mind as long as she lived. How would they return the girl's body to her family? Tempest frowned, making a mental note to speak to Madrid about it. No one else needed to imagine the horrors that had gone on in the princess's rooms.

Glancing at the window, she winced. Her time was up.

"I don't mean to be indelicate, but I really do have to go."

Juniper wiped her eyes and nodded. "Thank you for letting me know. I hope something like this doesn't happen again. It—it *won't* happen again, will it?"

"Of course not," Tempest reassured her. "Destin has

tripled the palace guards for now. And you always have me to protect you. Don't worry, everything will be all right. Just keep your head down and focus on your job."

"I won't draw attention to myself. Working at the palace has taught me many things. While advantageous, it is not always a safe place to be Talagan."

Temp nodded. "I promise to change that."

Juniper inclined her head. "I know you will. Let's get you dressed." She lifted the dress from the bed and shook it. "Out of that robe." A wry smile crossed her impish face. "It's such a change to see you in something so…"

"Feminine?" Tempest drawled, shirking her robe. Her skin pebbled, and she shivered as Juniper lifted the gown over Tempest's head.

"I was going to say so fine. Now, hold still while I get you wrangled into this dress and get your hair presentable."

Juniper was a master.

After ten minutes of fussing, tugging, and pulling Tempest into the tightly laced dress of onyx and smoke with trailing silver lace and too many pearl pins in her hair, she was finished. Juniper tutted quietly and adjusted a stray wave here and there.

Tempest stared at the mirror. She looked like a proper lady. Except for the hair. Women in court wore their hair in ringlets. Hers was wavy at best, not that she minded. She was proud of her periwinkle hair. It showed her off for what she was—a Hound of the Madrid line. Given that they had all put their lives on the line for the sake of the kingdom, she couldn't be gladder to belong to their ranks.

"You're going to start a new trend," Juniper said, taking a step back to admire her work. "You look lovely. Like a queen." She exhaled deeply after she finished fussing with Tempest's billowing skirt.

Tempest rolled her eyes. "Black and gray are my colors. They're dark, like my soul." She thought of the wintery dress Pyre had picked out for her for the masquerade ball. Its delicate swathes of silver fabric, and the tiny blue flowers weaved into her hair. The kitsune had given her a taste for pretty things.

"Given who you're marrying, I imagine you'll have to get used to it," Juniper said, pulling Tempest out of her own head. She squeezed her hand. "I best be off. I love you. And...be careful."

"Love you, too," Tempest whispered back, hugging her friend quickly. "Be safe."

Juniper nodded and left the room, casting a worried look over her shoulder before she shut the door behind her.

Her friend's final words echoed in Tempest's mind.

Be careful. Be careful. Everyone wishes you to be careful and do nothing.

She squared her shoulders and inhaled as deeply as the bodice would let her. Doing nothing had never been a choice. She had not accepted King Destin's proposal to sit at his side and look pretty, hoping that the odd word here or there would change his entire nation for the better. No, she had to be *active* in the rebellion.

Just so long as she treaded *carefully* while doing so.

With another look of resignation at the mirror, Tempest pulled on her black cloak and ensured it covered every inch of her gaudy dress.

Then she headed down to the dungeon before she could change her mind.

Chapter Fifteen

Tempest

"Damn this dress to hell," Tempest muttered under her breath, sweeping up its infuriating train of black and silver beneath her cloak for the fourth time in the last minute. A corseted, sumptuous gown was the worst possible item of clothing for what she planned.

This is stupid.

She gritted her teeth and picked up her speed, her hands full of the crinoline skirt. Her meeting with the Jester hadn't inspired any sort of confidence. She'd seen what he'd done before in the name of the rebellion. Could she trust him with Brine's life?

An image of the gruff wolf on the execution block, neck exposed to the sharp blade of a guillotine flashed though her mind. Her stomach rolled. The risk was too high to stand aside. The wolf shifter was her friend. Minutes prior,

Temp had told Juniper that she protected her friends. What good was being betrothed to the king if it did not afford her any privileges? If she couldn't save Brine from a court-sanctioned death, then what was she doing playing nice with the king?

She paused where the hallway leading to the dungeon bisected her own. Tempest peeked around the corner, her attention pinned to the ornate dungeon door. It still perplexed her that something so beautiful was the gate to hell. Maybe that was the point. The Crown was attempting to cover up their sins with something less unpleasant.

Her lips curled in a smile as she got a good look at the four Hounds stationed outside the door. The king was using his personal assassins to keep the rebels secure. One of the Hounds rolled his neck and glanced in her direction. She pulled back abruptly.

Levka.

How fortuitous. She was sure he would let her in without issue.

Is this a trap?

The Hounds were on her side, but had the king placed them there as a test or because he truly believed they were the best option of protection?

You've been among devious courts for too long.

It was possible. But she hadn't been caught yet. Paranoia had kept her alive.

Not much time. It's now or never.

She exhaled and rounded the corner, her head held high as she approached the door. All four Hounds stood to attention as she swept her hood back, revealing her hair. Levka broke out in a smile and met her halfway.

"Didn't expect to see you here," he murmured, his gaze sweeping her dress. "You're not dressed for battle."

She glanced over his shoulder at the three silent Hounds. "I hadn't planned on coming here. I'm due to see the king any minute. I need to get inside the dungeon. I wish to inspect the prisoners before their execution."

Levka sobered. "I'll let you in, but don't act foolishly. If any persons go missing, the Crown will come down hard on the Hounds too." He gave her a stern look. "That is something we don't need right now."

Translation: we're all committing treason, and if the crown investigates, heads will roll.

"I will keep that in mind." She chucked her chin at the other Hounds. "They are trustworthy?"

"I would trust them with my life. Who do you think has kept the guards from beating or starving any of the prisoners to death?" Levka spun on his heel and moved to the door, taking a set of keys from his belt. "Make sure you cover that hair."

Tempest pulled her hood over her locks and pulled the cloak around her dress once more. Her friend opened the door wide enough for her to enter. She squeezed his arm once as she passed by.

"Thank you," she whispered.

"I'm locking this behind you. Knock softly three times, and I'll let you out. If I don't answer, hide yourself," Levka said gruffly.

She nodded and began to descend the stairs. The door creaked as he closed it behind her, the snick of the lock seeming overly loud in her ears. Torches burned along the stone walls but did nothing to ward away the chill as she entered the bowels of the castle.

Tempest hoisted up the hem of her gown to ensure it did not touch the cold stone floor of the prison—an almost impossible task, but necessary. No one could know of her impromptu visit to the dungeon. Filth becoming stuck to the hem of her dress could condemn her, and King Destin had a way of noticing even the smallest details. Cobwebs, slime, and dust would be suspicious, especially given he believed she'd come straight from a bath.

Ignoring the other prisoners, she practically sprinted to Brine's cell. She skidded to a stop, her heart hammering with each second that passed. "Where's the lockpick I left here last time?"

The wolf in question leaned against the back wall, arms crossed over his chest. He arched a brow at her and shook his head. "You shouldn't be here, pup."

"I'm exactly where I should be. Where is it?"

His eyes glittered in the low light. "Don't test me, Tempest," he muttered. "It isn't safe for you to be here. You need to leave."

"And it isn't safe for *you* to be here, either," she retorted. She gathered her skirt into her left hand and pushed her right hand through the bars of the cell as far as she could. "Please, let me help you."

Brine eyed the space between them and sighed, closing

the distance. His cold fingers wrapped around her own. "You already have, girlie." A wry smile crossed his face. "Should have known Pyre and I couldn't trust you to do as you're told."

She bristled. "I've never been one to blindly obey without knowing all the facts. If you didn't want me to interfere, then don't keep me in the dark."

"He's going to be angry when he finds out you've been here," Brine drawled.

"Don't care. Your life is more important."

The wolf squeezed her hand. "You're loyal. I'll give that to ya, girlie. Could have sworn you'd been born a wolf because of that and your stubbornness."

"My best qualities I'm told."

He released her, a hard expression taking over his face. "Leave now. Stay out of the way while the Jester does what he does best."

"And what is that?"

Brine grinned, canines on display. "Cause chaos."

"Destin is out for blood. You'll die if you don't escape before you reach the execution courtyard. Trust in the Jester if you must, but if no escape comes before that point, you take that lockpick and escape."

"And what of the other members of the rebellion down here with me? What of them? You won't leave me. What makes you think I'd leave my men?"

She understood, she really did, but it didn't stop the pain that rippled through her at the thought of losing him. "I wish I could guarantee the safety of all of you."

"No one's life is certain. You cannot take responsibility for us. We've made our own choices."

He was speaking like he deserved to die. Like his life meant nothing. Like he'd resigned himself to death.

"Listen here, wolf. Your life is not over," Tempest hissed. "You're getting out of this."

"I may not. But it is better me than you."

She jerked. "Not true. Your life is worth just as much as mine."

"That's what makes you special, pup. If more people had your viewpoint, our world would be a better place. You're in a position of authority, and soon, you'll hold real power. Make sure that each decision you make reflects the sacrifices that have been given and will be given." He retreated until he leaned against the back wall. "Remember you can't win this war alone. Trust those around you and set your pride aside. The fox will get us out." His tone held certainty. Brine had complete faith in Pyre.

The wolf is an excellent judge in character. You trust him.

While her mind knew that to be the truth, she couldn't shake the kitsune's final words during their recent meet-up.

I will try.

There was an uncertainty about it, like she didn't know if Pyre could save Brine and the rest of his men.

"I swear to all that is holy that if you don't move your ass out of this prison, when I do get out, I'll paddle you something fierce. *Leave.* I will not tell you again," Brine threatened.

She nodded slowly. There was no changing his mind, and her time was up.

The dungeon door squealed, and Tempest stiffened. That wasn't part of the plan. Was Levka coming for her?

Brine's wolf ears pricked up to attention, and he growled, his silver eyes glowing. "The prince," he muttered just as Tempest heard the words *Your Royal Highness* echo down the staircase.

Wicked hell. Why was the prince coming down to see the prisoners?

Brine's eyes flashed to her. "Go," he urged.

She bolted into the same alcove she'd hidden in before. Her pulse hammered in her throat as she prayed it was dark enough to conceal her. Tempest just barely pulled the train of her damned dress into the protection of her black cloak before footsteps echoed across the stone floor toward her.

Don't look left, don't look left, don't look left.

Time slowed down as she released her dress and reached for the dagger secured at her waist. Her fingers curled around the cool hilt as she pulled it from the leather sheath. If Maven discovered her…

You'd have to kill him.

Her right hand shook, the tip of the blade rubbing against her dress. It was one thing to fight in battle, to defend herself. But if she attacked the prince…it was murder. Plain and simple. Her heart pounded, blood rushing through her ears. She'd be a murderer. A person couldn't come back from that.

Time slowed as Maven entered her view. He sauntered down the hallway, an expressionless Levka in his wake. The prince peered into each cell as he passed them as if searching for something. Or someone.

She almost jerked when all the prisoners began to scream and rattle the iron bars. Tempest held her breath as Maven passed. Levka didn't look in her direction but she was sure he knew she was there. She crept forward as the cacophony grew louder and louder still. Adrenaline rushed through her veins as her friend caught the movement and directed the prince's attention to a cell at the far end of the hall.

Now.

Tempest burst from her space, her steps silent as she sprinted from the hall and up the stairs.

No mistakes. Sweep the area.

She paused behind the closed door and peeked outside. Only the three Hounds stood there. No ambush awaited her.

With a stuttering breath, she nodded to the Hounds and ran as hard as she could. Tempest rounded the corner. The hallway was too long, too open.

"Is someone here?" Maven's voice floated to her.

She ducked into the nearest alcove as his voice grew louder. Tempest peeked out from behind the wall hanging. The prince had reached the junction of the two hallways. He swung his head left and right, his eyes narrowed. Levka stood silently behind him.

"My lord, there's been no one here but the king."

"No one?"

"Nobody, your highness," her friend lied smoothly. "There is nobody here but you and my men."

Maven did not seem convinced. For a horrible moment, Tempest was sure he was going to come down the corridor after her, but instead, he skulked back the way he'd come. "I want to see the leader. I have a few questions of my own before they're taken to my father…" His voice faded.

She caught her breath and forced her muscles to move, even though her legs shook. There wasn't time to consider what Maven was doing in the dungeons or whom he would be interrogating.

What if he's working with one of the rebels?

The horrible thought stopped her in her tracks. She shook her head and cautiously made her way up two levels before entering the servants' corridors. Her skin crawled the entire way back to her own rooms.

She smiled pleasantly at the guards outside her door and entered, closing the door softly behind her. With care, she examined her room for any intruders. What had happened with the king earlier couldn't happen again.

You were almost caught. Again.

Tempest kicked off her soiled slippers and tried to decide what to do. Should she hide, clean, or toss them out the window? Her gaze snagged on the fire. She'd burn them. She tossed them in the flames and added more wood to the fire, then she moved back to her wardrobe and put on another pair of black slippers.

On autopilot, she drifted back to the mirror, making sure not one hair was out of place. She met her gaze in the glass. Her actions had been brash. She'd allowed herself to be ruled by emotion, and it could have cost many people their lives. Madrid would kill her when he discovered what she did.

As you deserve.

It pained her to admit, but Pyre and Brine were right. She had to trust others. If she didn't, people would die, and that would be on her. It was against her very nature to do nothing, but maybe standing aside wasn't as passive as she thought. It was a choice.

She pulled the black cloak from her shoulders and stared at the woman in the mirror. A cold queen gazed back at Tempest. When had she become this distrusting, isolated person?

"Who are you?" she whispered. The backs of her eyes burned.

How would she help anyone if she lost herself in the process?

"Accepting the king's offer was a mistake." Her soft words reverberated right down to her marrow.

It didn't matter that the Jester and the Dark Court considered her position as queen to be a boon to their cause. Or that the Hounds were making a move to strike against Destin. Every day closer to her wedding felt like a noose tightening around her throat.

A bleak chuckle escaped her.

Chances were that the king would try to kill her once he'd gotten what he wanted from her. It may not be tomorrow, or in two months' time, but the inevitability was there. Every moment she was in the palace could be her last.

She'd been so focused on becoming a Hound, on securing a place on the war council, on ridding the kingdom of its underworld lord, on discovering the truth and securing freedom for all, that Tempest had forgotten why she'd started fighting at all.

For honor and vengeance.

There was no honor in marrying the king.

Tempest turned her back on the woman in the mirror and tossed her cloak onto her bed. She'd been naïve to think she could secure equality for all just by marrying a powerful king and becoming his queen. She'd have to fight for it like everything else.

Her uncles had given her many tools over the years. Dima constantly preached about the effectiveness of a mask or disguise.

The queen in the mirror was Tempest's mask.

She'd play the king's fierce new toy until the opportunity presented itself, and then she'd strike.

Chapter Sixteen

Tempest

Her heart beat in tandem with every step she took toward the throne room, but she wore a cool mask of indifference. Showing weakness in front of Destin was not an option. She had to remain stoic and strong.

Tempest felt anything but.

Two young guards opened the tall white-and-gold double doors that led to the throne room. Her palms grew clammy as she entered and gained the attention of the two royals standing near the throne.

Destin and his son.

The prince eyed Tempest with obvious disdain but schooled it into something more pleasant when his father looked his way. She ignored the prince and approached the king with confident strides. The prince was suspicious of her, but if he had any real proof of her wrongdoings, she'd be in chains already.

"You are looking well," the prince murmured. "Such dark colors against your pale skin. One could almost say you look like a ghost."

"I'm very real, my lord," she said, stopping before the two men and curtseying.

"No doubt. You'll fit right in. Ghosts haunt all parts of our castle, especially the dungeons. So many lost souls there." His smile became predatory, and the look in the prince's eyes dared her to spar with him.

Not today, demon.

Tempest risked a glance at the prince from beneath her lashes. "I don't believe in such things."

Destin glanced between his son and her, a small smile playing about his mouth. "My Lady Hound is far too reasonable to believe such nonsense."

"Very true, sire. I tend to believe in what is tangible. Ghosts don't leave evidence of their wicked behaviors. Humans do."

"How very astute," the king praised.

Tempest squashed her distaste for the condescension in Destin's tone. Let him talk down to her. It would be his undoing for underestimating her.

"I live to serve, my lord," she said dryly.

"Sarcasm. The lowest form of wit," the prince quipped.

Temp arched a brow at him. "Pot, meet kettle."

"You're starting to learn already," Destin commented, shaking his head, eyes crinkled in mirth.

"What, my lord?"

"Banter."

"Word play is just another form of warfare."

"Truer words have never been spoken."

The king held his hand out, and she took it. He maneuvered her until she stood between him and his son. The hair at the back of her neck stood on end when Maven stared down at her and pressed closer to her left side as Lord Betraz pulled the king's attention away from them.

"You may have my father beguiled, but I see you for what you are. Don't think I don't see what you're doing. You best keep your nose out of where it doesn't belong. It's a long way to fall from where you are."

"Two cleverly worded threats in one day. What have I done to receive such attention from the prince?" she murmured, while surveying the room. Several aristocrats stood around, yawning and looking disheveled. Had the betrothal ceremony only happened last night? Tempest flicked a look at the prince. "You're welcome to bestow them on anyone else."

His breath heated the side of her neck, and he leaned in closer. "You think you're so much better than me. You think you can refuse your Crown prince anything?"

"My allegiance lies with the king," she said lightly. "You are not king."

The prince hissed out a breath, and his face slowly turned red. "Enjoy your freedom while you have it," he bit out. "Soon, you'll be the one on the execution block."

He stormed away, and Tempest hid her relief. Her neck tingled, and she longed to wipe any evidence of the prince away from her. There was something wrong with him. He was unhinged. She'd have to look out for that one. Evidence of any wrongdoing on his part would be an asset. If the king had reason to doubt his heir, then any accusations the prince threw against her would look unfounded. But that was an undertaking for another day.

The king glanced over his shoulder at her and smiled, holding his hand out in invitation once again. How could he look so damn happy when he was about to attend a mass execution? The prince wasn't the only one unhinged—he came by it hereditarily.

Lord Betraz gave her a faint smile, his bloodshot eyes looking weary. Had he even gone to bed, or was he still drunk from the night prior? She smiled prettily as he took her hand and kissed the back of it, murmuring empty compliments. He released her hand and gestured toward the balcony.

"It will be quite a sight, no? The court always loves a little bit of blood sport." An unholy gleam entered his gaze.

With some difficulty, Tempest reined in her distaste for the hedonistic upper class. "Indeed," she commented, her tone bland. She'd heard of Lord Betraz's love for spilled blood, but she hadn't known if the rumors were true until now.

The doors to the throne room opened, pulling her attention. Tempest blinked and then managed to conceal her reaction as a huge, hulking man strode into the room. *A Kopalian. A giant!* She eyed him with intrigue. He was the largest person she'd ever beheld and that was saying something. The giant made Briggs look small. She eyed the muscles that strained the sleeves of his silk shirt and the size of his hand. He could probably crush her skull with just one palm. Intriguing.

"What a bestial man," the lord whispered. "How marvelous and barbaric."

"Brutes they may be, but strong allies they make," the king said softly.

The lord blanched and bowed deeply. "My apologies."

Destin nodded and held his elbow out to her. "My lady, shall we go?"

She dutifully linked arms with him, then led the procession toward the execution grounds alongside the king.

"What do you think of our Kopalian friend?" Destin whispered conspiratorially.

What answer was the king looking for? "I know a warrior when I see one," she replied honestly. "I would like to spar with him."

"Of course you would. Always ready for a challenge, aren't you?"

"I try to be."

They fell silent as they exited the palace and entered the Forsaken Grounds; Tempest had been there just once before. Dima had taken her there during her training, so she could understand what happened to those who were convicted of a crime and the seriousness of a Hound's duty to look at all the facts. No one wanted innocent blood shed.

She swallowed hard as her hatred for the place rushed

to break free. The smooth black granite of the ground seemed to soak up all the light from above. She looked around at the raised plinth with two thrones and a small ornate chair to the left of the center throne and luxurious seats in rows below. The thrones stood like a sentinels over the grounds. The wind tousled her hair, and snow drifted over the onyx ground. Her gaze moved to the guillotine with its wicked blade gleaming in the dull morning light.

Tempest lifted her skirts as the king escorted her up the plinth. Each step she took, her stomach knotted tighter. Sweet poison, how was she supposed to sit through this? What if Pyre wasn't able to get the men out? There was no way she could sit silently while innocents were executed.

Trust. Trust. Trust.

They reached the top of the plinth, and Destin patted Tempest's arm, a gentle smile on his handsome face. "You can rest after this, Temp," he said. "I imagine you're exhausted after everything that went on last night. Justice will be served this day."

The king's touch and his words made her skin crawl—though, in reality, his sentiments would have been comforting coming from anyone else. Anyone who meant them.

Bile burned the back of her throat. "I admit, it's been a trying few days."

"Don't fret, darling. Everything will be all right."

She swore her heart skipped a beat as she stared up into the king's face, so full of affection. Not because of his attention, but at the dangerous idea that planted itself in her head. One she wasn't even sure she should attempt to consider.

He led her around the thrones and sat her in the ornate chair, the prince taking up residence on the smaller throne to the king's right. Destin held her right hand loosely in his own when he sat in the huge center throne as highborn lords and ladies filed in around them. Wine was poured into goblets, and the sour stench was almost enough to make her retch.

Damn her, but her hands trembled.

The king ran his thumb over the top of her knuckles and glanced down at her, his tawny hair falling boyishly over one eye. "Tempest?"

Here's your chance.

"You are right," she stated softly. "I am tired. But, more than that, I am troubled. By the execution, I mean."

Destin frowned at her. "Whatever do you mean? They *must* die. They—"

"No, no, I agree with you," she reassured him. Tempest stared up at him with earnestness. "It is just…I fear that killing the rebels now will merely serve to rile the Talagans further." Tempest was disgusted at how easily the lies dripped from her tongue. "If we kill them now, then we would be making martyrs out of them. We could be dealing with even more assassination attempts within the palace as a result, and we might not be so lucky next time as to merely have the death of a handmaid on our hands." She squeezed his fingers for good measure.

"Why have you not said something before?" he asked carefully, his tone neutral.

"I did not feel like it was my place," she replied. "But I swore an oath as a Hound to protect you and yours with everything that I am. I cannot stay silent if a decision could put you or your family in danger, even if it earns me disfavor."

Tempest bowed her head like she was worried he'd cast her out.

Take the bait.

A finger slipped beneath her chin and lifted her head up. She willed herself to hold his mercurial gaze as he studied her face. Her heart thumped when the tip of his forefinger grazed her bottom lip.

"What would you have me do, then?" he asked, his piercing gaze never wavering from hers. "I've already announced the execution."

Seize the opportunity. You can't stop now.

"You could give them to me as a betrothal gift," she suggested. "It is an Heimseryan custom, after all, and I have no father for a bride price to be given to. It will paint you in a favorable light with the people and will give me peace of mind."

She held her breath as he leaned closer. His golden eyes locked on Tempest's, but he didn't verbally respond. Her heart began to throb in earnest, and a prickle of sweat dampened her forehead.

Only see what I want you to.

The moment was broken by the opening of the gates of

the Forsaken Grounds. A roaring crowd entered for the execution. Heimseryans from all quadrants of the city of Dotae had caught wind of the impending deaths of the rebels, and they had shown up in droves to witness it themselves. She swallowed hard, trying to keep the bile down. Were all people such beasts?

They know not the truth.

Destin straightened and kept her hand in his. She composed herself and adopted an air of aloofness as the square filled with people. Her head throbbed, and her stomach churned. These days, she always seemed to feel sick. Probably a side effect of living amongst a den of vipers. Even living as the Dark Court's prisoner had been easier than this. The thought almost made her laugh.

Almost.

She leaned forward as a line of guards marched into the Forgotten Grounds, followed closely by the prisoners. Sound ceased to exist. Brine led the ragtag group, his head held high despite how filthy and underfed he looked. His pointed ears twitched, and he growled at the crowd when they surged too close.

Please, please escape.

Her gaze scoured the crowd for any familiar face. She spotted none in the mayhem. Where was Pyre?

Trust.

Whatever happened now, she could no longer do anything about it without jeopardizing everything. Brine lifted his head and stared up at the throne with a snarl. Tempest met his gaze and didn't look away. All she could do was witness whatever happened next out of sheer respect for the rebels and out of friendship for Brine. She'd hold his gaze to the very end, so he wouldn't feel so alone.

"That shifter seems to want to eat you up," the prince drawled.

"He could try, but he'd be sadly disappointed." Temp curled her lip but didn't take her gaze from the rebels. "I'm not as sweet as perhaps he thinks."

"On the contrary, darling. You're a delight." The king lifted her hand and planted a kiss on the back of it. "Let's get on with this. I've had enough of that animal eyeing what is *mine*."

Chapter Seventeen

Pyre

His favorite cloak of forest green swirled around his feet as he moved slowly through the screaming crowd. It seemed as if the people of Dotae were as bloodthirsty as ever, but if one looked close enough, they could see the fear written on their faces. No one wanted to incur the king's wrath. It was easier to stand and scream in the crowd than garner attention. At one time, it would have disgusted him, but now, he understood what it meant just to survive. He dipped his head low, the cowl of his hood shadowing his face as the prisoners were led into the square. Brine led the procession, his head held high.

Pyre followed his commander's gaze and paused on the king—his father. Though he had tried to convince himself many times before that sharing the same bloodline did not make someone *family,* he still couldn't help but feel like he was tainted somehow because of his sire. He pushed down the urge to chuckle. What would Destin say if he knew his greatest enemy and eldest bastard son still lived?

He'd probably laugh before slitting your throat.

The king took a long pull from his wine goblet, completely at ease that innocent men were about to die while speaking to Maven. The monarch turned from the prince and smiled at the female holding his left hand. All sound ceased to exist as Pyre stared at the fierce beauty sitting on the throne, dressed in black and silver. Destin lifted her hand and kissed the back of her fingers, and she smiled. A low snarl rumbled in his chest, and he startled the child to the left of him. He took one step forward when the king used his other hand to stroke the apple of her cheek.

Mine.

Tempest put on a good show, but Pyre could see right through her mask. She wanted out. What had the bastard done to *his* mate?

She's not yours. Calm down.

A hand gripped his left shoulder tightly, holding him in place.

"Pyre," Briggs muttered. "Not the time. Calm yourself."

"I'm trying," he grunted, fighting every instinct in his body to attack the king and retrieve Tempest. With Destin right in front of his eyes, it was supremely difficult for Pyre to resist the urge to weave through the crowd, leap upon the plinth with his dual daggers in tow, and—

"*Pyre*!" Briggs warned again, jerking him.

Pyre turned his neck and flashed his canines at his friend. "He's touching her, and she's uncomfortable, which is rousing my beast. But I have it under control."

"Clearly," the healer retorted. "We have other priorities. You know she can handle herself. How many times does she have to prove herself to you for you to get that through your thick skull? If the king goes too far, I know for a fact she'll stab him. You're requiring her to trust you; you must reciprocate."

He nodded sharply and shrugged Briggs's hand off his shoulder. The bloody man was right. That's why Pyre trusted him so intently. The healer's wisdom had saved more lives than he could count. Still, that didn't make him feel any better. He *wanted* to protect Tempest. Wanted her to need him—craved it, even.

She's not yours.

Sweet poison, he wished she was. If she was, she wouldn't be on that throne, sacrificing her life to King Destin for the sake of every single person. Tempest wouldn't be alone. She would be loved.

She is loved.

Pyre shut that thought down. It was one thing to accept the inevitability of a compatible mate—it was another to choose to love.

Tempest's shrewd gaze moved over the crowd before focusing on Brine, who Pyre could see hadn't looked away. Long moments appeared to be passing between the two of them. It was as if Pyre could hear a silent conversation between the two: Tempest didn't want Brine to feel alone.

It made his heart squeeze at her compassion, but he also wanted to throttle her. Anyone with eyes could see the connection between the two of them.

"Look away," he huffed.

Destin laughed, and his eyes narrowed on Brine.

Not good.

The king's attention turned to Tempest, whose expression was one of cool disinterest once again. Brine's attention on them hadn't done her any good. She'd roused the devil in Destin, and she'd likely be answering questions after the execution today.

Well...after the thwarted execution. As long as Tempest didn't do anything rash, the rebels would get out safely.

As long as everything goes to plan...

The crowd around him pitched back and forth like waves, and their cries reached a new level as Destin stood from his throne. He pulled Tempest to her feet, and she stood regally next to him. The king took two steps forward and grasped the banister. When he raised his hands slowly and spread his arms wide, the crowd grew even louder. Pyre silently observed, thankful he'd taken his full human shape. The roar from the people was almost deafening without any enhancement.

This was the moment they were waiting for.

He turned his head and nodded. Briggs edged away, his hulking figure disappearing into the mass. Soon, all of Pyre's men would be on the move. Everyone was in place, positioned ideally for maximum chaos. They planned on low casualties, but if things turned to the worst, they'd fight their way out if necessary. Bloodshed was par for the course. He did not relish the thought, but death was a necessary evil at times.

Pulling in a slow breath, he tried to calm his pounding heart. Once they acted out today, there would be no turning back. Such a rescue was an obvious strike against the crown of Heimserya. Destin would no doubt retaliate against the Talagans, and the kingdom would fall into full-out war. The Dark Court had been preparing for this day for a long time, and while Pyre felt like they could use some more time, no one could be truly prepared for such a thing.

He scanned the plinth once again, noting each highborn lord and lady in attendance. The Crown prince was present but not Ansette. Was the princess in hiding, or did she hate her father's display? His spies had not yet been able to make out where the girl's loyalties lay. A grim smile crossed his face at the notion. Apparently, it was a family trait to keep one's goals hidden from the world. Tempest seemed to think the girl was smart and had a good heart, but only time would tell. Ansette had lived her whole life in the poisonous company of her father and brothers. Regardless, Pyre had no plan to hurt the girl. Whoever had attacked her and tried to pin it on the Dark Court would regret their actions.

His focus moved back to the prince. While Pyre liked the idea of having another sister, he hated the fact he shared blood with Destin's legitimate second-born spawn. Maven was clearly cut from a similar cloth as his father—

Pyre could see, even now, the way the prince's eyes roved across Tempest, though she was unaware of his attentions. While he shared blood with Maven, he did have dreams of hurting the bastard in the same ways the prince hurt his victims. Too many young maids had been maimed and hurt because of his proclivities.

Deal with him later.

"People of Heimserya!" King Destin called out.

Pyre gave the king his full attention while he prepared himself for what would come next. The hilts of his daggers found their way into his palms.

"*My* people. How pleased I am to see so many of you here to support your king. I know news spreads like wildfire in Dotae, which means many—if not all—of you must know of the attempt on my precious daughter's life in the small hours of the morning. Your beautiful princess Ansette. Just a wee girl." He pointed at Brine. "These *rebel scum* think it's fair game to harm a child! Do they deserve leniency?"

"No!" someone screamed.

"Send them to the grave!" called another.

"Justice for the princess!" cried a young woman, who seemed genuinely upset by the idea someone would harm Ansette.

For a moment, Pyre experienced pity for the people around him. They'd been fed lies based on reality in order to emotionally manipulate them for so many years that they couldn't tell the difference between fiction and truth.

Guards approached the prisoners and kicked them to

their knees. The prisoners held their heads up as the crowd cursed, threw rotten fruit and rocks, and spat at them.

It was time.

Pyre carefully wove through the crowd, knowing his men were doing the same. Brine held up his head, defiance clear as he stared down anyone who got too close. His expression faltered for the smallest of moments before a steely gleam entered his silver eyes. The wolf would never show any fear, even to death.

"And yet, to kill them now would only demonstrate that we are as savage as the rebels," King Destin announced.

Pyre froze as the crowd around him quieted in confusion. What was the king up to? Destin had never been known for his mercy. During his entire rule, every one of his enemies were executed, either publicly or privately.

Destin turned toward Tempest and held his hand out. Pyre's stomach bottomed out as she took the king's hand and glided to his side.

What. Have. You. Done? Tempest, what have you—

"Your good and gracious queen-to-be, in all her wisdom and mercy, reminded me that we are a civilized nation. The men you see before you did not commit the attempted assassination of my daughter, yet they are part of the group responsible for it. I have therefore decided that their lives will be spared and gifted to my betrothed for her to punish as she sees fit. I hope you all trust our righteous Lady Hound to seek appropriate justice."

Pyre couldn't believe his ears. How would the people react? It was as if the crowd inhaled at the same time. The pause stretched on and then...it broke.

The people screamed their approval, rapturous applause undulating through the masses. Pyre blinked slowly at the king who smiled smugly. Had this been his plan the whole time or did Tempest really have something to do with it? He'd bet his boots she'd arranged this, but what she obviously hadn't foreseen was that it would only make Destin stronger. Pyre's goal was to undermine him. This act of benevolence was nothing more than a ploy to get the common people on the king's side. They adored the female Hound. She'd become a symbol. One that the king was wielding for himself.

"Damn her bloody bleeding heart," he bit out, signaling for his men to stand down and recede. This was not how things were supposed to go.

The guards jerked Brine and the rest to their feet and led them away. Pyre watched as the wolf shifter cast a look of utter disbelief at Tempest and then resignation. She bowed her head to avoid catching his eye, a flicker of guilt moving across her face.

Pyre cocked his head and narrowed his eyes at her. This *was* her doing. His fingers curled into fists, and his jaw clenched. The stubborn wench was never going to stand back and let him deal with things his way. From the surface, her way *seemed* better. The rebellion did not have to ignite war immediately to save a handful of men. No innocent lives would be sacrificed. Tempest would be gifted the prisoners, and she would release them in the dark of night.

Only the prisoners would never reach her.

As he gazed up at the king, Pyre knew it in his soul. Destin made promises of all sorts but didn't follow through unless they benefited him. Pyre's men would befall some terrible 'accident' away from prying eyes—poison, overexposure to the elements, a mysterious illness. The fact of the matter was that the king would exact his revenge in private while the people believed him to be magnanimous.

Bowing his head and squeezing his eyes shut, he began to devise another plan. Brine had the tools to get out, and the Hounds were their allies, but getting a message to the wolf in time posed a problem.

He lifted his head and cast one more look up at the plinth. The tension in Tempest's body had disappeared. She'd made things more difficult and she clearly had no bloody idea.

You damn fool.

Pyre turned his back and stalked through the crowd. There wasn't much time to undo everything she'd done.

Chapter Eighteen

Tempest

He actually gave them to you.

Tempest could not believe it. Her pulse hammered in her ears, and she could barely hear anything around her. Not for one second had she expected Destin to go along with her desperate, last-minute plan. Relief washed over her. She'd done it. No one had been killed on either side, and the rebels would go free.

She caught sight of Brine's expression as he was led away from the execution grounds. His utter disbelief of what had just transpired was apparent, and Temp had to drop her head so she didn't catch his eye. If she did, there was no way she would have been able to keep the smile from her face. Euphoria bubbled in her chest, but she tamped it down. Looking gleeful wouldn't bode well for herself or the rebels, but she savored the win. For Pyre.

For the rebellion.

Destin's attention turned to the advisers pressing around the prince, giving Tempest a moment to take her first full breath in many days. She casually observed the teeming mass below for any sign of the kitsune. She hadn't dared look for Pyre during the last few minutes. Thanks to her, Brine had already caught the king's interest, and she didn't want to add anyone else to the list. Her gaze skimmed over a hulking man in a gray cloak, and Tempest paused when she spotted a glimpse of his face.

Briggs.

Temp forced herself to move on even as she grew angry. Why had Pyre brought the healer with him? Briggs's midnight skin was remarkable and rare this far south in the kingdom. He was sure to be noticed because of his beauty and stature. Unless that was the point? Draw attention to the healer while the Jester moved about unnoticed. The kitsune's hair was a shock of deep red and white. It was too recognizable, so he'd be wearing a cloak. She searched for anyone in forest green. It was a long shot, but worth a try.

Unconsciously, she drifted to the banister. Almost as if her thoughts conjured him, she spotted a figure in the middle of the crowd in a green cloak. Temp stared hard as the man lifted his head and met her gaze. Unbridled rage simmered in his molten eyes. Her muscles locked, and her fingers itched for her blade. Why was he looking at her with so much hostility? What had she done to deserve such ire? His upper lip curled back, revealing his canines before he spun on his heel and disappeared among the throng of citizens.

Her fingers clenched around the frigid marble banister and squeezed. Was his anger for her? Or for the men she was surrounded by? By all accounts, he should be relieved that they didn't have to fight their way out. Her gaze flicked toward the king. Was it really that easy? Her gut said no. Destin wasn't *nice*. He did things with purpose. Her euphoria wore off, and she began to assess the situation critically. The king's compliance with her wishes was unsettling. His generosity and forgiveness never extended to those he deemed to have wronged him, or to those he planned to use. The rebels were the perfect scapegoats for the Crown prince's death *and* the attempt on Ansette's life. So why did he give them to her? It wasn't because he liked her. Sure, the king wanted to bed her, but their union was just another political move.

What am I missing?

She released the banister and swiveled to face the king. She kept her expression placid when she noticed Maven was watching her. The new Crown prince was a problem. If she wasn't careful, he'd plant a dagger in her back when she wasn't looking.

Destin glanced at her from over his shoulder. "It's been an exciting day, has it not, my lady?"

"It has, sire." Tempest dropped into a deep curtsey, her head so low that snow settled on the nape of her neck. "You have given me a great gift."

Destin's polished boots came into view before he

helped her to stand. His lips quirked into a satisfied smile. "You are worth it, darling." He leaned close and dropped a kiss to her left cheek and whispered, "You have a dress fitting, but then, afterward, I'm sure you'd like to deal with the rabble?"

She nodded, hardening her expression. "I will make sure it's done."

"I know you will." A thinly disguised threat. "The guards will hold them in the barracks until you are ready."

"Of course, Your Grace," Tempest replied, forcing a smile to her face and bowing deeply again before leaving the plinth. She glanced toward the thrones one last time and frowned. Where had Maven gone? Probably slithered off to his lair.

Her mind turned back to what the king had said. The guards were holding the rebels in the Hound barracks. Sure, they had their own garrison, but why not the dungeon? Something wasn't right.

She held her head high as she descended the steps and strode across the black marble floor, the train of her gown whispering behind her. Snow fell from the bruised sky in small flurries, dampening her hair. A storm was a good thing. The city would be abuzz about the theatrics in the Forgotten Square and then would be boarding up their homes. The chaos would make it easy to smuggle out the rebels.

Keeping her strides sedate and even was a difficult thing when she entered the palace. Her gut screamed for her to hurry—to run. She glanced from left to right, making sure to move with the flow of the crowd until she made it to the lavish corridor that led to her rooms. She stepped from the staircase and slowed when she discovered a person lounging negligently against her door.

The prince.

What the bloody hell was he doing there?

She bowed her head, asking for patience, and continued forward, her gaze shuttered. "Your Royal Highness, to what do I owe this unexpected visit?" she asked, tone bland and uninterested.

Maven pushed from her door and closed the distance between them, once again towering over her. Did he really think that scared her? She'd fought bigger men and won.

He arched a regal eyebrow as he inspected her face. "Just making sure my new mum found her way back all right. You are new to the castle, and I know it's easy to get turned around and end up in places where you don't belong."

"How true you are, my lord. Good thing part of my training was to study the palace and memorize the layout." She cocked her head and arched a brow of her own. "It's been a long night for everyone. If you don't mind, I'd like to retire to my rooms."

He smiled, his mouth too wide. "My father said you had a dress fitting."

"Indeed, and yet you are lurking outside my rooms." She swerved around him and continued on. "Hoping to give your opinion on my dress? Or…" Tempest glanced over her shoulder. "Did you hope to catch me undressed? Because I can promise you, neither will happen."

Careful, Tempest. You've already pushed him twice today.

"It isn't being held in your room."

She reached her rooms and hesitated at her doors. "Excuse me?"

"Your fitting is not in your rooms." The hair on her arms rose at the evil twinkle in his pitch-black colored eyes. "Because I checked, of course. You're very organized. Not one mess anywhere."

"You will stay out of my rooms," she said softly, fighting to keep the last vestiges of her patience in place. "Or you will not like the consequences."

She'd threatened royalty. It was treason, but she didn't regret it for one moment. The prince was dangerous, but so was she. He was up to something as much as she was. Neither had proof, so they were on middle ground. She was his father's betrothed, and he was the king's new heir.

"Temper, temper," he called as he began walking backward. "You really have turned into a haughty little tart. Ever since my father made the mistake of elevating you above your rightful rank, you've forgotten yourself. And tarts get *eaten* in here." He saluted her once before turning on his heel and crawling back to whatever shadowed alcove he'd come from.

She opened the door to her rooms and locked it behind her. He'd invaded her space. It was probably a scare tactic, but it was better to be safe than sorry. She searched the room high and low for any mischief. For good measure, Tempest tossed out the water in her wash basin, the perfumes, cosmetics, and oils. Next, she dumped the meager spirits down the privy and pulled all the linens from her bed. No poisonous insects or reptiles to be found.

With that done, she struggled out of her black and silver gown, her pearl hair pins catching on it as she tugged it over her head. Tempest threw it on the bed, her heart racing as she jogged into her wardrobe and donned nondescript boys' clothes. She pulled out the top drawer of the dresser and grabbed the small leather pouch hidden behind it before putting the drawer back. Quickly, she tied the pouch to her belt, tucked a cap in the back of her trousers, and snatched her cloak from the top of the dresser. There wasn't time to pull out the pearl pins, so she nimbly braided her hair. It wasn't a great disguise, but it would have to do.

Unlocking the door, she opened it as much as she dared and observed the area. No one but a few guards. She closed the door and made sure her cloak was clasped shut so her clothes weren't visible. Temp smiled at both guards at the end of the hallway and swung around the banister and glided down the stairs. It was easy enough to pop into the seamstress's quarters and cancel with excuses of a long night and headache. After that little chore was completed, she tucked into a darkened corridor, wrapped her hair around her head and put on the cap. Paired with the hustle and bustle of the morning rush for breakfast, she managed to swerve through the servants' corridors relatively unimpeded until she reached the courtyard.

The snow had begun to fall hard, and her stomach twisted in knots as she jogged off the palace grounds. Once she was sure no one had followed her, her steps lengthened until she was in a full sprint. Heimseryans met in small groups as they prepared their homes and businesses for the oncoming storm. Some heckled her as she ran by, but Tempest didn't pay them any mind. Her breath puffed from her lips in small clouds, and her lungs ached as she pushed herself harder. Tempest didn't slow when reaching the dead-end of the alley she'd turned down. She sped up and used the wall of the apothecary to launch herself upward. Her fingers scrabbled at the roof, but she managed to climb up despite her cold, stiff fingers. Running across icy, snowy roofs wasn't the best idea, but it cut the travel time from the palace to the barracks in half.

Sweat slicked her forehead as she dropped from the blacksmith's forge and entered the Hounds' training grounds. She ghosted to the garrison and pulled the cap from her head as the initiate with a bowl cut guarding the prison straightened at her appearance.

"Any new prisoners?" she asked, hoping against all hope that the rebels were really there.

The boy frowned. "Just a drunk from last night."

Her blood rushed past her ears. They weren't here.

Tempest managed to thank the boy, then ambled away, not able to feel her legs. A group of trainees sparred in the ring, and Dima and Aleks were having breakfast with some of their comrades by a nearby fire. She blinked and blinked again, trying to make sense of everything. Maxim and Madrid were missing. They had been at the execution that morning, and the Hounds had been the ones guarding the rebels beforehand, but after… She closed her eyes and tried to remember every detail after the king had proclaimed the rebels as hers.

Her mouth gaped open as the realization slammed into her. Only the guards had led the prisoners away. No Hounds had been present. She gurgled and took a lurching step back the way she'd come, garnering the attention of Dima. He stood, and she shook her head once before sprinting in the direction of the palace.

Think, think, think.

The men hadn't been taken back into the castle. If they had, she would have seen it. They had been led out of the Forsaken Grounds in the direction of the Hound barracks. She scrambled on top of a cobbler's shop and eyed the city. A ruckus would have started up if they'd been led into the city at all, and the Hounds would have heard of it. The bobbing ships in the harbor captured her attention.

The bay.

It was the perfect place to dispose of bodies. Corpses were found weekly with the tides. But the harbor would be too public. The king's guards would need somewhere private and out-of-sight of prying eyes. With crushing certainty, she scurried south over slippery rooftops toward the rear of the palace. The immense castle was founded upon the craggy coastline which made it impossible for any ships to approach from the southern side.

"Hold on, Brine," she muttered to herself, ignoring the searing stitch in her stomach as she dropped from the nearest roof and kept moving.

It was easy to slip around the southern side of the palace. No one in their right mind went back there unless they had a death wish. The rocks were too slippery and sharp to climb upon, and the waves were relentless and brutal. Tempest slowed down and made sure to cling to the side of the castle as she crept around the edge, her boots slipping now and again.

"That's far enough!" a male voice barked.

She froze in place, her eyes scouring the area for the source of the voice. She spotted the red sash of a guard twenty paces ahead of her. His wide back was to her, so she slunk down into the huge, jagged rocks, making sure to keep her eye on the tide and the incoming waves. More male voices became clear as she tiptoed closer. She peered around the rock she was hiding behind and gasped, unable to smother the sound. The pair of guards nearest to her were so busy with throwing a body, restrained and weighed down with stones, into the sea to notice her.

Wicked hell, no! Oh no, oh no, oh no.

"The feral one said he'd rather rot in hell than be in our presence a moment longer," one of the men joked. "Well, now he can rot, but in the bottom of the black sea." Male chuckles filled the air before they began moving away from the sea.

Tempest pressed her back to the slick rock, dagger in hand as the guards climbed out of the rocks and entered a small metal gate near the base of the castle. It clanged shut, and the moment they were out of sight, she tore at her cloak, tossing the heavy wool to the ground. She tore her boots from her feet and haphazardly raced toward the sea. The waves began to pull back as she dove headlong into the dark water before giving herself any time to prepare for the shock of the water.

And it *was* shocking—bitterly cold and biting her skin like knives. For an agonizing moment, all the air was knocked from her lungs. She kicked up to the surface and gulped down a painful breath before diving back down once more.

The salt stung her eyes as she struggled to see though the churning dark water. She pushed herself deeper and spotted a pale, wriggling body. Tempest swam harder and pulled her dagger from her sheath and sloppily cut at his bindings. He tore free and kicked toward the surface as she spotted another body. Panic began to rise in her throat along with her failing air supply as she moved to him and cut him loose too, her attention darting to the surface.

Her lungs screamed as she forced herself to stay below as a wave rolled over the surface. Tempest kicked hard, letting her body float the rest of the way back to the surface. A sob caught in her throat as she gasped for air. Where was Brine? How long had he been under? Her body shook, and her joints ached, and only sheer determination made her able to force herself back under the ice-cold water.

Her sodden clothes became heavy as she searched the murky water. Out of the corner of her eye, she caught sight of a wolf struggling in seaweed, his paws firmly tied to rocks. His sharp teeth ripped at the spindly sea plant, and he writhed, making his predicament worse.

"Brine!" Tempest called out, the word forming bubbles in front of her face as she closed the distance between them.

His desperate silver vulpine eyes locked on her as she approached. There wasn't any humanity left.

Please don't bite me.

She dipped down and carefully reached for his first paw. He snapped at her, catching her forearm as she released his first leg. As if realizing what she was doing, he ceased struggling so she could cut him free. With astounding speed, he swam toward the surface without a second glance.

Tempest spied another body, but it was not moving. Her movements were slow as she cut him free and dragged him to the surface. Breaking the surface was a blessing and a curse. The wind and snow bit at her. A wet Talagan knelt on a rock to her left and held his shivering arms out. She swam over to him, and he took the unconscious body from her the moment she was in reach.

A wave rolled in, and Tempest ducked down, swimming as hard as she could, and anchored herself to a rock at the bottom as the tide threatened to tear her away and dash her against the rocks. The water seemed to take on a dreamlike state as the wave passed, and she blearily searched the sea for shifters. Could anyone survive this long without air?

Tempest pushed forward, her limbs fatigued and numb. The chill from the water didn't hurt anymore. Another wave crashed overhead, and a cloud of sand enveloped her, tumbling her about. She clawed at the water, and something slammed against her face. A flailing arm. Her vision went red and dotty. Her blade slipped from her fingers and Temp fumbled for her other blade, but her fingers were no longer moving.

She glimpsed the drowning man as her own lungs threatened to burst.

We're going to die.

An arm circled around her waist and yanked her upward. She stared at the flailing man as she was dragged away. He opened his mouth and a stream of bubbles escaped.

No, I can save him. I can—

She sputtered and cried hoarsely the second she was topside again. "I can save him!" she screamed. "I have to go back. He's dying. I can—"

A hand covered her mouth, quelling her screams.

"Shh," Pyre whispered in her ear, harsh and urgent.

She didn't have any energy to fight him, so she just stared at the spot where the man had been abandoned.

"Here, take her!" Pyre commanded.

Tempest didn't feel a thing as she was lifted the from the icy ocean. Small puffs of steam left her lips as she fought for breath, tears filling her eyes as the kitsune dived into the raging water.

"Oh, girlie," Brine whispered in her right ear as he pulled her away from the edge of the sea and settled her between two rocks that blocked the wind.

His hands rubbed up and down her arms, but she didn't really feel them. It seemed like ages that Pyre was gone. Another shifter popped above the surface just as a wave crashed over his head, tossing him against the nearest rock. A shifter cursed and nimbly dragged him from the surf, bruised and bloody, but alive.

Pyre surfaced a few seconds later and managed to haul himself from the water. He strode toward them, his face devoid of any expression.

"The rest?" Brine murmured.

"No others," the kitsune croaked. "All dead."

"That's—that's six of our men," Brine replied, voice so soft that Tempest barely heard him.

Stars flashed across her vision, and Pyre wavered.

Six deaths. She was responsible for the deaths of six men.

Hands cupped her cheeks, yet she didn't feel anything but the pressure. Pyre crouched before her, his molten eyes concerned. "Temp," he said firmly. "I need you to say something."

Her lips couldn't from any words. An inarticulate low wail escaped her, but that was it. She stared past him at the sea. Six lives. She'd ruined everything.

Chapter Nineteen

Pyre

Water dripped from Pyre's sodden clothes, but he didn't feel the frigid temperatures. He couldn't look away from Tempest's blue lips, so pale they almost matched her wet hair that hung in ropes over her cheeks.

"She's too cold," Brine growled. "We need to get her dry *now*."

"Briggs! I need your cloak," Pyre barked and then directed his attention back to Tempest. "We have to remove your clothes and get you dry." She didn't acknowledge him, her gray eyes empty of emotion.

The healer appeared at his side and pulled his cloak from his shoulders, his dark eyes creased in concern. "How long was she in the water?"

"I don't know," Pyre bit out as he worked at the buttons of her trousers. "Hold the cloak up."

Briggs held his gray cloak to give them privacy. Tempest flopped like a rag doll as they stripped off her clothes, not one sound falling from her lips. His panic ratcheted up a notch when he pulled her into his arms, her icy skin biting at his own exposed flesh.

Briggs lay the cloak over her naked body and held his arms out. "I can take her."

Pyre shook his head, his arms tightening around her limp body. "I'll take her. Make sure the rest of the men are ready to travel. We'll reconvene with the others ahead."

He wrapped an arm around her shoulders and the other beneath her knees and stood, holding her as close to his body as possible. Her eyes fluttered shut. *Hell, no.*

He shook her hard and glared down into her dazed face. "Do not go to sleep."

Brine stood on wobbly legs, naked as the day he was born. "How far?"

"Not far. Can you make it?"

The wolf nodded and strode after Briggs, his steps slower and less graceful than normal.

Pyre followed, his heart pounding in his chest as their ragtag group traversed the coast along the cliffside, unseen from prying eyes. Twice he stumbled and almost dropped his mate. Not once did she complain or fight him. It was like he held her shell: her body was there, but her mind was far away. Brine kept pace beside him, constantly flicking concerned looks at Tempest.

His steps picked up once their destination was in sight. He easily scaled down the rocks to a dry cave that hovered high above the writhing ocean. Smiles greeted him that faded to grim expressions as they spotted who he held in his arms.

"What happened?" Swiftly demanded, pushing through the men.

"The king," Pyre said as he made a beeline for the fire near the back of the cave. He knelt on a pallet and placed Tempest as close to the fire as he dared. He barely heard the happy reunions of his men as he opened the front of her borrowed cloak so the heat of the fire could warm her.

Briggs rounded the fire and dropped to his knees. He placed his large midnight hand on her forehead and then at the base of her neck. His lips thinned.

"She's gone into shock. Her pulse is weak."

"Is she going to die?" Pyre asked, feeling nauseous.

"Not as long as we're here. We need to work heat back into her limbs and keep her core warm." Briggs glanced around the group of men that were murmuring softly among themselves. "Brine! I need you to shift. Tempest will need your body heat."

A low groan sounded, and then a huge, black wolf edged along the side of the cave. He crept closer and hesitated, his tired, silver eyes flicking to Pyre who nodded, not caring if another male cuddled up with his mate, as long as she stayed warm.

"Lay her on her side," Briggs said.

Pyre was careful as he lay her on her left side, making sure she faced the fire. He lifted the cloak at her back for the wolf. Brine circled, dropped to his belly, and crawled up until he pressed against her back and thighs. Pyre dropped the cloak over them before taking Tempest's right hand to massage her fingers.

Swiftly and Briggs each took one of Tempest's pale feet and began to do the same. Slowly, his men took places around the fire. The men who'd survived the king's drowning were already in new clothes.

"Will she be okay?" Rayma asked, his wet, shaggy, blond hair hanging in his face.

"She's a fighter," Pyre rumbled. "A little cold water won't best her." He tried to smile, but it felt brittle on his face. Shifters could survive the elements with ease. Their makeup enabled them to adjust to different environments. Humans were so fragile in comparison. He swallowed hard as his finger traced over a blue vein in her hand that stood out against her white skin.

Please be okay.

As if his prayer was heard, she twitched in his grasp, and a small shiver worked through her body.

"That's it," Briggs grunted. "We want her to shiver. It means her body temperature is rising." The healer worked his hands up her leg, kneading the muscles. "Baby girl, you need to talk to us."

Another shiver worked through her body, and Pyre readjusted her head on his leg, fanned her wet hair out, and began working on her other hand, feeling sick. Why had she risked her life like that?

Rayma pulled a shirt from his pack, shuffled over, and began drying Tempest's hair.

Pyre glanced at the young man. “Thank you.”

“It’s nothing. She saved my life.” He frowned. “We should have known Destin would do this. It’s a miracle that half of us made it out alive.”

Dartain, a lanky man with curly orange hair, kicked a pebble, his expression hard. “If we’d been able to intercept the execution as planned—”

“There was no guarantee we would have all survived,” Pyre said sternly. “Lives still would have been lost.”

“Not *our* lives.” Dartain crossed his arms, his cat-like eyes shiny. “My brother would be here if it weren’t for *her*.”

Pyre resisted the urge to sigh. There were always going to be members of his faction who did not approve of her, no matter what she did. Tempest had brought the Hounds to their cause. She had placed herself at the side of King Destin to try to control him somewhat. So, while there might have been members of the Dark Court who did not approve of her, Pyre knew that nobody would betray him—or the cause—because of her.

A weighted silence settled over the group as Pyre mulled over what to say.

“I’m s-s-sorry,” Tempest’s voice rasped softly. “M-my fault-t-t.”

Pyre’s gaze flew down to her pained faced. “Love?”

She didn’t look at him but at Dartain.

The cat shifter stared her down. “You take responsibility for this?”

“Y-yes.”

Dartain glanced away and swallowed before nodding curtly. “You did your best in an awful situation. More lives would have been lost if you hadn’t arrived when you did. My brother knew the risks when he became involved.”

“Doesn’t m-m-make it okay.” Her words dripped with guilt and despair.

“No, but the king will pay.” Dartain stood and glared down at her. “Do better next time, but don’t hold on to this. There is only one responsible party: Destin. He’s the one who gave those orders. No one else.” He turned his back on the group, stormed to the mouth of the cave, and sat at the entrance, his head bowed in grief.

The group quieted, their eyes moving from the fire to Tempest like they couldn’t figure her out. Most of these men hadn’t met her before. Her shivers worsened as Rayma finished drying her hair and scooted back, his brow furrowed.

“What now, then? Do you know who attacked the princess? If that hadn’t happened, then we wouldn’t be in this position in the first place. It was the catalyst for all of this.”

“We have no leads,” Pyre hissed, hating that they’d been blindsided. “It certainly wasn’t anyone working for the Dark—”

“...prince,” Tempest coughed out, her eyes glassy as she stared at the fire.

Briggs released her leg and poured a cup of pine-needle tea. “Sit her up.”

Tempest moaned as Pyre hauled her up so that the

healer could give her some tea. She swallowed a mouthful sloppily, some dribbling down her chin. He wiped it away as Brine wiggled until his snout was free from the cloak and huffed. She turned her head away and coughed wetly. Briggs scowled at the sound.

"Don't like that one bit," he growled.

"Blood on his c-clothes," Tempest chattered. "He-he lurks about. Threatened m-me."

Pyre kept his expression calm, but inside, he raged. Maven's crimes were notorious, and yet, anyone with evidence ended up dead. If that bastard had hurt one hair on his mate's head...

"We'll set up some of our servants within the palace to watch him," he finally said, pleased that he was able to keep his anger from bleeding into his voice.

"Thank you," she whispered. "So cold."

"Brine, come around front," Briggs commanded. He glanced up at Pyre. "You can heat her back. Skin to skin."

Pyre set her head gently on the pallet, pulled off his damp clothes, and took Brine's spot. The wolf circled Tempest and wiggled into her embrace. Pyre hissed as her cold skin touched him from chest to knee. He threw an arm over her waist, making sure it wasn't too low or too high, and tucked his left arm under her head. She didn't make a sound but slowly melted into his embrace, her feet pressing to his shins.

How many times had he imagined them like this? In all his dreams, it had involved a lot more kissing and touching. But this? Pyre pressed his nose to the hair at her temple. This was everything. This was what he'd been looking for. Companionship. Intimacy. Love...

His heart hammered as he stared down at the woman in his arms. She was what he wanted. *Needed*. Emotion clogged his throat as Brine nosed her hand, and she shakily caressed his snout from his nose to the spot between his brows. His silver eyes drooped until he dropped into sleep. Pyre had never seen the wolf show that much affection to anyone. His kitsune counterpart didn't like another male so close to his mate, but Pyre knew there was nothing romantic between the two. Tempest was part of the pack to Brine, and she'd accepted the wolf as family.

Pyre wanted that.

Accept what she is giving you.

He pulled her closer as her shivers lessened and her muscles relaxed. This was the closest she'd allowed him without drawing weapons since the forest. He eyed the wolf and how Tempest slowly ran her hand along his fur. At some point, she'd let Brine in and shut Pyre completely out. He wanted in, wanted so badly to be let in.

You have no one to blame but yourself.

At every turn, he'd lied or kept her in the dark until she'd ended up taking matters into her own hands. He couldn't expect trust from her if he didn't reciprocate it. The broken part of himself rebelled at that thought. Being open meant he could be hurt, too. If he let her see everything, would she stay or run? He wanted to run from all the things he'd done in his life.

Be honest or let her go.

He lifted his head and eyed his men, then jerked his chin toward the entrance. They all took the silent hint and moved about the cave, giving him a little privacy. Sure, they could hear what he was about to say, but the illusion of privacy was more for his mate. Briggs scooted away and made himself comfortable against the rear wall before closing his eyes.

"Tempest?" Pyre whispered in her right ear. Her fingers didn't stop petting the sleeping wolf, and his hand itched to take hers, to slide their fingers together and never let go.

"He lied," Tempest croaked, the words so quiet that Pyre barely heard them over the crackling flames.

Pyre could only nod. "It's what he does."

"I feel so—no, I *am* so stupid." She tucked her chin down and pressed her face against his bicep. "I cost your men their lives. And for what? My own pride? I—"

"Enough," he said gently but firmly. "Did you not listen to a word of what Dartain said? There was no guarantee we could have saved *anyone* at the execution. Clearly, you knew this; otherwise, you wouldn't have tried so hard to save Brine on your own."

"But—" she choked out.

"The king cost them their lives, Temp, not you. Surely, you must be able to see that? The men he planned to kill had nothing to do with Ansette's attack. He knew that, and, yet, he condemned them and ordered their deaths."

Her body began to shake again, but in broken silent

sobs. He didn't think twice about hugging her tightly and kissing the crown of her head. He began to stroke her hair, and she cried harder. He wanted to tell her everything would be okay. No more souls would be lost. She didn't have to go back to the palace. She didn't have to go back to Destin.

But all of those things were lies.

After a few heart-wrenching minutes, her shoulders stopped shaking, and her sobs quieted. She sucked in one deep breath after another, as if trying to calm herself, and he did the same. There was something reassuring about how easily their breathing synced.

In. *Hold*. Out. Their hearts slowed but beat in unison.

This is right. This is where she belongs.

Her snowy shoulder was exposed, and he leaned closer to kiss the skin but paused, closing his eyes. He would not manipulate the situation. Instead, Pyre pulled the cloak over it and tucked her in.

"How does someone lose their way so much?" Tempest rasped.

He frowned, confused by the question. "Who are we talking about?"

"The King. Destin. How does someone become such a heartless...monster? Didn't he have people around who loved him? Why does he want people to suffer so much? Just...why?"

"I don't really know when my sire lost himself," he said, fatigue and contentment riding him hard. Winter's bite, he could fall asleep like this. "Perhaps he was always like this.

His father hated Talagans after the foreign princess tried to kill him. Maybe he was just a product of his environment. I didn't care enough—and still don't care—to find out."

He frowned when his mate slowly stiffened in his arms. "Temp, what's wrong?"

She tried to pull away from him, but he kept his arm around her waist. Pyre went over his words and wanted to bang his head against the stone floor at what he'd revealed. All it took was his mate's warm, pliable body against his and he was spilling all of his secrets. For a long, drawn-out moment, she said nothing. He gritted his teeth and resolved himself to stand firm. If he wanted her to let him in—if he wanted her to accept him—he had no other choice but to be honest.

She turned her head, her bloodshot gray eyes sweeping over his face. "Just who the hell are you, Pyre?" she whispered.

He smiled grimly. There was no turning back now.

"A prince, I guess."

Chapter Twenty

Tempest

Now that it had been said, she couldn't unsee the resemblance between Destin and Pyre. How had she not known—or at least *suspected*—that the kitsune was in some way related to the king?

You're a fool.

Pyre held her gaze as she stared at him. She'd never seen golden eyes on anyone else but the two of them. Just as her lilac hair screamed that she was resolutely a Madrid, the molten amber eyes should have given away the fox's heritage. How had she not seen it before?

Because people don't look beneath the surface.

She was a bloody Hound, for Dotae's sake. Tempest had been trained to look beneath the surface. Pyre blinked his amber eyes, warm and yet wary. But that was a difference—Destin's gaze was cold and calculating, whereas the kitsune was capable of affection and mercy. Or was he? Pyre was also just as ruthless as his royal sire when he took on his other personas.

Was the warmth just another mask?

I want you. It's not just a game.

Had he even meant those words or were they just another ploy, another way to get back at his father? Another shiver racked her body, and Pyre pulled her closer to his chest. Questions raced through her mind, but she could not decide which to ask first. A dull roar began in the back of her head, as well as a ticking clock. How long had she been gone? Surely, someone would notice her absence soon, if they had not done so already.

She swallowed and moved her attention over his shoulder, not able to hold his gaze any longer. Interrogating the Jester would have to wait. Time to return to the palace. Although...there was one question that had to be asked before she could, in good conscience, return to the palace.

"Do you plan to rule?" Tempest rasped, forcing herself to match Pyre's intense gaze. "You told me before that you have no plan to. Was that a lie?"

He shook his head slowly. "Not a lie. I have no intention of ruling."

Tempest examined his expression, which seemed to be open and honest, but could she trust it? Silence settled between them. It was clear Pyre was waiting for her to make the next move—to show that she accepted his origins, or wished to know more, or to outright reject him.

She didn't have the energy, nor the wits, to do any of those things. It felt as if she had sand in her eyes, ice in her veins, and thorns in her throat. Tempest laid her head down and continued combing her fingers through Brine's dark fur.

Pyre's breath gusted against the back of her neck as he sighed, causing more goosebumps to raise on her arms. Not from the temperature this time. She gritted her teeth as he eased his body away from hers and then tucked the cloak around her frame. Tempest heard him stand but didn't dare to look. While she hadn't protested the heat he'd provided, it wasn't until her limbs had warmed that she'd realized that his bare skin pressed against her own. Her cheeks warmed, and she rested her face against Brine, hoping it would go away.

Clothes rustled softly.

"You need to get back to the palace," he said. "You've chosen your path. You need to do your best not to ruin the progress you've made."

Her spine stiffened. How dare he.

"As if you had to tell me that," Tempest snapped. She released her hold on Brine and painfully sat up. Pyre stepped forward, as if to help. He only wore trousers, his dark skin rippling. She glared at him. "Don't touch me."

The wolf cracked open a silver eye and huffed, his snout pressing against her hand. She bent low and pressed a kiss to the musky fur on the top of his head, then stood on shaking legs.

Briggs rolled his eyes and frowned at her. "Where do you think you're going?"

"To the palace where I can do my duty," she bit out.

Tempest clutched the long gray cloak to her body and lurched toward the cave opening. She'd not stay another damn minute if it meant being in the same place as the infuriating kitsune. A hand curled around her right bicep, and she stopped. She glanced around the cave, noting that all eyes were on her.

"You can't think to go out there by yourself," Pyre growled. "It's snowing, and you'll catch your death!"

She slowly lifted her chin and locked gazes with the lying male. "I swam in the ocean in the middle of winter and didn't die. I won't die now. And I'll have company. Brine?" The wolf's wet snout touched her left hand. "Now, let me go or you won't like the consequences."

Pyre released her slowly, anger and irritation lighting up his features. "So damn stubborn." He grabbed a pair of boots from the floor and shoved them into her arms. "Your boots."

Tempest took them from him and swept from the cave as gracefully as she could. The winter wind sliced though her, and she staggered as she slipped on her boots outside. She hugged the cloak closer to her bare body and began trudging up the incline.

It would be a miserable hike home.

Chapter Twenty-One

Pyre

Every step she took hurt him.

Pyre followed close, making sure to stay far enough behind that she wouldn't notice her extra escorts. Briggs moved nimbly through the rocks beside him, a silent companion.

Tempest tripped and crashed into a large black rock near the peak of the coastline, and his heart ceased beating. There was too much space between himself and his mate. If she slipped and fell, he'd be too far away to catch her.

He sped up as she caught herself and a curse fell from her lips that almost had him smiling. Brine glanced in his direction, his serious gray eyes narrowing as if to say he had it under control. The wolf and his mate crested the hill, and Pyre watched as they ambled into the city.

"She's going to be fine," Briggs said from his left. "She may be abed for a few days, but the lass is healthy. I don't anticipate any long-lasting effects."

Pyre stared after Tempest until she disappeared into the city. He turned and began to slowly descend back to the cave, anxiety riding him hard. What if she was attacked on her way home? What if the king discovered her loyalties?

She has Brine. Calm down.

"I can smell your worry from here."

"How would you feel if your mate was engaged to another man and living in a den of vipers?" he shouted.

"I'd lose my mind." Briggs paused, his deep brown eyes full of compassion. "I thought you said you weren't going to pursue her. That she wasn't your mate?"

"Things don't always go to plan," he muttered. "How can I not want her?"

"She's prickly and rash, plus she has a mean mouth."

Pyre scowled at the healer. "True, but she's also kind, generous, fierce, and loyal."

Briggs grinned, his white teeth gleaming against his onyx skin. "Told ya so."

He blinked and then returned the smile. His friend was only trying to get a reaction out of him.

"So how are you going to get her to accept you? Do you have courtship gifts yet?" Briggs asked as they continued their trek, the snow falling heavily around them.

"No. Tempest has made her decision to be queen. She won't accept anything from me as long as she's betrothed to the king." He swallowed, feeling queasy at the thought of his father taking the one thing most precious to him.

"So, what are we going to do about it?"

Determination filled him, and his smile turned sinister. "We kill the king."

Chapter Twenty-Two

Tempest

There was no way she could enter the palace, not if she was a lady. If her lack of dress was discovered, any chance of marrying the king was out of the question. She was half-tempted just to chance it so she could get out of it. But that was a purely selfish thought. Brine licked her fingers and disappeared when they reached the Hound barracks.

In a haze, she entered the barracks courtyard, not able to feel her fingers or toes. No one was really about. That worked perfectly since she was about to steal a uniform from her uncles. Given the time of day—just before noon—she imagined that all the men would be currently out. Carefully, she opened the door to their home and popped her head inside. Nobody was around. She slipped inside and closed the door softly, looking for any sounds from the rear bathing room.

Nothing.

Tempest crept farther into the room, her attention pinned to Aleks's bunk. He was the shortest of her uncles. His uniform would have to do. As she reached his bed, the floor creaked and she froze in her tracks as a man materialized in the washroom entryway, dressed only in a towel.

Levka.

"Hello," she mumbled awkwardly, keeping her eyes firmly on his face. A shiver worked through her, and she gritted her teeth.

Levka blinked slowly and shook his head, wearing a small smile. "Is there any point in asking what you're up to, Temp?"

Her lips curled into the ghost of a smile in response. "I guess not."

"What do you need?"

"A spare uniform, if you have it," she replied. And then: "Perhaps a new cloak."

"I think I can manage that." His sharp gaze ran over her as he moved to his bunk. "You look like hell. Did you take a swim or something?"

"Something like that."

Levka frowned at her and then dug through the chest at the end of the bed. "You're starting to worry me."

"You and everyone else," she muttered.

"If I asked you what you were doing, would you actually tell me?" he asked softly, handing her the clothes.

She pulled them to her chest, holding his gaze, her

mouth in a firm line. "Let's just say it's not something to discuss aloud and leave it at that."

To her relief, he did not press for more information. She muttered a quick thank-you and scurried into the washroom. The steam from the warm pool immediately caused sweat to dampen her temples and the nape of her neck. She glanced longing at the water but grudgingly got dressed, shivering the whole time, despite the heat. Her hair was beyond tangled, but she was able to coerce it into a long braid that was passable at best. Levka's pants gaped at the waist, but she used a nearby belt to cinch them and loosely tucked her shirt in before exiting the room.

Her skin rippled, and she trembled as she left the washroom. Levka sat on the chest at the end of his bed and watched her approach. She held out the damp gray cloak, and he took it. Tempest wrapped his black one around her shoulders, the hem dusting the ground.

"Thank you. I promise I'll return your things."

He waved a hand at her. "Don't worry about it. I grew out of those a while ago. Keep them." He stared up at her. "You're a mess, and you haven't stopped shaking since you've arrived. I'm not sure I should let you leave."

She smiled faintly and headed for the door. "I don't really have a choice. See you soon."

"Wait!" he called out after her, and his hand on her shoulder urged her to stop.

She twisted and stared at him impassively, fatigue weighing her down. If she didn't get back to the castle and climb into bed, she might not make it back at all.

"I'm in a rush, Levka. You know I shouldn't be here."

He floundered on the spot, looking down at his shuffling feet before forcing his gaze back to hers. "Temp, I... Everything I said to you in the past. About selling out. And—well, just everything. I'm sorry. I—"

"You helped save me from the king's men when they cornered me by the gates," she cut in, a more genuine smile on her face now. "You're on my side, aren't you? So, there's nothing to apologize for. We all have made mistakes while trying to better our kingdom. Perhaps just...grow up a little bit."

Levka let out a soft laugh at her comment, looking more like his carefree father, Maxim. "Okay then. I'll accept that. Be—"

"If you say be careful, then I swear to Dotae, Lev, I will kill you."

"Then I won't say it." A pause. "Good luck, Tempest. Don't get killed."

She rolled her eyes and pushed him good-naturedly before sneaking from the barracks. She huddled in her cloak, the snow crunching beneath her boots. Everything was white, and the storm looked like it would not stop anytime soon.

Her mind wandered back to Pyre as she slogged to the palace, each breath and step a labor. Had she managed *anything* good thus far? Her heart sank. It seemed all she had done was get people killed. And now, to discover that the man she had been working with—the man she had come to like, despite everything—was King Destin's son?

It was all too damned much.

Pyre was older than both the first-born prince and the now-Crown Prince. The king wasn't Talagan, so it was clear the king had taken a shifter lover. If the kitsune hadn't been bastard-born, then he would have been the heir to the throne. Could his words be trusted when he said he didn't want the throne? Pyre liked power, that was apparent, but he didn't seem like he was scheming to become king. Why hadn't he told her?

Tempest chuckled darkly and began to cough. It was because she was prickly and had a temper like a badger. No wonder he hadn't brought it up. He probably trusted her as much as she trusted him.

A few of the guards exchanged glances when she returned to the palace, but none questioned her. No one questioned a Hound. Her ascension to her room was thankfully unimpeded. Her throat burned, and her limbs shook as she arrived in the royal wing. Thank the stars her bed was close. It felt as if her legs would give out any second. Tempest managed to open the door with shaking hands before the sound of footsteps behind her gave her pause.

Please don't be the king or the prince.

She steeled herself and turned.

Madrid stood a few paces away, his expression unreadable. He eyed her from head to toe, his expression thawing into something softer that she couldn't understand. "Tempest," he said. "A war meeting has been called in the council room. We must go."

She dropped her head and nodded. "I need just a moment."

As fast as she could, she entered her room, changed, and forced herself away from the comforts of her bed and the fire. She locked her room and dutifully followed Madrid to the east wing of the palace. The silence grew between them, becoming more and more awkward with every passing second.

He glanced at her from the corner of his eye. "You don't look so well."

"You're not the first to make that remark," she grumbled, feeling even more ill. Tempest wrapped her arms around herself. The memory of the icy water caused more ripples to break out along her skin. Did the Hounds know what the king was planning to do? "Did you know?" she whispered. "About what would happen to the prisoners after I asked for them to be gifted to me?" She studied her sternest uncle.

Madrid nodded, and she swallowed. Why hadn't anyone said anything? If they had shared even a scrap of that information with her, lives could have been spared.

It goes both ways. You should have gone to them for help.

She hung her heavy head, feeling the weight of failure on her shoulders.

"Tempest."

Madrid's serious tone caused her to lift her head and meet his gaze. He gently placed his hand on her left shoulder and steered her toward the inner wall, far enough away from the door to the council room that nobody would overhear them. She surveyed the man, the head of the Hounds. He looked tired and *older*. Silver littered his lilac hair near his temples, and there were lines around his eyes. While he was still a man in his prime, it was startling to realize that he wouldn't be young forever, and, sooner or later, someone would replace him. The thought alone had her heart clenching.

"Why are you looking at me like that?" he asked, frowning.

She grimaced. Sweet poison, she hated the fact she was so transparent.

"I just..." she began, not quite knowing what to say. She sighed. "I don't want anyone else to die, I guess."

Madrid barked out a humorless laugh. "Then you're in the wrong profession, lass."

"I didn't exactly have a choice in that matter, did I?" Tempest muttered before she could stop herself. She held up the end of her braided hair. "I was found out—smoked out, really—and had no choice but to be a Hound. Isn't that the way of it, Madrid? I've always belonged to the Crown."

The man flinched. The Hound who never balked at any situation flinched as if she'd struck him. She almost put him out of his misery as he struggled with what to say. The door to the council room opened, and they both pulled away from the wall. The royal treasurer stepped out and waved them in, annoyance plastered all over his sallow face.

As they approached, aggravated voices reached them and became louder as they entered the chamber. Tempest observed the room, her stomach sinking as she noticed the prince. Maven had never been to one of the war meetings before, as far as her knowledge went. It was reasonable for him to be there now that he was the heir, but it still bothered her. She hovered near Madrid and hid her mirth as the king growled something at his son, his face ruby red.

Somehow, the prince had earned the king's ire, and that pleased Tempest more than it should have. She hid her smile.

"What happened?" Madrid asked, calm as ever.

"There's been an attack in the northern province of Fiergone," the treasurer informed them. "The rebels are responsible, apparently. But intelligence suggests that the rebels in question are *giants*."

That was an interesting piece of news. Hadn't the king sent the princes to be ambassadors to the kingdom of Kopal? What were the giants doing working with the rebels? There'd been a Kopalian ambassador in attendance for the execution that morning. Something wasn't right.

The king glared at his son. "Just what in Dotae's name have you done?" he demanded, his voice raising to almost a shout. "What were you doing while you were there? You had *one* job. One. God, what I wouldn't give for different sons."

Tempest kept all emotion off her face and directed her attention to the table with a map strewn across it in the middle of the room. She peered through her lashes to gauge Maven's reaction. The prince looked like he was about to launch over the table and attack his father. Was this why Maven had turned out the way he did? Without any paternal affection, did it always create monsters?

She eyed him, theories running through her head. Was the giants' attack a ploy from the rebels or from the prince? Could the Kopalians be colluding with Maven?

Don't let your imagination go crazy. Not everything is the prince's doing.

"How would you like to proceed, my lord?" Madrid asked King Destin. "The Hounds are ready to do your bidding."

"Mobilize the army into Fiergone," the king replied immediately, thrusting a pointed finger down onto the map on the table. "We need to hit them hard and fast. They can't be given a chance to retaliate with their full numbers. This needs to be nipped in the bud *now*."

Tempest held her breath.

"We don't have enough men," one of the councilors pointed out, his long gray goatee quivering. "Most of them are still in the south. We—"

"Then get more men!" Destin hollered. "Draft them from every household if necessary. We've already begun the process anyway."

She blinked slowly. He'd been drafting men for his army? Tempest glanced at Madrid from the corner of her eye. His expression was blank. How long had he known?

"We do not have the money to pay for new soldiers," another councilor pointed out. "The Crown cannot afford this."

"Our men should *want* to sacrifice their lives for the kingdom! This draft is not optional—it's compulsory. Send out the order now."

She kept her mouth shut as the horror of Destin's demand sunk in. Anything she could have said would have been treason. She didn't agree with this decision at all, and, going by the faces of everyone in the room, they all agreed with her. War was one thing, but a draft without compensation for the families? It would lead to a riot in and of itself.

A riot.

Would this be the straw that broke the people who were still loyal to the Crown? While horrible, it was the perfect solution to unite all the people—those of Heimserya and Talaga.

Tempest's attention moved to the king, who hadn't looked away from his son. Her heart picked up speed as she saw Pyre's angry sneer in his expression. It was ironic that Destin desired different sons when he had a powerful, scheming son already. What would the kitsune have been like if he'd been raised as the heir?

The idea made her colder than she already was. If he'd been raised in the palace—under the king's direct tutelage—then any of the good, honorable traits Pyre possessed would have been completely snuffed out.

It was better that he was a rebel. Better that he was the Jester. Better that he worked with the Dark Court.

She curled her hands beneath her armpits to keep her fingers warm as she came to another epiphany. It didn't matter that he was Destin's son. Blood meant nothing. Only the actions.

You should have said something.

Judging a person's parentage, which he had no say in, was as bad as someone judging *her* for her lack of a father. Shame washed over her. She'd have to make amends. Well, after they dealt with the pressing issue at hand.

War was coming.

Chapter Twenty-Three

Tempest

She didn't remember much of the trek back to her room as the chill from the sea seemed to seep as deep as her bones. The bath burned her skin, but it still wasn't warm enough to dissipate the cold that lingered in her blood. Tempest shivered as she climbed from the bath and wrapped herself in a fluffy robe, her eyelids almost too heavy to keep open. Only a few more steps and she would be in her bed.

Swinging open the door, she released an embarrassing squeak when two newcomers surprised her with their presence. Maxim and Dima sat by her southern window. She scowled at them. Hadn't she locked the door? What was up with everyone invading her privacy?

Her uncles stood, and Maxim rushed forward, wrapping his burly arms around her.

"Girlie," Maxim breathed, "Levka just told me about you showing up in the barracks looking like a half-frozen, drowned rat."

"That sounds about accurate," she mumbled against his chest, his familiar scent of leather and mead curling around her. Tempest turned her face to the side and gave Dima a weak smile while soaking in Maxim's heat. "What are you both doing here?"

"What was said at the meeting?" Dima asked instead of answering her question. His serious face was uncharacteristically haggard. She frowned. Clearly, something was troubling him.

Join the club.

"When was the last time you slept?" she asked, eyeing her bed longingly. They all could use a bloody nap or two.

"It's been a while," Dima muttered before continuing on. "Now, the news."

"There's been an attack in Fiergone," she replied, reluctantly releasing Maxim. "There is to be war."

"We knew that was coming. He's been mobilizing soldiers around the kingdom for the last four months." Dima nodded slowly. "The king is going to put a draft in place."

Tempest wrapped her arms around her waist as another shiver worked through her and she moved toward the fireplace. "Not only that." She sat and stared grimly at her uncles as they joined her. "He plans to draft from the people without compensation."

Maxim cursed loudly, running a hand through his long

light bluish-purple hair. "That complicates things. What is that bugger thinking?"

"Watch your words," Dima chastised softly.

Maxim rolled his eyes but kept silent.

"How does this complicate things?" she asked, holding her frozen fingers out to the fire. The heat hurt a little bit, but it was better than being cold.

"I guess you'll find out this evening," Dima answered. "Madrid's called a meeting among us and the rebels. Say you feel too unwell to be at dinner and sneak along to see us."

Tempest chuckled, the sound rusty. She winced at the pain in her throat and pulled a wry smile. "That shouldn't be too difficult as I feel like death."

"Look like it, too," Maxim commented as he retrieved a blanket from the foot of her bed and laid it over her shoulders.

Tempest gave him a grateful smile and huddled into the blanket cocoon. "Okay. I'll be there." She stared at her uncles and swallowed hard. Now was the time to ask her questions. Who knew the next time she'd get them alone? "I know you're both lying to me," she said softly.

Dima blinked slowly and Maxim frowned.

"What do you mean?" Dima asked carefully.

So, he was going to play it that way.

Temp sighed and rubbed at her throbbing temple. She didn't want to play mind games. All she wanted was answers. "I heard you in the village in Merjeri. I know you're keeping secrets about my mum." She stared at

Maxim, letting her hurt and desperation shine through. "I need you to tell me the truth."

Maxim's expression crumpled and he ran a hand over his beard. "I don't know what to tell ya, girlie. She's gone and nothing we say will bring her back."

Her attention moved to Dima who was doing his best impression of a marble statue. "Don't pretend you can't hear me or that you don't know what I'm talking about. This is *my* life. I've formed pieces together, but I don't know everything." She swallowed and looked between her uncles. "I know my sire hid me away to protect my mother and I. Which one of you is my father?"

Both men said nothing. They weren't going to tell her the truth.

Maxim held his hands out, his eyes pleading with her to understand. "You are a daughter to us both. What does it matter who sired you? We raised you as our own. We love you."

She knew they did, but it still hurt that they wouldn't be honest. Her gaze strayed to her bed and she willed herself not to cry. It would just make her head and throat worse.

"I don't want to be rude, but I've had a very, very long day—and night—and I could do with some rest for a while," she said woodenly. "If I don't get some sleep now, I won't be going anywhere tonight, or I very well may pass out on my way to the meeting tonight."

"Of course, lass," Dima said, breaking his silence. He patted her on the shoulder on his way out of her room.

"You're loved. Don't let this build a chasm between us.

One day we will tell you everything, but today is not that day." Maxim bent down from his towering height and kissed her on the top of her head. "You need to take better care of yourself, girlie. You've scared many years off Dima's and my lives."

"I'll try," she mumbled, turning her attention to the fire when Maxim straightened and left the room, the door clicking shut.

That didn't go as she wanted but she was too tired to agonize over it.

Temp dragged herself from the chair, locked her door, and crawled into bed on the off chance that she might actually manage to snatch a few hours of sleep.

She opened her gritty eyes and groaned, snuggling deeper into her bed. Her head felt like it was full of cotton. Weak light spilled through her windows. What time was it? Sunset? It wasn't fully dark yet, but storms always made it difficult to discern the time of day.

Tempest flopped onto her back and sighed. Her body still ached, and the chill hadn't left her, but it was better than before, at least. A servant knocked on the door, and Tempest forced her groggy carcass from the bed. The maid's eyes widened when she got a good look at Tempest.

"My lady, are you all right?"

"Just some fatigue and a headache. I wish to rest tonight. Please pass on my regrets for not making it to dinner. I also don't wish to be disturbed."

The maid sketched a curtsey and moved along.

Tempest closed the door and leaned against it. She rubbed her brow, noting how clammy her skin felt. That wasn't a good sign. Her legs carried her back to the bed, and she stared at the covers.

If you get back in that bed, you won't get out.

Tears burned at the back of her eyes. Winter's bite, she was so bloody tired. With strength she didn't know she possessed, she stiffly donned her Hound uniform, folded the spare one that Levka had given her beneath her arm, and left her room. It was a surprisingly quiet journey through the palace. People tended to settle in when a storm raged outside. Her legs felt like noodles by the time she reached the entrance hall. Two familiar figures caught her attention, and some of her worry faded away. Maxim and Levka waited for her. She joined them, feeling lighter by their sheer presence. Family had that effect.

"Thanks for the clothes," she told Levka once they were within throwing distance of the barracks. She held out his uniform. "They really saved me."

He nodded. "No problem."

"Look at the two of you finally getting along!" Maxim bellowed, wrapping his humongous arms around both their shoulders to hold them tight. "The impossible has happened. Who knew it would take fifteen years for you to not argue with each other? Not me!"

"Get over it, Dad," Levka muttered, though a bashful smile crossed his face at his father's approval.

Tempest grinned, her heart filling with warmth that

she'd not experienced in ages. Sweet poison, she missed her family. She missed the Hounds. She missed Juniper.

Tears once again began to burn at the back of her eyes, and she blinked repeatedly.

She missed Briggs and his sister and her little fawn boy, and Nyx, and Brine, and…even Pyre.

She longed to be home. To feel safe.

The snow fell heavily around them, swallowing their footsteps. Tempest got a hold of herself as they strode past the barracks, the garrison, and finally entered the multi-hall of the Hounds. All conversations were better when served with a warm meal and some mead. It was surreal to enter the room full of jovial men. She surveyed the Hounds and their trainees. These were the men who had served the Crown for generations or would in the future.

Forced servitude.

The thought left a bitter taste in her mouth.

Tempest gazed at her family in a new light. How many had been torn away from their families? How many mothers had lost sons or daughters to the king's machinations and selfishness?

She skirted around the edge of the hall as Madrid stood. Several Hounds took their places near the doors, making sure to shut and lock them. Maxim pressed a hand to her back and directed her to a nearby bench. She wordlessly sat down, her focus locked on Madrid.

"You all know what happened in the small hours of this morning and what has now occurred in Fiergone. The king has called for war and is forcibly drafting all able-bodied men to fight. You know what this means." Madrid cast his gaze across the entire group. "It means we must move our plans ahead."

"How far ahead?" Dima asked, who was sitting with Aleks two benches in front of Tempest.

Unease skittered up her spine when Madrid's gaze moved to her and held. All eyes turned to her. She resisted the urge to withdraw; she had never shied away from her Hound brethren before. She would not do it now, despite how uncomfortable all the attention made her.

"In three weeks' time," Madrid answered.

Her heartbeat whooshed in her ears.

"On the day of Tempest's wedding to King Destin." A pause. "We will not be alone in our endeavors. Each leader will be given an assignment for his group. Be ready." With that, Madrid sat back down at the head of his table and the room lightened once again, as if they hadn't been planning treason.

A shadowy form pulled her attention to the left-rear corner. She blinked. Briggs and Nyx. The curvy shifter waved Tempest over. On wobbly legs, she stood, giving Maxim and Levka a parting smile before shuffling over to the shifters.

Nyx pulled her into a huge hug, her scent of violets and snow filling Tempest's nose.

"Let's go somewhere quieter," Nyx murmured in her ear.

She released Tempest and reached for her hand. Briggs led them from the dining hall back to the quiet barracks.

Her lungs burned, and she coughed as they entered her old home.

Nyx directed Tempest to her old bed and made her sit. Briggs knelt on her floor, his dark eyes sweeping over her face. He pressed the back of his hand against her forehead and tutted, clucking his tongue when she coughed again.

"I'd ask how you're feeling, but I think I know," he muttered.

"Tired, that's how I'm feeling." And beat up.

He gestured to her shirt laces. "I'd like to listen to your breathing."

Tempest waved a hand at him. "You've seen me naked before. Go ahead."

Briggs unlaced the top of her shirt and crowded in, pressing his ear against her chest. "Breathe in and then out."

She did so. "Do you not have a tool for this?"

The healer pulled back with a twinkle in his eye and tugged on his right ear. "Talagan hearing, lass. No need for human tools."

"That's convenient," she mumbled.

"It is." He clapped his hands together. "I have some tinctures for you, but you'll be all right." Briggs smiled, the tilt of his lips a little devilish. "I knew you'd be all right, but *someone* insisted we see you."

Tempest managed a smile. "You telling me you didn't want to check up on me?"

"Always, but he's been a little demanding."

Her stomach flipped as Briggs stood and held his elbow

out to Nyx, who took it.

"We'll take our leave." They waved and exited the barracks.

Tempest stared at the closed door for a long time, knowing she wasn't alone.

"How long are you going to pretend you don't know I'm here?" a sensual voice crooned.

She exhaled and swiveled around, eyeing the kitsune lying across on the bed next to hers. He hadn't been there a moment before.

"How?" she growled as she made to stand up.

Pyre snapped upright, his feet hitting the floor as he reached for her. Tempest stared at his burnished hand curled around her pale wrist. She settled in and gently pulled her arm from him.

"The usual way," he joked. When she didn't return his smile, his amber eyes sobered. "I came to explain."

"Explain what?"

The kitsune glanced away, his throat working as he gazed blankly at the wall behind the head of the bed. "Everything, I guess."

"Like how you have royal blood running through your veins?" she asked evenly. "Are you sure you want to talk about his now?"

He chuckled and ran a hand through his hair, his fox ears nowhere to be seen.

"What other time is there but now? A few weeks from now—hell, a few *days* from now—one or both of us could be dead." He winced and fully faced her. "Sorry."

Tempest shrugged. "You speak the truth. When I took my oath as a Hound, I knew my life would be short."

"You will not *die*."

She startled at his snarled words and cocked her head as Pyre worked to calm himself.

He exhaled heavily. "After I sent you off earlier…I regretted my words." His amber eyes locked on Tempest's gray ones, and he leaned forward, erasing most of the space between their bodies. "You deserve better than to be kept in the dark. About me. I should have been honest with you the moment I knew I could trust you."

The air seemed to flee the room.

Trust.

He trusted her. It felt…big.

"When did you decide you could trust me?" she managed to ask without emotion leaking into her voice.

He let out a self-deprecating chuckle and moved to the foot of her bed. The bed dipped, and she leaned toward him, her pulse picking up speed.

"It seems like the moment I met you." He ran a hand over his face and rolled his eyes. "It sounds ridiculous, right? I told myself I had to put you through your paces—it was idiotic to trust someone so blindly. And the enemy, no less!" Another chuckle. "When you set foot in that tavern with coal in your hair and watchful gray eyes full of secrets, I knew what you were."

She stared at his handsome profile, barely able to breathe. For a minute, neither of them said anything. Tempest wasn't sure what she *could* say, anyway. From the first minute she'd met the handsome rogue who was playing cards, she'd been intrigued. She glanced at her lap and struggled to keep her feelings bottled up. If she let them out now, all hell would break loose. She was betrothed and had to keep a level head.

Betrothed to his sire.

The thought made her feel ill.

Pyre flopped backward, jostling the bed. She twisted to face him, but he kept his unsettlingly beautiful, dangerous eyes on the ceiling instead of on her, as if he knew the last thing Tempest wanted to see was the most telltale sign that he was related to the king.

"My mother was a pretty maid," he began, voice singsong and far away as if he was recounting a tale that happened to someone far removed from him. "She had fire, charisma. Her hair was a deeper wine than even mine. The king, of course, took a liking to her," he continued, his face slowly creasing with rage, "and snatched her up without her consent. He kept her locked away. Like a bloody prisoner, he locked her away. At some point, she realized she was pregnant, and my mother—well, she was fierce of spirit. A fighter." Pyre paused in his story, and the look on his face told Tempest everything she needed to know: his mother's nature was both her saving grace and her downfall.

Temp swallowed hard, already knowing how this story ended. She almost told him not to continue, but she kept silent. If Pyre was sharing his pain with her, she owed it to him to listen.

He glanced at her out of the corner of his eye. "You can imagine how much Destin loved that spirit of my mother's. But, one day, she went too far. Her fighting with the king got her thrown in the *actual* dungeon, and he left her there to die." His jaw worked. "It was Madrid who discovered her and sent sympathetic guards to watch over her, you know. He's a good man."

"All the Hounds are," Tempest whispered, realizing tears were already filling her eyes.

"Not all," Pyre argued softly. "At least, not at that time. Things are better now." He blew out a breath, ruffling the white streak of hair that lay across his forehead. "Anyway, Destin left my mother in there for so long that she gave birth to me. He didn't know. For three years, she and Madrid somehow managed to conceal my birth."

Tempest's heart ached at what his mum must have gone through. The dungeon was a horrid place. Imagining a child spending the first few years of their life there… "I'm so sorry," she whispered.

He nodded and kept going. "But they couldn't keep it a secret forever. He caught wind of it—his wife was pregnant at the time with their first son. Madrid got us out. To this day, I still don't know how. I remember snippets as we ran. We found solace in a small house in a remote village at the edge of the forest, and my mother met a man who treated me like his own son. His family accepted us, and then Nyx was born." He closed his eyes, his brows slashing together as if in pain. "And then…"

"The king found you," she murmured, knowing it in her

heart.

Pyre nodded, opening his pained eyes. "My mother handed me Nyx, who was a baby, and told me to run. I was five."

The same age she had fled her own burning house. Empathy for Pyre, plus her old pain, wrapped around Tempest, and she swallowed back the lump in her throat.

"We escaped, but I made the mistake of looking back." A cluck of his tongue. "At least Destin had the decency to strangle my mother with his own hands."

Her hand found his before she knew how it had gotten there. She had thought her origins were sad. She lay down and pulled him into her arms, his face buried against her shoulder. Tempest ran her fingers through his silky hair, a tear leaking from the corner of her left eye. They'd both lost part of their family at the age of five. What a sad pair they were.

After a moment, he threw an arm around her waist and hugged her hard, his lips brushing her forehead in a tender kiss. "Please don't let your guard down around him," he begged, his breath tickling her scalp. "You witnessed firsthand what he does even when he promises something else. Never trust him. *Never.*"

Numbly, she nodded. Then, Pyre lifted her chin so he could stare down into her eyes. *How could I have believed his eyes and Destin's were the same?* Tempest thought, ashamed of herself. There was compassion and kindness in his eyes that she doubted Destin was even capable of.

"If you get in too deep, you run, do you understand me?"

"I can handle it."

"I know you can. I just want you to know that you will always have sanctuary with us, with me, if you need it or want it."

She glanced away, seeing more emotion in his gaze than she could handle. If he wanted to, he could break her in a way Tempest didn't think she could come back from.

"I am truly sorry for bringing monsters into your life," he murmured.

It would have been easy to cry. Instead, she grinned. The Hounds had been feared for generations. "Good thing I was *raised* by monsters."

Chapter Twenty-Four

Robyn

"We can't keep avoiding the subject," her father said softly.

Robyn glanced up from her mashed potatoes and locked eyes with her papa. So, he wanted to have it out at the dinner table? She pushed her plate away and braced herself.

"What did you want to talk about?" she managed.

He rolled his eyes and pointed a fork at her. "Stop pretending. Tomorrow, I have to leave. We need to discuss what will happen should I die."

She stood abruptly, her chair screeching across the polished floor. "This is *stupid*. You can't possibly go!"

"We have no other choice. If I do not go, the soldiers will come and drag me from the house, or worse they'll look for John."

Her heart squeezed at the mention of her twin. Only a

year since his death. Only a year since everything began to truly fall apart. "There has to be another way."

"There isn't, dearest."

"Who will care for Mama? She needs you." It was a low blow to bring up her mum, but Robyn was desperate.

Her father's expression faltered. "She'll have you and Maya. I'll be home before you know it."

She placed her palms on the table and stared at its shiny surface. If her father joined the king's army, he wouldn't be coming home and he knew it. "So, what happens if you don't come home?" Robyn lifted her head, gazing over the tips of the flickering candles that ran down the middle of the long table. "What am I supposed to do?"

"Protect your mother and yourself."

"What of the people of Locksley?" she asked.

"Just do the best you can."

"As John or Robyn? Do you want me to pretend to be your son or your daughter?"

Her papa stood slowly. "As yourself of course."

She pushed away from the table and shook her head, pacing behind her chair. "People will ask questions. I won't be able to keep this secret if you go."

"Our people have always known John is sickly. It's why we've kept so isolated. There will be questions but nothing we can't handle."

Robyn chuckled, and her throat began to tighten. All of this was wrong. "We won't be able to hide the truth forever. Your son is dead." Her papa flinched, but she carried on. "We've hidden the truth for over a year to protect our people and our home. I can't live as two people. I live as my twin." She rubbed at her brow. "If you don't come home, John will be expected to marry—*I* will be expected to marry. Women will come from all over to seek the heir of the house of Locksley. Except they won't find him. They'll only discover a fraud in his place and when that happens the Crown will seize everything we own, and Mama and I will be locked up, or worse, hung. If you leave, this is our future." She took a deep breath and soldiered on. "But if you let me go in your stead—"

"Out of the question!" her papa interrupted, shaking his head. "I will not have you head to battle."

"I am well trained," she answered evenly. "I can fight as well as any man. You made sure of that."

"You'd be living with men. It wouldn't be proper."

She snorted. "I have been impersonating my brother since I was a child. I've grown up with the menfolk in our area with no one the wiser. I wear boys' clothing more than I wear dresses these days. I've long since abandoned what is proper."

His face flushed red. "It's not safe."

Robyn threw her arms in the air. "We are on the verge of collapse. One mistake could bring our lives tumbling down. Nothing is safe in Merjeri, *nothing*."

"Enough, Marian Robyn Locksley!" he barked, his voice booming.

She flinched. He rarely raised his voice.

"We've done what is necessary to keep our people safe, but I will not sacrifice anything more. I will not sacrifice my only child."

"Your last child," she whispered, her eyes heating.

Her father limped to her side and pressed a kiss to her temple. "I love you, Marian. You are the bright spot in my day, and I'll be damned if you take one more thing upon your shoulders."

He stiffly hobbled out of the room, and Robyn gulped down air as she tried not to cry. Life had never been easy in their home, but as a family they'd made the best of it. They had achieved happiness despite adversity. All of that seemed to disappear when her twin died. It was as if he'd taken the light from the world with him.

She angrily wiped the tears from her face and glared at the lavish dining room. Sometimes, she wished they'd been lowborn. No one would be eyeing their holdings like a plump goose to pluck then.

Her twin's health had been concerning growing up, but they'd been able to keep it mostly under wraps. Their servants were fiercely loyal and never spoke about the young master's frailty. His delicate figure was scorned in the world but was a blessing in disguise. It made it that much easier for Robyn to go for rides, play with the children of the holdings, and train with weapons growing up, all the while pretending to be John. Living as two people hadn't been easy but it had afforded her more freedom, and her brother loved hearing the stories of her adventures.

His death had changed things.

Their ruse had been a source of protection over the

years, but now it was more necessary than ever. Locksley had always been a profitable fiefdom. The lords of Merjeri had been salivating over it for years. They imposed unreasonable taxes and caused all sorts of mischief to get their hands on her father's lands, but it all came to nothing because of her father's careful planning.

John's death changed that. Without an heir, their land and people were completely vulnerable. Robyn pressed the heels of her hands to her eyes. For the last year, playing her twin wasn't a fun pasttime, but a duty that rested heavily on her shoulders.

She lifted her head and gazed at the mirror across the room, her splotchy reflection staring back at her. She pushed her hair over her shoulders, and it was as if John was looking at her. Their resemblance had always been striking.

You only have one choice.

Robyn swallowed and steeled her nerves. The fact of the matter was that they could not lose her father. She had no choice but to fight in his stead as John.

"And the fairies settled into their beds..." she trailed off, peeking over the edge of the book. Her father sat in his chair, chin to his chest with eyes closed, snoring softly. He usually read to her mama, but tonight he wasn't up for it.

Robyn closed the book softly and stood, setting it on the high-backed leather chair. She moved to the large bed and pulled the covers up over her mum's shoulder. Her mother blinked sleepily up at her and smiled before her hand snuck out and grasped Robyn's.

"Thank you, daughter, for all you do."

She froze and peered down at her mum, noting the lucidity in her eyes. Dropping to her knees, she pressed her mum's palm against her cheek. "I love you."

"As I love you. You and your brother are my greatest gifts." Her mum smiled softly. "I see a restlessness in your spirit, and I see what you do for our family. Don't let duty rob you of your joy or living your own life."

"I promise," she whispered.

Her mum's expression changed, and she patted Robyn's cheek. "Make sure to tell your brother I wish for him to visit tomorrow and that I know it's him getting into my sweets."

The lucid moments were few and far between. Robyn swallowed heavily. "I promise."

She stood and tucked her mum in once again before placing a blanket over her father's lap. On light feet, she left their chambers and snuck to her own. Quickly, she began to pack. If she left within the hour, she would arrive at the northern regiment by dawn.

Dressed in her boys' clothes, she moved to her mirror and pulled out her dagger.

One last thing to do.

Robyn grabbed a handful of her waist length hair and cut it. A chunk of black hair fell to the floor. There weren't any tears. With each cut, she left behind the girl she was and became a new person. She eyed her work. Her hair brushed the top of her shoulders and with her breasts bound and dressed in male clothing, she looked exactly like her brother.

There wasn't time to mourn. She swiped the sheared locks of hair from the floor and tossed them into the fire. Emotion swelled in her chest, but she shoved it down ruthlessly.

Today, Robyn ceased to exist.

Only John remained.

Chapter Twenty-Five

Pyre

Seven days until the wedding

"You don't want us to attack now?" Maxim asked, his thick brows furrowed together. The big man crossed his arms as he stared at the map on the small table in the center of the room.

Pyre shook his head. "No. The palace is a poor place to strike. We won't be able to smuggle in enough men for a strong attack."

Dima picked at his nails. To anyone else, he'd seem disinterested, but Pyre guessed the man had already figured out ten ways to kill everyone in the room. He may be shorter and of slighter build, but Pyre knew a viper when he saw one. Out of all the men, Dima caused his hackles to raise. The assassin was the kind of danger you didn't see until it was too late.

"The Hounds are an army in and of themselves," Maxim argued.

"He's right," Madrid said softly. "Even with our skills, we wouldn't be able to take on the king's army by ourselves."

"It would be easy to kill Destin," Dima commented, his tone flat. "He'll be on display for all to see on the day of the wedding."

"True, but then we'd have to contend with Maven," Madrid countered. "He is unknown to us."

Pyre snorted. His half-brother wasn't an unknown variable. He was a psychopath who thrived of sadism.

"Something to add?" Brine asked, his silver eyes narrowed on Pyre.

"I agree with Madrid in this instance. As much as I would love to wipe Destin from this earth in less than a week, it would be to our detriment. Maven isn't stable, and we don't want him on the throne. If Destin died, the prince would have Ansette assassinated that very night and that wouldn't go over well with anyone. We'd have civil war on our hands. The lords of this kingdom are only united by their greed and selfishness. They'd all fight for power."

"Civil war isn't something any of us wants," Chesh muttered from his slouched position from the east wall. He glanced away from the window and scanned the room, uncharacteristically somber. "The Hinterlands have been salivating over Heimserya for ages. If you think Destin is a tyrant, he's nothing compared to the Empress of the

Hinterlands. Your kingdom will be painted with blood if she invades." The cat yawned and then went back to staring out the window, as if he was bored.

Pyre watched his friend for a moment. Chesh had a dark past with the Hinterlands and he rarely shared anything about his former homeland. The kitsune moved his attention back to the map and ran his finger along the border of Talaga and Fiergone.

"Destin expects the rebellion to come from this area. I ensured that his attention will stay focused there."

Maxim ran a hand over his mouth. "We've received word that the workers on the farms are rebelling. That's your doing, not a product of the attacks in Merjeri?"

Pyre nodded. "Yes. The extremists in Merjeri were dealt with, but it gave us the perfect opportunity for the workers on the farms to execute their part of the plan. Nothing they do is down to chance."

"And you can trust these men?" Dima asked.

Brine shared a glance with Pyre before addressing the Hound. "I have family on the farms. They are as loyal as they come."

The Hound sheathed his blade. "Wolves are known for their loyalty. We are lucky to have their support."

"Where I go, they go," Brine said gruffly.

"And your lady commander has the attack on the palace well in hand?" Madrid asked, his dark gray eyes holding no trace of his thoughts.

"Nyx has everything well in hand," Pyre answered.

Chesh snorted. "That female is the best commander I've

had the pleasure of meeting. If she demanded that the mountains bow to her, they bloody well would. Everything will go according to plan."

"And if it doesn't?" Madrid arched a brow.

"Then she has a hundred backup plans." Chesh flicked an amused look in Pyre's direction. "She comes by it naturally, it seems. Like brother, like sister."

Maxim clasped his hands together. "So that settles it. We hold position."

"We hold," Madrid echoed. "Until the battle, then the king will be dealt with."

"One last thing," Dima murmured. His chilling gaze locked on Pyre. "Tempest."

"What of her?" Pyre held the assassin's gaze.

"She's ours."

His hackles rose, and his nails began to pierce his fingertips.

Reel it in.

"She belongs to no one," he said evenly, proud that he kept his expression blank.

"True, but we raised her. Tempest is a Madrid and belongs to the Hounds. She may be working with you, but she's not of the Dark Court. She's not one of you."

"What's that supposed to mean?" Brine growled, his silver eyes flashing. "Is that a dig at our heritage?"

"No." Dima's attention cut to the wolf. "We respect those of shifter heritage. My meaning is that we protect our own, and, if anyone hurts her in any way, well…" Dima cracked a small smile for the first time. "We'll kill them."

Pyre smiled, his canines showing. “On that we can agree.”

Anyone who hurt Tempest would die.

Painfully.

Chapter Twenty-Six

Tempest

The wedding day

War had begun, and she was being pampered. Men had been forced from their homes to fight a battle they believed nothing in. She stared at the crackling flames as women nattered about everything and nothing.

By the end of today, she would be married.

To the king.

She blinked slowly. At least they only had to share one night together before he moved to the front lines. Hysterical laughter caught in her throat. Just enough time for Destin to bed her and possibly sire an heir.

If you survive the night.

Ice trickled into her veins, numbing her. She would

handle what was coming. Tempest had to.

In the three weeks that had led up to her wedding, it had been a flurry of festivities, war planning, and subterfuge. It was a bloody miracle she hadn't blown her cover. Maven had been a constant thorn in her side, but nothing she couldn't handle.

Numb, she glanced around the room filled with servants and fashionable women of the court. She knew who they were but not why they were there. None of them were her friends, save Ansette, who chatted animatedly with Lady Dimpleton.

Whooshing filled Tempest's ears, and it felt like her head was underwater. The sounds of the world dampened until she could only hear her own heartbeat. It was as if the day was happening to someone else and she was merely an observer.

Snap out of it.

She couldn't *afford* to be a mere observer. She had to keep her head in the game—see everything and miss nothing. One wrong slip today meant death…for more than just herself.

Her thoughts turned to all the secrets she held.

Pyre was the king's first born.

The Hounds were rebelling against the king.

The Talagans were prepared for the army the Crown had amassed in the northwest.

She hated the king and…cared for another.

At that last thought, she shook her head, ignoring how a maid pulled her hair. Tempest rubbed at her temples and tried to keep calm. She'd not heard from the kitsune since their time in the barracks. It unsettled her. It was smart to keep isolated until the wedding, so mistakes couldn't be made, but the lack of information was bothersome. She wanted to know what was going on. What was being planned for today?

Do you really want to know?

Temp rolled her neck and popped a small tart into her mouth, hardly tasting it. While she was a creature designed to gather intelligence, she wasn't sure she could handle one more thing. Playing the perfect queen-to-be had been more difficult than she'd expected. Every decision she made, she questioned. Tempest ran over every conversation with the king and paid special attention to everything she said. It had been like walking on knives.

A hand touched her shoulder, and she blinked, glancing to her left as Ansette sank onto the nearest chair.

"Such a grim face for a blessed day," the princess said, taking a sip from a glass of iced wine.

"Much is on my mind," Tempest murmured. "Today is a serious occasion."

The girl eyed her and then waved away the servant brushing Tempest's hair. Ansette set her wine down and picked up the abandoned brush. "Let me help."

Tempest obediently scooted her stool over and sat in front of the princess, the mirror to her left catching part of her profile. Ansette gently pulled the brush through Tempest's hair.

"You are like no one I've met before."

"I was raised by men," she replied, eyeing the girl's reflection.

The princess laughed. "That is true, but not what I meant." The girl sobered. "You care for others and truly believe in the Crown."

If only the princess *knew*.

"I appreciate what you did for those prisoners."

She didn't know what to say.

"Tempest, can I ask you a question?" Ansette murmured.

She glanced at the room from the corner of her eye. No one was seemingly interested in their conversation. She turned to the younger girl and reached for her hand.

"What do you want to know?" she asked.

Ansette stared down at her with serious, knowing eyes. "Are you going to leave me?"

Tempest blinked at the princess. That was not what she was expecting. She found herself pulling the girl into a hug before she could stop herself. The princess felt delicate and fragile in her arms. It would be so easy for someone to kill her.

I will not leave her.

It was one of the easiest decisions she'd ever made. If things went badly and she had to flee, she would take Ansette with her. The girl didn't deserve to live the rest of her life in this viper's nest. The princess might not understand what Tempest was doing, but, in time, she would. The girl wasn't blind to the monster her father was and the havoc he caused. It wouldn't be easy, but she'd see the truth. She had no other choice.

"I won't leave you. I promise."

Ansette pulled away, her lips twisted in wry smile. "Don't make promises you can't keep."

"You can trust me," Tempest whispered.

"I know."

They fell into silence as Ansette continued brushing Tempest's hair until it was dry and shining. The next few hours passed by in blur of ice wine, primping, and unsolicited marital advice.

Her fingers brushed over her wedding dress as Ansette set a delicate silver crown onto her head and the servants wound her hair through and around it. Tempest shivered as a collar of clear diamonds and white gold was placed around her neck.

The women cooed in awe.

Tempest stared at the mirror. A queen stared stoically back. Oh, how far she'd come from the little forest imp she'd been as a child.

"That king will not be able to take his eyes off you," Lady Dimpleton commented.

"Or his hands!" the Duchess of Fiergone crowed with a smirk.

Tempest blushed. She'd grown up with bawdy uncles, and a few older women were getting to her. She'd been gone from the barracks for too long.

Ansette stood to her right, her dress a pale lilac, complimenting Tempest's hair in a way that was clearly deliberate. The princess smiled. "We look quite nice, don't we?"

Tempest smiled warmly at the girl. "You are beautiful, Ansette. You better be careful, or you'll overshadow the bride."

The princess laughed. "I highly doubt that. Shall we go?"

Tempest lifted her heavy dress and glided toward the door as the women crowded around, throwing compliments her way. A maid opened the door, and Tempest's mood soured as Maven swept into a low bow. She curtseyed back, keeping her placid mask in place. He straightened, his eyes unashamedly roving up and down her body as if she'd dressed just for him. Bastard.

"My soon-to-be stepmother," he drawled, holding his hand out to her. "I am here to escort you and my lovely sister down to the ceremony. Shall we head down?"

He was a snake who needed to be beheaded. Her skin crawled at the thought of touching the prince, but there was little choice. She couldn't mess up today. Tempest placed her gloved hand in his and allowed him to guide her down the hallway. Ansette followed in their wake, along with the horde of ladies, their excited chatter a dull roar.

"You look the part of a bride and queen," the prince murmured, pulling Tempest closer to his side. His breath ruffled the hair around her temple. "He's even dressed you in diamonds and jewels. The question is, can you play the part?"

"There's no question of me playing the part, Your Royal

Highness," she replied calmly. Maven was a toad, and he wouldn't get to her. "I *am* a bride, and, by the end of the ceremony, I will be queen. No playing about it."

He smirked. "We'll see how long that sticks. My father's tastes vary often."

That was a damned truth.

They lapsed into silence as they descended the grand stairway, and Tempest was half-prepared for the prince to trip her or toss her down the stairs. He did neither, although he caught one of her looks and grinned, as if he knew exactly what she was thinking.

Her pulse hammered as they arrived at the gargantuan wooden doors that led to the ceremony. Two footmen bracketed the entrance. They watched her, waiting for the signal to open the doors.

She was really doing this.

Maven released her arm and smiled, but it wasn't friendly. "Don't get comfortable," he warned under his breath before sliding one of the doors open to join the ceremony. The highborn ladies smiled and wished her well as they also entered the room. The door slid shut, and Tempest tried to regulate her breathing.

Oh, God. She really was marrying the monster.

Ansette appeared at her side and squeezed her fingers. "It's okay to be nervous," she said, handing Tempest a beautiful bouquet of white and blue lilies. "It's your wedding day. But maybe take a breath and put a smile on your face."

Tempest nodded and curled her lips into a small smile.

"That's better." The princess kissed her right cheek and stepped to the other side of the footman, gathering Tempest's train. "It's now or never."

She smoothed her hands over her dress one more time, and then nodded, her fingers practically crushing the stems of the flowers. The footmen swung the heavy doors open, and she inhaled slowly, her soft court smile in place. Her eyes threatened to water as the blinding lights from the ceremonial hall hit her eyes.

The aisle stretched out before her and the music began.

There was no turning back.

Her steps were smooth as she slowly glided down the aisle. She caught Ansette moving to her seat from the corner of her eye before she focused on the altar. Her stomach twisted as she stared at Destin, who waited for her at the base of the stairs. He looked resplendent in claret and gold, with a sumptuous, deep-burgundy, fur-lined cloak adorning his shoulders. The man was handsome, there was no doubt about it. She met his gaze and inwardly quailed. It was as if Pyre was staring at her from Destin's face.

Focus.

The king smiled, his eyes full of pride, possessiveness, and heat. She was going to be sick. Her legs trembled, and, for once, Tempest was thankful for the damned dress that hid her weakness. Her palms began to sweat as she reached the middle of the long aisle, where all eyes were on her. The space between her and the king seemed to shrink to almost nothing. Soon, he would own her. What had she done?

Someone, save me.

As if a deity heard her, an explosion rocked the room, and the music screeched to a halt. Tempest froze as the crowd screamed and chaos ensued. Assailants dropped from the rafters, and soldiers rushed into the fray. Highborn men and women rushed toward the exits, clawing at and tripping over each other.

She slid her hand through the hidden pockets she'd had added to her wedding dress. Her fingers slipped through the layers to the daggers she had strapped to each thigh. A high-pitched whistling cut through the air, and she dove for the ground as another explosion went off. The floor groaned, and small pieces of stone fell from the ceiling. Screams of terror echoed around the room.

Tempest lifted her head and peeked over the nearest pew. A soldier launched at a man dressed in black and tore his mask off. She stiffened as serpent-like eyes connected with hers before the Talagan opened his fanged mouth and bit the soldier on the shoulder. The man's squeal was cut off.

She rose to her feet as the serpent man stared her down and wiped his mouth. Tempest held her ground, her fingers curling around the knives in her hands. Was this a shifter insurgent or someone from the Dark Court? Was she still supposed to appear like the queen-to-be? Or was the attack on the wedding her go-ahead to act? Sweet poison, someone should have clarified what her role was.

Your only goal is to marry the king.

Tempest bared her teeth at the man as he took one step in her direction. She'd have to take her cues from those around her. Unless provoked, she would not attack. The serpent hissed as another soldier rushed him. Tempest spun on her heel and gathered the train of her dress. She quickly cut the excess off and began pushing through the crowd toward the altar. Her eyes locked on her king. He wielded a crossbow in one hand and a sword in the other, his long fur cape long gone. Blood spattered him from head to toe, and he smiled as he cut down his attacker.

She could take him now.

All sound ceased as she advanced on Destin. He neither heard nor saw her as she battled her way toward him. His reign would end now.

You're not a murderer.

She faltered. An arrow whistled past her nose, and she blinked. Her life literally flashed before her eyes. A shifter barreled over to the Duchess of Fiergone, knocking the woman to the floor. Tempest snapped out of her stupor, when he snarled at her and closed the distance between them. He took a swipe at her with his broad sword. She ducked and slashed him from elbow to shoulder, cutting deep. Not a killing blow, but bad enough that he dropped his sword.

He growled, eyes narrowed on her. The shifter meant to kill her. Definitely not Pyre's people.

Her attention once again returned to the altar. Destin had disappeared. She needed high ground. Tempest grabbed handfuls of her dress and ran for the altar. It would give her the greatest vantage point, but she'd be exposed as well. She had to be quick.

A soldier caught her about the waist, and she tossed her head back, breaking his nose. He yelled. She stomped the heels of her slippers on the top of his foot and slammed the butt of her dagger into his groin. The man collapsed in a moaning heap as she kept moving. She caught glimpses of periwinkle hair amongst the writhing mass. Hounds.

Before Tempest could work out what to do next, however, she was swept into the large and burly arms of Maxim.

"What?" she yelled as he wasted no time careening through the bloody chaos of the hall to get her out.

"Thought it was high time you escaped," he shouted back, smiling grimly. "Don't want to ruin your dress any further, after all."

Tempest huffed out a laugh. The dress was now covered in blood, torn, and missing its train. "I'd call these alterations an improvement," she joked as they bowled over a man wearing too many feathers in his cap. "You can put me down."

Maxim loped away from the bloody chaos. "No. I have orders."

"What orders?" she said sharply.

"You're to be protected."

"I am the protection," she said flatly.

"I'm taking you to Destin's quarters."

Tempest wrapped her arms around her uncle's shoulders and stared at his dirty face, a knife in each hand.

"Who attacked us?"

Maxim's gaze flicked to hers for a moment. "Us."

She blinked slowly. "But they tried to kill me."

"It had to look good. Today was never meant to be about defeating him in the first place; it was simply about getting the first strike in. Steel yourself, girlie. He's going to be in a mood."

She nodded and swallowed hard. She'd almost attacked the king. If he'd died…then Maven would've become king.

Tempest shivered and closed her eyes for one second.

Chapter Twenty-Seven

Pyre

He'd broken his own rules.

Idiot.

He wasn't supposed to be at the wedding. Nyx was taking care of this part of the plan—they'd already agreed to it. Plus, he was a liability, and everyone knew it, himself included. But every time he thought of his bloody sire getting his grubby, bloodstained hands on Tempest, he could hardly breathe. His damned emotions had been out of control since he'd hauled her freezing body from the sea. She'd almost drowned trying to save his men. She could have died. It changed things for him. Over the years, vengeance had been his sole focus. Pyre had given everything to the cause, but now he found there was something he wasn't willing to give up.

His mate.

It had taken him far too long to admit it.

Nyx is going to kill you.

His life had always been far too dangerous for a wife and kits. It wasn't a risk he could take until now. He smiled grimly. Who better to claim than a fierce assassin? Tempest fitted in his life, whether she realized it or not.

Pyre shifted slightly, his body hidden in the shadows above the ceremony.

Nyx's men hovered around him, their gazes trained on the procession below. The sumptuous crowd of strutting peacocks and fine ladies whispered and gossiped as they waited for their soon-to-be queen. His jaw clenched beneath his black mask as Maven slipped in the far door. What was his slimy half-brother doing out and about? Maven sauntered down the aisle and took his place near the front.

Pyre eyed the king when his flinty gaze turned on his son. Trouble between the ruler and the heir? How very useful in the coming times. The kitsune tried not to let it bother him how well his sire looked. King Destin stood on the altar, dressed head-to-toe in reds and golds, his chin held high, legs braced apart. He cut a powerful figure. Pyre stifled a growl. While he mostly took after his mother, it was still difficult to see some of his own features on the king's face.

The musicians struck up their music, and Pyre's attention snapped to the rear doors of the cathedral as they opened. All thoughts of his father disappeared as he caught sight of Tempest. His chest seized as she took her first step down the aisle.

Agony. That was the only way to describe how she affected him.

She looked stunning. *Too* beautiful, almost ethereal. Her elaborate gown trailed behind her like fresh snow, and the cold diamonds encircling her neck glittered in the light. The silver crown upon her head looked like it was meant for her. She looked immaculate, polished, and elegant. Everything a queen should be.

The placid expression she wore didn't fool him. Tempest was cataloging the room. Always a Hound. As she neared the center of the room, her footsteps slowed a touch before she resumed her speed. He glanced back at the king and froze. The predatory grin worn by Destin and the possessive glint in his eyes sent Pyre over the edge.

Nyx's first explosion rocked the building.

That was their cue.

Pyre signaled the men to attack. *No one* looked at his mate like that. No one.

Their men dropped from the rafters, into the screaming throng of courtiers and onto the backs of unsuspecting guards and soldiers. The crowd screamed, trying to get to their feet. They rushed toward the exits, slippers, wigs, and fans abandoned, as well as those they crushed in their mad dash to escape the carnage. Pyre had no interest in them.

No, he only had eyes for King Destin.

Pyre crept around the room, closing the distance between himself and the altar. A guard rushed him, but he ducked under his arm and swung around, slamming the pommel of his sword into the man's temple. The guard dropped to the ground like a sack of potatoes. Pyre stood, his focus moving back to the altar. Destin had moved away, farther down the dais and into the crowd, wildly swinging his sword around at whoever dared come close, friend or foe. A balding man with a portly belly yelped when he caught the receiving end of one of the king's swings. The man scrambled away as Destin cut down one of Nyx's men.

Red descended over Pyre's eyes as he prowled closer. The king would die this day. He didn't care about anyone but himself, and Destin would destroy the kingdom brick by brick.

He's your father.

Pyre faltered for a moment and shook his head. No. The monster had only contributed to his creation. This man was the demon who strangled a young woman to death simply because she'd had a child and fled to keep that child safe.

He stalked closer to Destin, his eyed locked on the king.

Pyre's keen ears caught the whisper of a blade slicing through the air barely in time. He darted to the right, cursing as the dagger sliced across his left cheek, tearing his mask from his face. He spun and faced his attacker, his hood falling back, his white hair visible. He'd chosen his Mal form for today.

The prince sneered at him, a sword in his hand.

Maven, his half-brother, spat on the floor. "I'm going to

kill you, you filthy mongrel."

Pyre rolled his neck and eyed the prince. His younger brother certainly had the look of their father in him, but where the king was all brawn, the prince had a physique like a serpent. Fast and limber. There was something simultaneously weak and cruel about his disposition. One could almost pity him if it wasn't for the hateful, scheming gleam in his eyes.

"Get back, boy," Pyre snarled at the prince, parrying his next blow before attacking with his own dual daggers. Maven avoided them both, moving like oil.

The prince grinned, the sight chilling. "I don't think so, fox. Your blood is mine."

Pyre kept his rage banked as they danced around each other, intermittently attacking and defending, slashing and ducking, stabbing and backing away. He didn't have time for this rabble. He needed to be done with him. Just kill him and be done with it.

He's your kin.

He growled, hating the thought that the slimy bastard held any relation to him. From the corner of his eye, he caught a flicker of white. His gaze darted toward Tempest as she battled an assailant who was twice her size. Pyre took a step in her direction.

"Look what you're doing, you idiot!" Nyx screamed as she seemed to appear from nowhere, swinging a club.

She bashed Maven on the head, and his eyes rolled up before he collapsed on the ground, his sword skidding across the stone floor, pausing at Pyre's feet.

His sister glared at him. "You almost got your fool-self gutted!"

"Not the first time," he replied.

Nyx shook her head. "I should have known you wouldn't be able to stay away. Now, get your head in the game. Her uncle has it covered. Tempest won't be hurt."

He grinned. "She doesn't need him."

"True." Nyx grabbed his arm and began towing him toward the exit, her fine clothing spattered in blood. "Time to retreat and *actually* follow the plan."

He dug his heels in. Destin needed to be dealt with.

Nyx glared at him. "He's gone, brother."

Pyre glanced over his shoulder and scanned the chaos. The king was nowhere to be seen. *Damn it.*

"You can't go rogue on me now. We've spent too much time on our plans," his sister growled. "Even in this form, you could be recognized."

Today had been a show of how weak the king's defenses were—to cause mischief and havoc and, coincidentally, destroy his wedding day. Even though he longed to hunt the king down, it would be a suicide mission, and Pyre planned to live a long life. Soldiers flooded the cathedral, battling through the panicked courtiers. Nyx was right. It was time to go. They were outnumbered. He inhaled deeply and focused on shifting his white ears completely out of sight. It hurt, and his hearing dulled, but it was a necessary evil. He dropped his black cloak to the floor, revealing gaudy clothing, and clutched Nyx's hand.

"You ready?" he murmured.

"Yes."

They both ran for the door, stumbling and screaming. It was easy to move through the people when they were only feigning panic, not truly terrified. Pyre held his breath as the soldiers pushed past them, not sparing one glance in their direction as they emerged from the ceremonial hall. People only saw what they wanted to see.

They moved through the crush, and as they reached the top of the stairs, the skin between his shoulder blades tingled. He slowed and carefully glanced around the chaos to find whoever was watching him. From beneath his lashes, he glanced up and paused as he locked eyes with the king who stood two stories above. His sire blinked slowly and then smiled before moving away from the banister.

Nyx tugged at his arm, pulling him down the stairs as he tried to digest what had just happened. There was no way Destin could have recognized him. He had been just a child the last time the king had seen him.

As they fled, Pyre couldn't help but feel like something had gone wrong.

Chapter Twenty-Eight

King Destin

The Jester was alive.

Bloody hell.

Of all the things Destin had imagined for his wedding day, discovering that his bastard son was alive rankled more than the damned rebel attack. The Jester didn't think that Destin knew about his other form, but he did. His spies had made sure of it. He stormed to his rooms, shock and anger rolling through him. The bastard had infiltrated his home!

Blood dripped from his sword as his Hounds followed silently in his wake. Clearly, Tempest hadn't given him the heart of the Jester. The question was if she'd knowingly betrayed him.

How was that blasted blighter alive? Any other child would have died in the woods years ago, but somehow the whelp had managed not only to survive but *thrive* and take control of Heimserya's underworld. If he didn't hate the boy so much, he'd actually be impressed at his tenacity.

Tenacity that's now focused on your crown.

His fingers clenched on the pommel of his sword.

It was clear the boy had scented blood with the death of Destin's heir, but the knave would never claim the crown. Maven was as deceptive and slippery as an eel, but he was better than the Talagan pup of a maid. Destin would die before he allowed shifter scum to dethrone him.

His lips twitched. And he had no intention of dying any time soon.

His mind ran over the attack as he ascended the stairs to the royal wing. Why strike today? The palace was a poor target. The rebellion was outnumbered ten to one. An assassin would have had an easier chance murdering anyone from the royal family than a bold-faced attack. Was it a fear-mongering gambit? If so, it wouldn't work.

He reached the top of the stairs and paused, his eyes narrowing before he continued on to his rooms. The Jester was supposed to be dead. He picked up his speed. A mistake had been made, or he had a potential liar and traitor on his hands.

He slammed through the doors leading to his chambers, finding several Hounds guarding each window and his queen-to-be standing stoically next to the fireplace. She was bloodied and disheveled, her perfect gown torn and her hair in disarray. His Lady Hound looked delectable. Irritation pricked him at the thought.

"Leave," he ordered.

Maxim took a step forward, concern plastered across his ugly mug. "Your Grace, it isn't safe to leave you al—"

"Leave," he repeated, his voice thick with warning. "Now." His bride moved to follow, but he held up a hand, his gaze pinned to her face. "My future queen stays."

Maxim glanced at Tempest askance, and Destin almost took a swipe at the Hound. The only person he should obey was his king. Maybe her ties to the Hounds weren't as useful as he'd thought. Her dismissal of her uncle's concern was the only thing that comforted him. She clearly knew her place.

As she should.

Destin slammed the doors shut, the force rattling the lanterns that bracketed the entrance. He heaved a breath and slowly faced the room. Tempest had drifted to his west window, her profile facing him. The light illuminated the painted panes of glass, casting colorful patterns across her pale skin and ruined dress.

He leaned against the door and observed her. Ever dutiful. If only she knew what a prize she was. Every moment she spent in his presence was another blow to her father. Destin covered his mouth with his hand to hide his smile. No one deceived him without repercussions. It would have been easy to have Tempest executed as a child or sold to a Hinterland barbarian, but revenge was so much more satisfying as he watched it play out year after year.

His attention moved to the diamond choker encircling

her throat. Flecks of dried blood spattered the gems. It made a barbaric but appealing vision. Was such a deadly beauty also deceptive?

Did she betray you?

He pushed away from the door and tossed his sword onto the nearest chair, then moved to the mahogany cabinet where he kept his spirits. Destin watched his intended from beneath his lashes. Spending time with Tempest had taught him one thing: she wasn't a very good actress. She loved Heimserya and hated shifters as much as he did, which was ironic, because Destin was really the root of her pain. As for the Jester—Destin's dirty fingers squeezed the glass he pulled from the cabinet—he was known for his trickery. It wasn't a far stretch to reason that the Dark Court had pulled the wool over her eyes.

In all honesty, the king didn't think she had it in her to deceive him, but women... They were tricky creatures. They betrayed as easily as they crooned sweet nothings in one's ear. It was in their very makeup. Women could not help it. He liked to think his Hound was better than the women he'd formerly engaged with, but she was still female—expendable—no matter her assets.

He carefully pulled a bottle of fire whiskey off the shelf and took a long draught straight from the bottle. It had always been the plan to use her as a martyr, framing either the rebels or the South Isles. Destin had hoped for the latter. He'd wanted to at least have some fun with her first. He needed a new heir. That meant a year, minimum. But if she had tricked him...

Her time would be cut short.

"You should sit," he murmured, nodding toward the chairs and table that sat in the center of the room. Delicacies were set artfully across the surface, along with fine wine. The perfect meal for newlyweds. "After the ordeal we've been through, the least we can do is recoup our strength."

Tempest pulled away from the window and rubbed at her bare arms. "If it doesn't trouble you, my lord, I would like to sit near the fire. I can't seem to get warm these days."

He sauntered to the table and smiled as she passed him, her hand gently touching his bicep. His body heated at the innocent touch. Destin plucked several choice items from their post-wedding private dinner: sliced meats, an assortment of cheeses, flaky crackers, tiny pastries of caramel and cinnamon, and a single apple and set them on a small china plate.

He dragged a chair across the floor, managing to balance the plate of food in his other hand. Destin groaned as he sat. He flashed a smile at his betrothed. "I'm getting old, dearest."

She cocked her head, her crown sitting precariously on her brow. "My lord, you are hardly decrepit, as you know. You're a fine male specimen, to be sure."

"Such compliments," he murmured. "What a lucky man I am." He held out the plate after plucking a few pieces of meat and cheese and popping them into his mouth, chewing and then swallowing. "You should eat something.

I doubt you've had much of anything today."

"I'm not very hungry." Tempest held up her filthy hands. "Plus, I'm hardly in a state to touch anything that I'll eat."

"We both need a bath. I'll give you that." He pulled a dagger from his waist and observed her as she watched him set the food on the small table between them, unsheathed a blade, and begin cutting the apple. The knife glinted in the firelight as he focused on his work. "The attack was distressing, to say the least. Violence turns anyone's stomachs, even if they've had training." He peeked at her from beneath his lashes.

Her eyes tracked his movements as he carved the apple. His spies had informed him that she had a weakness for the simple fruits. Destin leaned closer and held the piece out to her. "Take a bite, dearest. I can't have my fierce bride going hungry. And it would settle me to see you eat something."

Her stomach gave a small growl, and he couldn't help the small chuckle as she rolled her eyes. Any other lady would have likely been mortified, but not his Hound. He wiggled the apple slice, daring her to take it.

Tempest bent closer, her teeth clamping on the apple slice, her lips brushing his fingers. Sweet poison, it was sexy. She chewed the morsel before swallowing it. Destin suppressed his smile as he wiped his knife and hands on a cloth before replacing it in its sheath. Now all he had to do was wait. His poison blade was his favorite. Tasteless and odorless—a poison refined from his favorite source. The mimkia plant.

If she was innocent, she had nothing to fear. He'd interrogate her and then administer the antidote. If she'd betrayed him, well, then she'd signed her own death warrant and he'd enjoy what fun he could get from her before she expired. Just a few minutes and the poison would take effect. Sleepiness. Heavy limbs. An inability to fight.

He ate tidbits from the plate, relaxed into his seat, and noted as her lids began to droop and she leaned her chin on her palm.

He rose from his chair and reached for her hand. "You are tired, my dear," he crooned. "I think you need to lie down. Come, I'll help you to my—"

"No, thank you," Tempest cut in, frowning as she staggered to her feet. She braced a hand against his chest, swaying slightly. "I feel—I need to return to my own room, I think. You are right: I'm in shock. I just need some time to…recover. Today is not what I expected."

She staggered around him, and he let her go, casually stalking after her. He placed a hand on the door above her hand as she fumbled with the lock.

"No need. What is mine is yours. We were to be married today anyway."

"I think I should return to my rooms."

He leaned closer and pressed a kiss to the back of her neck. "You aren't going anywhere, Tempest."

She stiffened. "My lord, it is unseemly. I must go."

"No."

Tempest spun to face him, her gray eyes narrowing on his face. Destin grinned. He loved when her feistiness came out. His kitten liked to scratch and he, for one, enjoyed each and every moment.

"Move aside, my lord." She swayed, but held her ground. "I'm leaving."

He leaned down, a smirk playing about his lips at her sass. "You are not the master here."

His words triggered a response. He saw the mutiny and determination flash though her eyes a second before she jerked to his left, beneath his arm. He grabbed her forearm and yanked her back. She twisted toward him, and he caught the glint of a blade a moment before pain slid across his nose and beneath his right eye. Destin hissed and released her, gently probing his face.

"You bitch!" he growled.

She'd actually cut him. None of his partners had ever dared raise a hand to him. He bared his teeth in a smile, arousal rushing through his body. This was going to be more fun than he'd anticipated. She took a stumbling step away and tripped on her dress, crashing to the floor. Destin launched himself at Tempest as she twisted and kicked. He wheezed and dropped to the ground, his hands cupping his crotch. It *hurt*. Tears blurred his eyes, and he blindly reach for his lady, snagging some of her hair in his fingers, his other hand digging into her thigh to hold her in place. She grunted and kneed him in the face

He opened his mouth to yell but choked on his own pain. Tempest crawled away from him, and he glanced in shock at his fist. She'd sliced off some of her own hair to escape him. Tempest stumbled to her feet as he wheezed. With clumsy fingers, she managed to open the door and fled. He gurgled on a laugh as more tears squeezed from his eyes. Poisoned and outnumbered, she still thought she could escape his wrath.

"Guards," he huffed.

Two men appeared in the doorway of his chambers and stiffened when they spotted him on the floor. Destin hauled himself to his hands and feet, then retched. He slapped away the helping hand of one of the guards and clambered to his feet as his stomach and groin cramped with pain.

"Bring my future queen back to me," he growled.

They were far from done.

Chapter Twenty-Nine

Tempest

That bastard had attacked her.

Tempest stumbled into her closet as the world lurched beneath her feet. She crashed into the dresser, her fingers clinging to the edge as she leaned heavily against it, her head swimming.

He drugged you. Get it out.

Tempest shoved her fingers down her throat. She trembled and retched, spitting bile and chewed apple onto the gleaming wood floor. Her eyes watered, and she wiped her mouth with the back of her hand. Her legs shook like they were on the verge of collapse.

This is the first place they will look for you. Move.

She tugged on the dress but couldn't get her fingers to work well enough to remove the buttons or laces. Tempest clumsily groped for her dagger and sliced the skirt. Grabbing handfuls, she cut the soiled fabric from her body until only the corset-like bodice was left. There wasn't time to do anything about it. Good thing she always wore hose beneath her dresses. They would pass for trousers. She blinked hard as the room waved and she swayed, bumping her hip against the cursed dresser. When the hell had she lost her shoes?

Tempest wiggled her bare toes and lurched toward her boots. She had to get out of there. It was a bloody miracle she'd gotten away from the king in the first place. Jerkily, she managed to get her boots on and collected her emergency bag, sword, and weapons. A huge wave of exhaustion hit her, and she could barely keep her eyes open. Wicked hell, what had he given her?

She stumbled from her closet and fought to keep her balance. Her body was shutting down. If she didn't get out now, she'd pass out and be at the mercy of the king. Movement from her window caught her eye. She sloppily held a dagger and squinted, trying to make out who was in her room.

The princess's face swam into view. "You—Ansette, what are—"

The girl seized her arm, eyes wide. "What is wrong?" A cool hand touched Tempest's brow. "You're burning up and spattered in blood. You need to get into bed now."

"Can't," Tempest gasped, grabbing the princess. She closed her eyes and tried to get her balance. "I need to leave." Opening her eyes, she focused hard on the girl. "I need...no. *We* need to get out of here, Ansette. Now. There's no time."

Ansette's gaze narrowed, and she propelled Tempest to

the door. The girl checked the corridor before navigating outside. The princess steered her into a dark, empty room three doors down from her own. The girl locked the door, towed Tempest through the dusty room, and pulled back an old tapestry, revealing a hidden passage.

"Before we go any further, I need you to be honest with me," Ansette murmured. "Are you with the rebels?"

Tempest shook her head, a lie on the tip of her tongue.

"Just be honest with me. I'm not some little girl you have to protect from the truth."

She had no doubt of that, looking at the princess standing there with her head held high. Whatever the king had given her was clouding her mind. Her tongue felt too slow and thick in her mouth as she replied, "I just want a better future for Heimserya. Better for everyone." Her head drooped.

"None of that!" the girl whispered harshly. She shook Tempest. "Do not go to sleep. I'm not sure what you've been dosed with, but sleeping is the last thing you want to do." She huffed. "Even drugged, you're a vault of secrets. I can't imagine what your training must have been like."

Tempest smiled widely. "Hound."

Her head lolled to the side as she registered shouting and the thunder of steps. Ansette pulled her into the hidden passage, made sure the tapestry was back in place, and began guiding them down the narrow dark passage.

Tempest's boot slipped, and it was only Ansette's strong grip that kept her from tumbling down the steps headfirst.

"I wish you had told me sooner," the girl whispered.

"Things could have been so much easier for the both of us."

Tempest blinked. "How—"

"You're not the only one who sees the suffering and wants things to change for the better." She paused. "I kept waiting for someone to reach out. Not all royals are bad."

"Never thought you were," Tempest slurred. There was a reason she liked the princess. "Where are you taking me?" She didn't really care where it was, as long as she could lie down and sleep.

Weak light shone between the two stones on the wall, illuminating Ansette's profile as she glanced over her shoulder. "The palace is full of secret passageways. This one is only known to those of royal blood."

"Not even the Hounds?" Tempest asked, her voice sounding loud in her own ears.

"Our family is secretive. Hush, we will be passing some of the guest rooms. Sound echoes in here something terrible, and we must get you out before it's too late."

Tempest closed her mouth, hardly daring to breathe. She focused on putting one foot ahead of the other as time slowed. Every step was a fight. Frowning, her mind went back to their conversation and she struggled to process the princess's words. There was something wrong about them. And then it clicked.

"Must get *me* out? What about you, Ansette? It isn't safe for you here," she muttered.

"And you think it's any safer for me out there?" the girl countered. "If I go missing, you and I both know my father will blame the rebellion for my kidnapping."

"But the king is already at war with the Talagans. How

much worse could things possibly get if you leave—"

"My place is here." A pause. "To act as your contact inside the palace. You cannot tell me you don't need one."

"It's not safe," Tempest argued, feeling her nausea return. Sweet poison, she was going to vomit. "Your father isn't who you think he is."

"I've grown up with him my whole life. Do you think I'm blind to his machinations? Do you think I don't know what he did to my brother?" Her voice broke on the last word.

Way to go, Tempest. You made the princess cry.

"I'm sorry."

"You didn't kill him. My father did. He was the one who released the information. We're just pawns."

"He cares for you," Temp offered.

"Only as long as I fall into line. If he knew what I'd been up to for the last year, he'd have had me executed already."

"What have you been up to?" Tempest asked, her words slightly garbled.

"The same thing you have been up to, it seems."

She wanted to question Ansette more, but it was too difficult to speak and to walk. They twisted and turned down narrow passage after narrow passage. When they finally reached the end of the passageway, Tempest almost cried in joy. The girl paused at the end of the corridor and leaned her ear against an old, plain wooden door. A bitter draft whistled through cracks around it, and Tempest shivered at the haunting melody it created.

"I think the coast is clear," Ansette said softly. "You need to go now."

Tempest sagged against the slimy wall and scowled. "I

don't want to leave you, but I know it's the smart thing. You need to be careful."

"I always am."

"I can't prove it yet...but I believe your brother might have had something to do with the assassination attempt."

Ansette's expression turned grave. "I'm not ignorant of his sadistic ways. I'll keep my head down and keep out of his way." She straightened and threw her shoulders back, her lips forming a sharp smile. "Living with such a family has given me many skills. I can handle myself, make no mistake." She pulled Tempest from the wall and hugged her fiercely. "Be careful, and if you need to send any messages to me, send them through Maibeth, the cook."

Tempest nodded, her head bobbing. Bloody hell, she hoped she could remember that.

She pulled back and gazed down at the resourceful royal. This was who should be on the throne. Ansette was the ruler the kingdom needed. Heimserya already had their queen—they just didn't know it yet.

"Stay safe and be careful," the girl said, opening the small door.

"You as well."

Tempest stepped from the passageway, the bitter wind waking her up the tiniest bit. She blinked. It led completely outside the palace gates. Useful, but only if she could remember where it was.

Move.

She made sure that her hood was secure and stumbled north toward the city gates. The king would expect her to go to the Hounds for help. It wouldn't be safe there.

Staying in the city wasn't an option, either. The people knew her face—Destin had made sure of that. Each step she took felt like it would be her last. Tempest dug deep and pressed on, determined not to slip in the snow and fall asleep.

A wagon trundled past her, and she hopped on, tucking herself under a blanket. She gagged at the stench. Someone was emptying privies. That alone should keep her awake. Tempest wiggled in between pots, and her nerves were strung tight as the wagon stopped.

"What's the meaning of this?" a thready voice whined.

"The king is missing his betrothed. We're to check everyone."

"He has himself a runaway bride, eh?" the wagon-owner said with a chuckle. "Women are flighty things."

"This one is dangerous too," the guard mumbled.

Damn right.

Tempest pulled her dagger from her waist with a trembling hand as several heavy steps crunched in the snow near her. She squeezed her eyes shut and prepared herself. If they discovered her, she'd fight her way out or die trying.

The blanket rustled near her feet, and she didn't dare move as it was lifted the tiniest bit. A man gagged as the blanket was lowered.

"That's disgusting. How can you stand the smell?" the soldier asked.

"You get used to it. Am I allowed to go?" the wagon-owner whined. "Got places to be."

"Get on with you," the soldier barked.

The wagon jerked, and Tempest winced as something wet sloshed over the edge of the nearest pot onto her leg. She dry-heaved and tried to stifled the sounds. But once she started, she couldn't stop. Her throat felt too thick, and the air was dry and scratchy as if she hadn't drunk in days.

Tempest scooted to the back of the wagon and peeked out. It was the wrong move. Her sober self knew it the second she locked eyes with a soldier on the top of the wall.

"I see her!" he cried, lifting his bow. She retched and rolled from the wagon, crashing to her knees. She shoved to her feet and ran past the wagon toward the woods, her feet catching on rocks.

Zigzags. Don't give them an easy target.

Half stumbling and half running, she made her way toward the dense forest. Sweat coated her body, and her lungs were on fire. She could barely breathe. Tempest tripped and fell, her right leg taking the brunt of her weight.

An arrow whipped past her ear. Another.

Get up and run.

She lurched to her feet and darted into the woods, thankful that the snow wasn't as deep. All sound ceased to exist as she ran for her life. In the back of her mind, she knew she was leaving a trail straight to her and that it would have been better if she took to the trees. But there was no way she could climb. Even if she did manage it, she'd have broken her neck on the first jump. And it wasn't as if she was in control of her body any longer.

Glancing over her shoulder, she couldn't see anyone,

but that didn't mean they weren't still pursuing her. They would likely send the dogs after her.

Fatigue weighed her down like a boulder on her back, crushing the air from her lungs and begging her to close her eyes. She tripped, and her arms wind-milled as she tried to catch her balance. Tempest crashed face-first into the snow. She lay there and slowly lifted her head, whispering a prayer of thanks. The entrance to a burrow of some sort was right in front of her. Hopefully, the beastie wasn't home or wouldn't mind her presence.

She yanked her knife from her waist and crawled through the small hole. It was blessedly empty. Tempest turned onto her back, panting, and stared at the ceiling. Two large bushes had grown next to an oak tree and formed a bower of sorts.

"Just f-five minutes," she stammered, scooting until her back was pressed to the tree trunk and she was nestled between the roots.

The blade fell from her fingers, and she couldn't pick it up again.

Her eyelids fluttered closed, and her mind went blank.

Only five minutes.

Chapter Thirty

Pyre

"Get ready to move," Pyre ordered his men.

They all moved into action to pack up their makeshift camp. Destin's forces were moving into action as they spoke. The king's army had been gathering troops and steadily moving through the province of Merjeri toward Betraz. Pyre smiled as he gazed down at the map in his hands. The king expected the rebels to attack from the farms in Talaga as they had two times before. The Kopalian giants causing mischief along the borders of Betraz and Fiergone were a bonus. While Destin would be looking to the east for the next attack, the shifter forces would attack from the west.

Pyre rolled up the map and tucked it into his back pocket, his attention moving to the south. The towering trees of the thick forest blocked the capital from view, but he felt himself pulled in that direction. Pyre growled and pulled his hat from his head, slapping it against his trousers. He'd left Tempest again when all his instincts had begged him to steal her away. Coming to terms with what she'd meant to him had been difficult, but standing aside while she made her own way was even harder. It seemed like all they did was walk away from each other when they were stronger together.

But sentimentality didn't win a war. Neither of them could afford weakness now. The stakes were too high. It was lucky Nyx had gotten to him before he'd made a grave mistake that he couldn't take back.

Pyre stuffed his hat back on his head and huffed. The damned woman was turning him into a fool.

His sister approached from his left, her boots crunching in the deep snow. She pushed her dark braid from her shoulder and paused next to him, her gaze trained to the south. Nyx hadn't said much to him since they'd left the capital. She had a nasty mouth when provoked and had learned to keep quiet until she was calm enough to have a conversation. Her self-control was impressive. She glanced at him from the corner of her eye, and Pyre squirmed. She was still angry.

"She can fend for herself, you idiot."

"I know."

Nyx rolled her eyes and crossed her arms. "Then why are you brooding over here, hmmm?"

"Just because I comprehend a fact, doesn't make it any easier to ignore the scratchy feeling beneath my skin."

"You alphas," she groaned. "So dramatic."

"Just you wait until your mate comes along," he retorted. "Most men don't have a tenth of my self-discipline and patience." Well, fraying self-control.

"On that, we can both agree." She spun and placed a hand on his shoulder. "Tempest is a distraction."

"I know," he bit out, pinching the bridge of his nose.

"You can't live in this in-between space. You need to put her completely out of your mind, or you need to claim her."

"And how do you suppose I do either of those things?"

"By making a bloody decision. The Jester I know would never let anything come between what he desired."

"The bloody woman is engaged to another man!"

"She is not married. You made damn sure of that today. And when have you ever cared about such things?"

"It's Tempest," he said softly. She made him want to be better, to do better.

Pyre groaned and ran a hand over his face. Not for the first time, Pyre wished Tempest wasn't so damned *good.* He'd been so close to kissing her in the barracks. She'd read the intent on his face and had scrambled out of there like a frightened hare. But it was one of the things he loved about her. She was loyal. When Tempest gave her word, she meant it. His sire may be the devil, but she still upheld her vows. That type of honor was attractive and admirable.

"It will all work out, brother." Nyx patted him. "The men are ready to move. We're just waiting on the scouts to return."

Pyre nodded as she strode away, his head swimming with thoughts of his mate and the battle ahead. His ears twitched as he picked up the sound of running footsteps headed their way. Brine loped into view, a limp figure in his arms. A weary traveler or one of their people? The figure looked too small to be one of their scouts.

He inhaled deeply, scenting the air. Pyre staggered, his heart racing. It was Tempest.

"What's wrong?" he demanded as Brine skidded to a stop.

The wolf's ears were flat against his head, and worry carved lines into his face. "One of the scouts discovered her and called for me. We found her in a burrow beneath the snow."

Pyre pushed back her hood and scanned her pale face. "Any injuries?"

"A few minor scrapes but no blood." A pause. "I can't... I can't wake her up. She won't wake up."

"Nyx!" he barked. His men gathered around them as his sister appeared at his side. "She needs help."

His sister placed her hand over his mate's forehead. "She has a fever, and her breathing is labored." Nyx frowned. "She couldn't have been out in the elements for long. It wouldn't have caused this reaction. Was she sick at the wedding?"

"Not that I know of," Pyre said. He inhaled deeply near Tempest's cheek and frowned. "She doesn't smell right." Another inhale, and his nose wrinkled. Her breath was bitter.

Nyx leaned closer and inhaled. Her eyes widened, and the color drained from her face. "Poison," she whispered.

His stomach bottomed out. His claws slid from his fingertips, but he barely felt the pain. Someone had poisoned his mate.

"Her clothing is wet," Brine said. "We need to get her warm."

"Not until I know what she's been given. Different types of poison react to temperatures. The cold might be the only thing keeping the poison at bay," Nyx said. "I need my herbs and a place to test and treat her."

"Where is Briggs?" Pyre snapped, tremors running up and down his arms. Someone had tried to kill *his* mate.

"He's in the village ahead of us."

"Swiftly," he called. The horsey man stepped forward. "I need you to carry us to Briggs." He glanced at Brine. "Can you carry my sister?"

"I can."

Brine held Tempest out, and Pyre pulled her into his arms and held her close to his chest. Terror threatened to overwhelm him, but he forced it down. He had to be calm for Temp's sake. "Everyone, move out. We'll meet you at the village."

Pyre felt neither the cold, nor the wind, nor the snow against his face as they finally arrived on the outskirts of the village. A howl cut through the air, letting him know Brine was close with Nyx. Pyre vaulted from Swiftly's back, Tempest limp in his arms, and leaped up the steps leading to one of their small holdings. He kicked the door open and swept inside.

Briggs held two curved, wicked-looking blades and stood in the middle of the room. The healer cursed. "How about a warning next—" he bit off his words as he spotted Tempest in Pyre's arms. "What happened?"

"Nyx says poison," Pyre responded, his voice shaking as he moved. "Brine found her in the woods."

"How in the hell did she end up in the woods?" Briggs growled and grabbed a towel from the small table at the end of the room before moving to the fireplace to retrieve the boiled kettle. "Place her on the bed."

Pyre strode across the room and laid her down on the mattress. He pushed her hood from her face and ran a hand over her cheek. Her skin was hot to the touch.

Boots thumped against the porch, then Nyx came bustling in, followed by Brine and Swiftly, who both only wore trousers. The wolf slammed the door behind them. Nyx stripped her gloves and cloak off and tossed them into a chair on the right side of the bed.

"What are we dealing with, Nyx?" Briggs asked as he nudged Pyre out of the way.

He growled and glared at the healer.

Briggs held his hands up. "I only wish to help. You need to move so I can do so."

Pyre nodded and moved to the foot of the bed. This wasn't happening.

"Poison," Nyx said sharply.

"Damn it." The healer opened Tempest's mouth and inhaled. "Bitter, but sweet. What are her symptoms?"

"Shallow breathing, fever, sweats, and unconsciousness," Nyx replied, stripping Tempest of her cloak.

Pyre stiffened as he got a good look at her clothing. She still wore the bodice of her wedding dress. Jagged scraps of the skirt clung to the soiled hose she wore. Weapons were strapped to every part of her body.

She ran with only the clothes on her back and her blades. Dread churned in his gut.

"Pyre?"

He blinked at his sister.

She gave him a stern look. "Take her boots off. We need to check every inch of her skin to see if she was injected or if she ingested the poison, perhaps both. It will narrow it down."

Woodenly, he yanked her boots off and hissed when he caught sight of her feet. They were bloodied. She didn't even have socks on.

"I need to turn her onto her side."

Briggs helped turn Tempest over, and Nyx used a knife to cut through the laces on the bodice. Her skin was red and bruised. Pyre snapped a look in Swiftly's and Brine's direction, but both men had their backs firmly to the bed. Shifters didn't care about nudity or privacy, but Tempest appreciated privacy.

Be honest. You don't want anyone looking at your mate unclothed.

He was a jealous brute.

"If you don't strop growling," Nyx warned, "I will toss you outside or gag you. You're putting everyone on edge."

His upper lip curled, and he snarled at his sister. He was barely keeping it together.

Nyx slapped a warm wet rag against his chest as she passed by. "Clean her feet."

He took the rag between his numb fingers and did as he was told. His mind raced as he cleaned Tempest's heels, and Briggs and Nyx began scouring his mate's body for needle spots. Where had her uncles been? Why had there been no one to help Tempest? How had she been exposed?

He blinked, and the rag fell from his nerveless fingers. A whine escaped him, and he began to shake. "It's my fault," he whispered.

Nyx frowned at him. "She made her own decision. Don't take this upon yourself."

"He saw me," Pyre mumbled, his eyes glued on Tempest's frozen, unconscious face. He wanted nothing more than for her to open her eyes. "Destin recognized me. He knew I was the Jester. Tempest was tasked with giving him my head." He wheezed as if kicked in the gut and braced himself on the mattress.

"He wouldn't have let her live," Nyx said, more to herself than anyone else. "He wouldn't—"

"He likes suffering, and she was his trophy." His claws sliced through the bedding, and he shook.

"No punctures on my side." Briggs said. "You?"

"None," Nyx huffed. "So, ingestion. I'll swab her mouth

and test it against any of the antidotes I have on hand. Also, we need charcoal."

Pyre lifted his head, tears burning in his eyes as his sister ran small strips of linen along the inside of Tempest's cheeks. Nyx collected the strips and strode purposefully to the table and began mixing potions together in little cups before dropping the linen into each cup. She hissed and slammed her hand against the table, rattling the contents.

"What is it?" he croaked.

His sister turned to face him, her expression pinched. "Mimkia."

"You can fix it, right?" Mimkia poison was common.

"You don't understand," she whispered. "It's the poison the king used on the villages."

He flashed hot and cold. Nyx had been searching for an antidote since the beginning of 'the plague.' The people afflicted by the drug in the villages and towns throughout Heimserya and Talaga had been fed a diluted version of the drug: all the better to get them slowly addicted to it, even as their internal organs failed and they fell into a never-ending sleep. Everyone who drank the poison died.

"No," Pyre rasped. His lungs seized, and he couldn't breathe. He stood there, frozen to the spot, until Briggs removed his shirt and began unlacing his trousers.

Pyre lunged around the bed and grabbed the healer by the throat. "What the hell are you doing?"

Briggs slowly placed a hand over Pyre's. "She needs to be warmed up. Now that we know what the poison is, we can move forward. If you can control yourself, take your clothes off and get in the bed."

Pyre slowly pulled back, frowning at the small punctures around the healer's neck. Then he fumbled with his clothes, fingers uncharacteristically clumsy. Pyre crawled into the bed with Tempest, wincing at how cold her skin was. It was as if she'd been carved from a block of ice. He moved her hair out of the way and wrapped himself around her. This was the second time within a month he'd found himself naked with his mate but not in the way that he wanted.

Pyre shuddered and clutched her tighter, his ears focused on her labored breathing and slow heartbeat. Nyx and Briggs moved to the other side of the bed. They opened Tempest's mouth and slowly fed her charcoal water.

"I'll head back to the capital," Brine muttered, his back to them as he watched the flames. "Aleks created this abomination. He has the antidote."

"That will be two days journey round trip ," Nyx said. "She's progressed faster than anyone we've come across. The poison wasn't diluted. Two days is too long."

Two days.

Pyre pressed his face into the crook of Tempest's neck and forced himself to take deep slow breaths. "What else can you do?"

Nyx poured a few drops of the purple tincture between Tempest's lips, followed by a bright yellow one that smelled sharp and astringent. "This should help with the fever, and the other will help keep her lungs open."

"And what of the poison?"

She slowly met his gaze, her eyes filled with sorrow.

He bared his teeth. "She's not going to die. I won't allow it."

"I don't think... Pyre, I don't think we have anything that'll—"

"Don't you *dare* give up," he growled. He tightened his arms around his mate and glared at Nyx. "There must be something you can try. Anything. You're a poison mistress. Heal her!"

His sister held his gaze and then walked around the bed. Glass bottles clinked together softly before his sister came back. She held a small bottle with inky liquid.

"You're out of your mind," Briggs uttered in a low tone. "You'll kill her."

Nyx ignored the healer and sat on the chair next to the bed. She held out the tincture. "This is Midnight Kiss."

Pyre glared. It was one of the deadliest poisons. It burned its victims from the inside out and caused their hearts to beat so fast that they exploded. Pyre opened his mouth, and she held up a hand.

"You know I've studied both Midnight Kiss and Mimkia. The poison in Tempest will slow her bodily functions until her heart completely gives up. Midnight Kiss does the opposite. It accelerates the heart and heats the body up to ferocious temperatures."

"This is dangerous." Briggs ran his hand over the top of his head. "But she's dying, Pyre. It's our only chance at counteracting the drug. The choice is up to you. You're her mate."

Pyre lifted his head and gazed down at Tempest's unconscious face. What would she want? He swallowed hard and pressed a kissed to her cheek. The Hound had never shied away from a challenge in her life.

"Give it to her," he murmured.

Nyx carefully administered three drops of black liquid into Tempest's mouth and then poured a little water between her lips.

"How long will this take?"

"I don't know."

"Leave," Pyre whispered.

Nyx, Briggs, and Swiftly all filed out of the large main room into a small room. Brine approached on the opposite side. The wolf bent at the waist and leaned his forehead against Tempest's, a pained whine escaping him.

"You are strong," Brine growled. "You will not slip away in sleep. That is a cowardly way to die. You are a warrior. Fight, pup. *Fight.*"

Pyre watch as his second then straightened up and followed the others into the adjacent room and closed the door behind him. He ignored their muffled voices and gently turned his mate in his arms. He gazed at her lifeless face. His heart broke.

"I've been so stupid," he whispered to her, his breath fanning onto her lips. He stroked her cheek, the wing of her eyebrow, and the slope of her nose. "If I'd only been honest with you from the very beginning... When you wake up, I will never leave your side again." A tear tracked down his cheek. "You are mine, and I am yours."

He cupped her cheek and brushed his lips across hers.

Pyre pulled back and settled Tempest against his chest. He counted each of her breaths and prayed that the next one wouldn't be her last.

Chapter Thirty-One

Pyre

"We have to leave. It's been two days, Pyre. Damien is holding the line, but you are the leader. You must be there," Nyx said, her tone brooking no argument.

He nodded, brushing a sweaty strand of hair from Tempest's pale face. "I know."

"We can leave her with the village healer—"

"No. Where I go, she goes," he cut her off brusquely. "Tempest can handle the journey, right?"

"If she was going to die from the poison, it would have happened already," Briggs said stoically. "She can travel, but you need to be mindful of her body heat. It would be easy for her to become too cold and for fluid to gather in her lungs."

"Brother," Nyx began in a low tone.

"Enough," Pyre said and stood from the bed, the frame

groaning. "She comes with me." His attention turned to Brine who stood quietly in the corner, staring out the front window. "Brine."

The wolf eyed him. "Yes?"

"Have Swiftly go ahead of us and make sure sleeping quarters are ready for Tempest when we arrive at the war camp. I don't want her exposed to the elements any longer than need be."

"Consider it done," Brine said softly before exiting the cottage, the door clattering shut behind him.

Pyre looked at his sister. Her somber expression spelled mutiny. "Speak your mind, Nyx."

"I care for Tempest, but she is a distraction. Your focus should be on our people, our warriors, our cause."

"It is."

"Is it?" She arched a brow.

"I've given everything to our people, and I will continue to do so." He pointed at his unconscious mate. "But I will not leave my other half alone among strangers."

Nyx nodded. "And when we arrive at the camp?"

"I will fight with my men and leave her in the loving care of Briggs."

The quiet healer shallowly bowed. "I will care for her as if she was my own."

"Good. Let's move," Pyre commanded.

Chapter Thirty-Two

Tempest

So bloody tired.

Her eyes flickered behind her eyelids, and Tempest began to rouse. Tingles ran up and down her arms and legs as she tried to move into a more comfortable position. Only a few more minutes of sleep. She grunted when her body didn't immediately obey the command to roll onto her left side.

She shivered, goosebumps rising along her skin. Winter's bite, it was bloody cold. A thread of unease curled in her belly when the chill didn't abate. Something was very wrong. Flashes of memories skipped through her mind, and she stiffened. The burrow. Sleeping in the snow. She had to get moving now.

Temp moaned as she opened her gritty eyes and blinked at the white snow ceiling of the burrow. She frowned and rubbed her blurry eyes before once again focusing on the ceiling. The roof consisted of strong wooden beams with canvas stretched over them. Her heart began to pound as she painfully sat up and massaged her throbbing temples. The room waved, and she shivered as the cold seemed to cut straight to her bones. She tugged the blanket up around her shoulders and ears as the canvas walls of the tent fluttered in the bitter wind.

A tent.

A lavish tent.

Colorful carpets covered the floor, and luxurious pillows formed seating around a low-set table to her right. A woodstove sat in the far-left corner, and the glow of red coals peeked out between the grates. A long table lay to her right, flush against the wall, maps and weapons scattered haphazardly across its surface. Dread filled her as her eyes latched on to a decanter full of fire whiskey. There was only one person she knew who religiously drank fire whiskey.

The king.

Terror skittered down her spine, and she glanced to the left, toward the entrance that led to what appeared to be a larger section of the tent. How much longer did she have before he returned? Tempest flipped back the blanket and checked for restraints. Nothing. He must have thought her too sick to try to escape. Painstakingly, she inched toward the right side of the bed, determined to get to the weapons table. Her body cried out in pain, and each movement was stiff and awkward.

She hissed as her feet touched the floor, her toes curling. She was so damned cold. Her legs shook when she tried to stand, and Tempest collapsed back on the mattress, her breathing labored. Sweat dampened her brow, and her pulse kicked up. There would be no escape in this condition. Her attention moved back to the table covered in knives. If she couldn't run, she could at least protect herself.

Tempest lowered herself to the floor and painstakingly crawled on her hands and knees to the table. Sweat dampened the nape of her neck and her palms as she reached the table. Carefully, Temp stretched her arm up and groped for the first blade she could find. Her fingers curled over a cool hilt, and she pulled it back. It was a simple dagger, but it would do the job. Her body shook as she clawed her way back to the bed. She placed the weapon on the mattress and grabbed fistfuls of the sheets, praying her muscles would hold long enough for her to get back into the bed.

Her throat burned, and her belly cramped as she huffed and puffed, barely managing to flop herself onto the mattress. Shivering, she scooched toward the headboard with silky pillows and propped herself up, wheezing. She needed a drink, badly. A small pitcher sat on the ornate circular side table to her left. She licked her chapped lips. Was it worth it?

He poisoned you.

She shoved down her need for water and wriggled down into her covers, the blade safely in her possession.

Destin hadn't wanted to kill her after all. The drug he'd given her had made her lethargic and rendered her unconscious. But for what purpose?

Her heart skipped a beat, and she focused inward, assessing her body for the type of pain she was experiencing. She wiggled her hips and trembled when nothing pinched or ached in her groin. Surely if he'd raped her, she would feel something? Her uncles had explained to her what happened when a woman lost her virginity, and it wasn't usually pleasant for the woman the first time.

Nausea rose high and fast, and she turned her face to the left, heaving. Bile dripped from her lips but nothing else. She shook as she wiped her mouth with the back of her arm, and tears flooded her eyes.

Don't cry. Once you start, you won't stop.

She clenched her fists and sucked in a shuddering breath before collapsing back on the pillows. Tempest couldn't afford to be emotional. Emotions led to mistakes. And mistakes led to death. She wasn't ready to die.

Calm yourself. Think. Don't feel.

For a while, all she did was stare at nothing. Finally, she looked at the ceiling and began to count her breaths. Her eyes slowly dried, and her racing heart slowed. Grim determination replaced her initial fear. She palmed the knife. Destin would come for her, and, when he did, she'd strike hard and true. He'd never hurt another person again, and he'd never get to have her.

Footsteps crunched in the snow, and she snapped her attention toward the entrance to the right. Tempest closed her eyes and made sure her breathing was regulated. She cracked open her eyes just a sliver as the flap to the larger part of the tent was pushed back. From her angle, she could only see the man's boots. Her muscles threatened to lock up, but the boots disappeared from view. Fabric rustled, and hinges groaned.

A trunk opening, perhaps?

The light steps whispered over the carpet, growing louder as the person drew closer.

Everything stopped as the intruder paused in the entrance, his head bowed as he fiddled with the buckle on his chest plate. His armor was splattered with blood and mud.

She gasped; a gurgle stuck in the back of her throat. His head snapped up, and icy blue eyes locked on her.

Mal. The Jester.

Her bottom lip trembled. She didn't care what form he wore. He'd found her.

A choked sob escaped her, and then everything broke free. He rushed to the bed and pulled her into his arms. She cried, not caring how his armor pressed harshly against her.

He swaddled her in the blanket and deposited her into his lap, soft crooning sounds falling from his lips. Helplessly, she clung to him.

"It's okay, love," Pyre said, rocking them back and forth. "You're safe."

"I thought you were the king," she sobbed.

"He will never hurt you. I've got you."

Tears ran down her cheeks, and she realized she wasn't the only one shaking. "Pyre?"

His arms tightened around her, and he lifted her chin, peppering kisses along her cheeks, jaw, temples, and hair. A small whine escaped him as he pressed his face into the crook of her neck.

"Almost lost you," he rasped, his breath heating her neck. "I didn't think you'd wake up. I thought—" He pulled back and stared down at her face, his blue eyes wild. Even with Mal's appearance, she could still see the kitsune she'd met in the woods beneath everything. "You almost died. I can't—" Another shudder rolled though him. "I can't lose you."

Tempest tucked her head beneath his chin and hugged him as hard as she could. Pyre squeezed her and leaned back against the pillows with his nose resting against her temple. She licked at her dry lips, tasting the salt of her tears, then swallowed, her dry throat screaming.

"Water," Tempest whispered feebly.

Pyre jostled her around, and then a wooden cup pressed to her lips. She greedily drank the liquid as it quenched her parched throat.

"Slowly," he murmured pulling back the cup.

Tempest tipped her head back and stared up at him, the tears on her cheeks beginning to dry. "Thank you."

He set the cup on the nightstand without taking his eyes from her. His jaw clenched, and he swallowed hard. His eyes glossed over, and one tear trailed down his left cheek. Tempest lifted her hand and wiped it away, cupping Pyre's cheek without being fully aware of what she was really doing. He nuzzled his cheek into her touch, then turned his face slightly to plant a kiss on her palm.

It was by far the most intimate touch she'd ever received. She inhaled sharply, and Pyre pulled away, dropping his forehead onto hers. He held her gaze.

"From here on out, we do everything together or not at all."

He brushed his nose against hers and laid a gentle kiss between her brows. She found herself nodding, even as her eyelids began to droop. Finally, she was warm but so tired. So many questions had arisen in her mind, but she couldn't remember a single one of them. Tempest pillowed her cheek against his bicep and closed her eyes, already sinking into sleep.

"Sleep, love. I'll be here when you wake." His fingers skimmed her cheek.

She clutched at his hand. "Don't let me fade away."

"Never," he whispered fiercely.

Chapter Thirty-Three

Tempest

"Why won't *anyone* let me fight?" Tempest grumbled. "I swear, I'm fine!"

Five days had passed since she'd almost died, but it felt like a lifetime.

Miserable days of being fussed over like a small child—of being watched like a hawk every time she ate or drank or needed to relieve herself. Five days of being told to get back into bed whenever she ventured outside of the tent, even though she'd steadily regained her strength.

"Sure thing, pup," Brine muttered, rolling his silver eyes for the umpteenth time. He pushed her shoulder softly, indicating for her to get back inside the tent. He'd barely tolerated her stretching in the morning. Apparently, sparring was still not on the list of okay things to do when one had been poisoned.

Tempest scowled as she let him maneuver her back inside the warm tent. She thought she'd known headstrong men growing up in the barracks, but the shifter males she was now surrounded by were a whole new level. "I can't afford to lose my edge. I need to train. I'll be careful."

"I don't believe you for one second." The wolf snorted and crossed his arms over his wide chest. "You almost died. Poison isn't something to take lightly. Even *I* would take it easy if I survived what you've experienced."

She huffed, blowing a strand of hair out of her face in the process. Now that her mind was clear and strength had returned to her body, she was itching to get back to normal. Staying still was never one of her attributes. Fighting was all she knew how to do. "*Taking it easy* isn't in my vocabulary."

"I noticed."

"So, spar with me!" she needled, gesturing to her sword leaning against a nearby stool.

"Not a chance, lass."

"Brine—"

"I'll fight you," a deep baritone voice offered.

The tent flap lifted, and Damien stepped into the room, his green hair a shock against the bland color of the tent. He held the canvas open for Nyx. Tempest blinked at them. Whereas the dragon lord was dressed impeccably in silk, leather, and brocade, Nyx was muddy and sopping wet. She waved haphazardly at Tempest and then shuffled toward her own quarters that branched off from the main room of the large tent.

Damien smiled, his teeth a little longer than normal, and winked. "I'm always in the mood for a battle or two."

Her eyes narrowed as she reflected on the night of the masquerade ball and the subsequent murder of the Crown prince. "I strictly remember you turning tail and abandoning me when I needed your help."

"It was not my fight."

"What are you doing here, then?" she challenged, feeling prickly.

"This is my battle. Destin's greed is far-reaching and will not stop."

"Lives were lost," Tempest said. Her thoughts flashed back to the moment the prince died in her arms.

"People die all the time."

"That's a hell of a way to think."

The dragon shrugged. "It is the way of life. Now, how about a sparring session?"

Brine growled, but Tempest ignored him. She eyed Damien carefully. Tempest didn't like his outlook of the world, but that didn't stop her from seizing the opportunity. "You will? This isn't some ploy to grab me and forcefully throw me back into bed?"

Damien threw back his head and roared in laughter, the scaled surface of his neck exposed. He caught her gaze, his green eyes twinkling. "I always did enjoy a bit of bed sport, but I didn't know you liked to play rough."

"Oh, for Dotae's sake," she muttered, swiping a hand over her burning cheeks. Of course, he had to go there.

"That's not what I meant, and you know it."

"You're so much fun to tease," the dragon said, smiling. "I forget how much innocence intrigues me."

"I'm not so innocent," she blurted, her head held high. "I was raised by men. Nothing has been kept from me."

"There's knowing and then there's *knowing,* lovely," Damien murmured.

"Bloody hell," Brine groused, glaring at the dragon. "I'm not sure if you're trying to rile her up or seduce her, but stop it. She was in a coma and should take it easy. Plus, I'm sure her *protector* won't appreciate your interest."

Protector?

"Indeed?" Damien's brows rose, and he inhaled deeply. "She has no protector yet. If he doesn't want anyone to encroach, he should take care of that. You never know when someone might come along and steal your treasure." He grinned at Tempest.

She rolled her eyes. "Stop making mischief. Will you, or will you not, spar with me?"

"If you're sure you can handle me," the dragon said, "then I'd be happy to fight you."

Tempest grinned and snatched up her sword from where it had been leaning against a nearby stool. "Lead the way."

She followed Damien from the tent and huddled deeper into her cloak. The snow and cold had never bothered her before. But since her swim in the ocean, she still hadn't been able to get rid of the chill. It was as if the cold had rooted itself in her bones. They rounded tents and lean-tos until they reached a makeshift training ground that was encircled by bales of hay. Tempest rolled her eyes as Brine stomped behind them.

"Stop pouting," she called over her shoulder.

Her friend cursed. "He's not going to be happy with you."

She snorted. "He is not my owner."

Pyre's constant attention since she'd woken had been simultaneously overwhelming and endearing. But she would not stay abed while he waged war against the king. The kitsune would just have to get used to it.

She scooted between two bales of hay and entered the ring as the dragon lord sauntered to the other side of the space, stripping his vest and shirt from his body, leaving him bare-chested.

"Is that necessary?" she drawled, pulling her sword from the scabbard. "Aren't you cold?"

"Ice dragon. We love winter."

She rolled her neck and settled into her stance, Damien mirroring her.

"Let me know when you're ready, lovely," he said, his sharp teeth gleaming in the winter sunlight.

"No sword?"

He held up his hands, and wicked claws sprouted from his fingertips. "Don't need any."

Arrogant bastard.

"Come and get me," she whispered.

The dragon smiled, and it was all the warning she got before he surged forward. Tempest backpedaled and swung her sword as he made a grab for her. It was by the skin of her teeth that she avoided his claws, letting her knees buckle beneath her in order to skid across the muddy ground.

She leapt to her feet, the movement clumsier than she would have liked. Tempest circled to the left with her eyes locked on Damien.

"You'll have to do better than that to beat me," he said.

"Oh, I'm just getting warmed up, I promise."

Her blood heated, and her nerves sang as he launched a few more attacks and she managed to keep out of his grasp. Sure, he'd shredded part of her shirt, but he hadn't gotten a solid hit yet.

Adrenaline coursed through her veins, making her more daring with every strike she tried—and failed—to land against Damien. The man was bloody quick.

"You going to actually attack sometime soon?" His feline eyes danced with laughter.

She smiled, enjoying herself too much to rise to his taunt. It didn't matter who won. All she cared about was getting back to optimum shape. No one would ever render her helpless again. Some of her joy slipped away at the thought, and her jaw clenched. If she'd been more dedicated to her training, such a thing would never have—

"*Ah!*" Tempest yelped, when her feet were knocked out from beneath her. She wheezed as she landed on her back in the mud and snow. Where had that come from? She lifted her head and caught Damien's tail slowly sweeping across the snow. "That isn't fair."

"Fair?" he teased, huffing out a laugh.

Her nose wrinkled as the tail slowly shrunk and disappeared behind him. "How does that work? Does it hurt?" she asked, clambering back to her feet.

"It's painful at first, but our bodies eventually learn what they're supposed to do."

"Old stories used to say Talagans were born of magic," Tempest said, brushing the snow from her arms.

Damien closed in on her, and she swiped at him, catching him on the arm. Her eyes widened, an apology on her tongue. He knocked her back down, slamming her into the ground and keeping her there with the thick trunk of his forearm.

He smirked. "Do I seem like I'm made from magic?"

"No."

"People label things that are beyond their comprehension as magic. Our bodies are different from yours. When your body heals, do you call it magic?"

"No, it's just how our bodies work."

"Much like how shifters change."

"Interesting." Her gaze stayed locked on his face as she drew her dagger. "Sorry I cut you."

"You didn't. Scale, remember?" Damien smiled. "Did you really think you could hurt a dragon, lovely?"

She smiled as she pressed the tip of her knife to the inside of his thigh. "This seem familiar to you?"

"You little minx. No wonder he's besotted."

"Yield." Tempest pressed harder.

He smiled and then tossed her through the air. A shriek

caught in her throat as she was airborne. She tumbled onto a bale of hay and rolled over the side, miraculously landing on the balls of her feet. She lifted her head, breathing heavily, not sure how she'd managed the feat.

Damien began a slow clap, and the two shared a grin.

"Well done," he called.

Her smile slid from her face as Pyre jumped into the ring, his face a mask of rage. She blinked as the dragon lord faced the kitsune and held his hands up. "She's fine."

"If you ever lay a hand on her again"—the kitsune sucked in a sharp breath—"I'll kill you."

"So, it's to be that way?" Damien muttered. "Wondered how long it would take you." He glanced over his shoulder and inclined his head politely before leaving the training ring without another word.

What was that all about? Tempest rolled her shoulder and clambered back over the bale of hay, her attention pinned to Pyre, whose gaze was locked on to the dragon lord's retreating back. He'd run off her sparring partner.

"Why'd you chase him off?" she demanded. "I was doing just fine."

Pyre's attention snapped to her, his amber eyes narrowed. "Did you, or did you not miss the part when he threw you across the *entire training ring?!*"

"And? I need the training, and Damien was willing to help. I may have a few bruises, but he didn't risk my life. He knew exactly how far he threw me."

"And you know him so well?" Pyre bit out.

"As well as anyone." She shrugged and frowned when

Brine shook his head at her, his eyes uncharacteristically wide. "What am I supposed to do now? I need training, not to be coddled."

The kitsune cursed and ran a hand through his ruffled deep-red hair. "Fine," he hissed, pulling out his daggers. "I'll spar with you. Let's see how long you manage."

Brine kicked the nearest bale of hay. "You're not supposed to *indulge* her, Pyre! She needs to—"

"If she needs to fight, she'll spar with me."

That was presumptuous. Tempest swung her sword in a lazy arch. "Weapons?"

"Doesn't matter what you use, you won't hurt me." His tone was saturated with arrogance.

He was trying to rile her. She sank into a defensive pose and arched a haughty brow. "When you're ready."

"Just go for it, love." He smiled, and a strange light entered his eyes. Pyre looked almost eager for her to attack him, as if he meant to teach her a lesson.

Tempest schooled her expression.

It was his mistake to underestimate her.

She wasted no time in slashing her sword forward, using the momentum of Pyre's resulting parry to spin around and attack him from the back. He avoided her and threw one of his daggers in her direction.

That was his second mistake. One never got rid of their primary weapon.

He danced around her, darting in and out to test her guard. Her breaths came heavier than before, and her muscles burned with the strenuous activity. She glowered at the kitsune. He was just trying to tire her out.

"Are you going to play games all day, or are we going to crack on?" she murmured.

"You're the one who wanted to spar," Pyre insisted, almost lazily avoiding another attack from her in the process. "If you can't keep up, you shouldn't be in the ring."

Now *that* got under her skin.

"You *bastard*," she snarled. Forget proper swordplay. He didn't want to play fair? She'd give him a dose of his own medicine.

Pyre darted in and swung his dagger. She ducked under his arm, and, instead of sliding away, she tackled his legs, knocking him to the ground. Tempest shimmied up his body and straddled him, attempting to immobilize his arms with her knees. She squeaked as he tossed her to the side. She scrambled to her hands and knees and growled as his arms wrapped around hers, pinning them to her body as he hauled her to her feet. Tempest tossed her head back and bucked against him as something began to unwind in her chest. Her breathing sped up, and the world began to turn blue on the edges.

"Let me go!" she demanded.

"Yield," Pyre's calm voice whispered in her ear.

The ugly feeling of helplessness uncoiled further, and she began to fight wildly. "Let me go! Let me go!"

"Calm down, and I will."

She registered tears on her cheeks and began to shake. All she could feel were Destin's hands on her body. "I—I can *feel* him touching me. I can't get him off my skin. I can't—I can't—"

Pyre spun her around and pulled her into a tight hug. She sucked in a breath, his spicy scent grounding her some.

Tempest's fingers grasped at his shirt, and she released a shuddering cry. "How am I supposed to get rid of Destin if I can't fight? I have to be ready. I can't let myself be caught unaware again. I can't."

"Shhh..." he crooned, resting his cheek on the top of her head. "You are one of the strongest women I know. You are powerful. I vow that he will never touch you again."

She believed him.

Another sob escaped her, and she just let it all go. All the fear, pain, uncertainty, and guilt she'd been carrying for months. Pyre rocked her back and forth, humming softly. She turned her face to the side and noticed Brine and Briggs hovering on the outskirts of the training ring. Instead of feeling embarrassed, their presence somehow, inexplicably, helped calm her. She wasn't trapped in the palace with Destin. Tempest had her uncles, her Talagan friends, and...

She had her kitsune.

Her fox.

When had she decided that? Sure, he was handsome and fun, but he was also dangerous and mercurial. Pyre was all sorts of gray, where she was black and white. Her skin tingled as she realized how intertwined they were right now. She swallowed hard, hoping he couldn't scent her change in emotions. Time to get away from him.

"If you're ready, we can start again," Pyre murmured in her ear, affection infusing his tone. His grasp on her loosened. "Or perhaps we can try tomorrow. Allow some time for you to work your strength back. I promise to be gentle with—"

In one quick movement, she turned around and nimbly tossed him over her shoulder. The kitsune landed in the snow and mud. Brine's booming laughter brought a smile to her face. Pyre grinned as he rolled over and hopped to his feet, brushing at his clothing.

"I don't do gentle," she stated. "Let's go again."

Chapter Thirty-Four

Tempest

War was ugly. Tempest had only seen the battlefield from afar, and the horrors of that wouldn't leave her anytime soon.

She left the war meeting and tried to clear her mind. What had made her think she was ready for this? Her body ached from her recent sparring session with Brine. Winter's bite, the wolf had a mean right hook. Her gaze was drawn back toward the battlefield. Were her uncles all right? The Hounds were gearing up to make their move. It had to be at the right time, or the king and his army could pull back to the capital, and it would be almost impossible to bring about a siege.

Please be okay.

Tempest reached her tent and moved through the outer room, then into the smaller sleeping area. Sitting on the bed, she stared at the gaudy carpets and then ran her hand along the luxurious blankets that covered the mattress. Her attention moved to the open trunk at the end of the bed that held both Pyre's and her clothing. Something about the combined mess felt right.

Alarm ran through her at the thought. They were not together. The kitsune flirted and cared for her, but he showed affection to most women. What was she still doing here? It wasn't her tent, and it wasn't her bed. It was Pyre's. What did the rebels think of her? She'd seen the looks thrown her way. Did they think she was a loose woman? Hopping from one man in power to another?

You need to get out.

She lurched from the mattress and grabbed her rucksack from beneath the bed. It was time to move. She couldn't stay here anymore. But who could she speak to? Briggs or Nyx could probably find her a place to stay. Her heart ached as she yanked her belongings from the trunk and stuffed them into her bag. Pyre's things looked forlorn all by themselves.

Stop being a ninny.

Since she'd woken up, he'd become more of the playful attentive fox she'd first met, rather than the Jester of the Dark Court or the cold-hearted Mal or even the king's bastard son. Pyre had become her friend, and she liked having her meals with him every night before he would remove himself to the outer room to sleep on the floor in front of the entrance of the room where she slept. Becoming accustomed to him would be problematic in the future. If they both survived, she'd still be a Hound and Pyre would still be the lord of the underworld.

It was necessary to set some boundaries now, so no one got hurt.

You're already in too deep.

She swiped the leather ties for her hair from the side table and ignored Pyre's rings and comb. She and Pyre were already far too tangled, and the war should be her priority. Distraction cost people their lives.

Tempest closed the drawstrings on her bag and then swung it over her shoulder. She turned away from the side table and cringed.

Pyre stood in the entrance to her sleeping quarters.

Former sleeping quarters.

"What are you doing?" he asked slowly, his gaze missing nothing as it lingered on her bag. He raised an eyebrow. "Is the princess fleeing her cruel and vicious captor? And just when he was bringing her lunch. How ungrateful," he said lightly. He held up a basket filled to the brim with breads, cheeses, meats, and apples. "Nothing fancy, but it should do the job. Are you hungry?"

She was.

Tempest shifted awkwardly. "I was just packing."

He stepped inside the light room, the flap closing behind him. The kitsune strolled to the other side of the bed and placed the basket down carefully. "I can see that. Were you just planning to flee without saying anything?"

"I just—I need my own space," Tempest murmured with a weak smile. "I can't exactly keep expecting you to sleep on the floor while I take up your bed. That's not right. It's downright rude. I should have moved to my own tent days ago."

"You know what is mine is yours," he said softly and held out a bit of cheese.

Tempest took it from his fingers, ignoring the tingle of awareness that lit up her body when their fingers touched. "That's awfully generous coming from the Jester. You better be careful with your words or some woman will steal the Dark Court from your own hands." She popped the cheese into her mouth.

"You don't have to steal it. I'll give you it," he said gravely, his expression completely serious.

She choked and swallowed hastily. What was she supposed to say to that?

"And there's the issue of what your people think..."

Pyre tore a chunk of bread off and held it out, his expression one of bland interest. "And what exactly do they think?"

"Oh, come on. Like you don't know." She took another bite and almost sat on the bed but decided better of it before closing the trunk and perching on the lid. "They know I was betrothed to the king, and now I'm staying in your quarters."

"As is my sister," he replied.

"I am not your sister."

His gaze pierced her. "You are not," he whispered softly. Pyre held out an apple slice, and she jerked back. He glanced at his offering and growled. Quickly, he gathered up the apples and tossed them into the stove. "I'm sorry, I wasn't thinking."

Tempest waved him away. "Not your fault." She took another bite of her bread.

"Are you worried that the others think you're warming my bed?"

"Yes."

He set his meat down and studied the bedspread. "And that bothers you?"

She gaped at him. "Yes!"

"Because of who I am?"

"No!" she exclaimed and then lowered her voice. "It has nothing to do with you. For months I've let Destin dictate everything I've done. He encouraged me to use my *feminine* wiles to get my way. I look like a whore."

"Don't ever refer to yourself like that again."

"I look like one. You and I both know it," she replied stubbornly. "Which is ironic since I've never even been with a man."

Pyre froze. "Excuse me?"

She colored. "I never trusted anyone enough. Despite my somewhat hedonistic upbringing, my uncles raised me to uphold certain guidelines and morals. One of them was not to sleep with anyone I wasn't bound to. I know many don't adhere by that standard, but it protected me from being used by careless men, from disease, and children before I was ready."

"You don't have to explain yourself to me."

"Of course, I needed to." Temp laughed sarcastically.

"Even you didn't imagine I was untouched. What do you think your people see when they look at me?"

"You know what I see?" he asked, ignoring her question completely.

"What?"

"Someone worth a kingdom. Someone worth protecting."

Her treacherous heart fluttered at his pretty words. "I don't need protecting."

His ears twitched, before he rounded the foot of the bed and sat on the opposite corner of the trunk. He dusted his hands off and then looked her squarely in the eyes. "All the precious things in life deserve protection," he murmured, cupping Tempest's face with both hands. He rubbed his thumbs along her cheekbones, his touch feather-soft against her skin.

"I was never meant to be protected," she whispered. Her breath caught as she scooted closer, her belly erupting into a million butterflies. "I'm a warrior."

He chuckled, his molten eyes creasing at the corners as he smiled. "Trust me, I know. You are the fiercest creature I've ever had the pleasure—and displeasure—of meeting. But you must know that those who love you will *always* protect you."

Love?

He leaned closer, and her lips parted. He was finally going to kiss her. Her eyes closed as he pressed the gentlest of kisses first on her left cheek, then on her right.

Her eyes fluttered open when he pulled away.

"Tempest Madrid, I love you."

Her heart stopped.

"You are my match in every way. You're proud and stubborn. Your sense of honor knows no bounds, and you have a mischievous streak that runs deep. Let your guard down and let me love you. Trust that I won't ever hurt you. I will always choose you."

"Why?" she blurted, feeling stupid as soon as the word escaped her.

"Because you are everything." He brushed his nose against hers. "You, love, are my mate."

"And I have no say?" she said faintly, trying to conjure up any information about Talagan matings.

"You will always have a say. But know this: I will *never* stop fighting for you. You are mine just as much as I am yours."

Oh. *Oh.* There would be no getting rid of him.

She blinked when he released her and stood. "Where are you going?"

"Out. If I stay here much longer, I don't think it will be wise." His eyes swept her from head to toe and Pyre quirked a smile. "I plan on leaving you innocent for now."

Her belly flipped and Tempest realized she was staring at his lips. Time to change the subject. She glanced toward the fire. "I still need my own tent."

"My people know who you are to me. No one thinks anything improper."

She tossed a droll look his way, and he held up his hands, wearing a small smirk.

"Well, I'm sure there are some rumors. But if you get your own tent, I'll just sleep outside that one."

He was crazy.

"You'd sleep outdoors in the snow?"

"Shifter, love. I run hotter than you do." He clapped his hands together. "So, I vote you stay in here one final night. Tomorrow is likely the day the Hounds will attack. We will need everyone at their best. Disrupting your sleep pattern will hinder you for the battle. You need to keep your strength up if you're going to ride into the fray with me tomorrow."

"Why tell me this now?" she asked, her stomach knotting.

"No time like the present. I want no regrets, and you deserve to know, whether you decide to accept my feelings or not."

It was on the tip of her tongue to admit she wanted him, but the words wouldn't come out. She swallowed. "Do you think it wise to fight together? I don't want to be a distraction."

"We're better together than apart, right?"

They did make a magnificent team.

"Yeah."

"Then goodnight, my mate."

"Not your mate," she called after him as he moved toward the exit.

He paused and winked over his shoulder. "Yet, you're mine. You just haven't admitted it to yourself yet."

She picked up her half-eaten bread roll and took a bite,

not willing to admit anything out loud, even though she already knew it in her heart.

Pyre was right.

Chapter Thirty-Five

Pyre

Pyre's pulse thundered in his ears as his horse galloped toward the chaos.

Years of planning had led to this moment.

Talagan warriors in all shapes and sizes were by his side as they charged toward Destin's army. Pyre glanced to his right and grinned. It was everything and nothing like he imagined.

A Hound rode beside him.

My mate.

Tempest's periwinkle hair streamed back from her intense face in a tangle of braids. She stood out in her Hound uniform, silver armor gleaming. He'd tried to get her to wear something else—she drew too much attention—but she wouldn't have it. She'd vowed to protect the Crown as a Hound, even from wicked kings.

Today, she'd wear her uniform proudly.

She glanced at him and jerked her chin toward the enemy line as if to tell him to get his head in the game. The grin he gave her was feral as he urged his horse forward. She flew ahead on her dappled gray mare, hands twitching around the reins of her horse.

For one second, he wanted to chase after her, but he tamped it down. She was a warrior, and this was war. The incident with Maven at the wedding ceremony flashed through his mind. The prince had almost cut him because he was distracted by Tempest. Too much was at stake to make the same mistake. If all he did was worry over her, he'd end up getting them both killed.

A soldier charged at him on his own gray war horse, brandishing his sword. Pyre ducked and slammed his own blade into the man, knocking him from his saddle and into the writhing fray. Pyre kept on going, felling one enemy after another. He pulled on the reins of his mount and scanned the battle for Tempest.

He grinned as he watched her pick off a king's man with her bow. She was a machine. Every shot she took found its target. A soldier swinging a huge axe raced toward her, his face a mask of rage. Pyre's blood went cold. Tempest didn't see him until the last second. She turned and loosed two arrows in succession into the man's chest. He slumped forward and crashed to the ground near the hooves of her prancing mount. She was a goddess. A fierce, beautiful, deadly goddess.

He pulled his attention from her and scanned the

battlefield. Where was his wretched sire? If they cut off the head of the snake, the Hounds could take it from there. His ears twitched at the sound of a horse screaming, and his attention snapped to his left just as Brine was tossed from his wounded horse and the mount crashed to the ground, crushing the enemy soldier.

Pyre crashed through the soldiers to Brine's side and nimbly swung off. He held out the reins as the wolf clambered to his feet with a curse. Blood ran down his brow and into his face, but he smiled.

"Take the horse," Pyre commanded. "We both know you're the better rider."

"Damn right I am!" his commander muttered before he swung up into the saddle, brandishing his axe. "Have you spotted him yet?"

"Not yet, but I will."

Brine bared his teeth, a wild glint in his eyes. "Take his head off, Pyre. Only, make him suffer first. For what he did to our people. For what he's done to *his* people. And for what he did to our lass."

They shared a look of understanding before Brine took off into the fray.

Pyre spun to meet the next attack. His sword clanged against the enemy's sword with a sound that made his teeth rattle. He tore his dagger from his chest sheath and slashed at the man's torso. The soldier cried out and dropped to his knees. Pyre kicked him and moved on.

Pyre waded into the chaos, hardly hearing anything around him. The world surrounding the Jester faded, and all he could focus on was the next opponent, the perfect strike point, and the safest route for escape.

His sword bit into the flesh of his newest foe, and he watched, completely unfazed, as life drained from the man's gaze. He released the warrior and lifted his own head, once again scanning his warriors, searching for who needed help.

Talagans used the trees as protection, darting in and out, attacking the soldiers. To some, it might have seemed cowardly, but it was the smart way to fight. It was the shifter way to fight. War was ugly.

Owls, lions, and wolves fell on the soldiers, and Pyre didn't look any closer. He took no pleasure in death or in the doomed soldiers who were only doing their jobs.

The hair at the nape of his neck rose as he spotted Nyx battling a warrior who was twice her size. Terror seized him.

His sister was sweating and fighting with everything she had. Pyre dug his toes into the ground and pushed forward, racing toward the duel. While Nyx was faster, her opponent had worn her down with his brute strength. Pyre cut through the swathe, his heart pounding. Only a little farther. If he could reach them, it would be a fair fight.

Big heavy snowflakes fell from the sky like someone had cut a feather pillow and dumped it from above. The soldier swept Nyx's feet out from under her, and Pyre put on a burst of speed as the man slammed his boot down on Nyx's knee. She screamed, her face paling.

Pyre's focus honed in on the enemy as he lifted his

sword. Nyx retched but managed to slash wildly at the man's Achilles tendon. The soldier bellowed, his eyes squeezed closed. The Jester smiled darkly, sprinting the last few steps.

The soldier opened his eyes just in time to see his death. Pyre drove his sword into the soldier's chest. The man teetered and gasped for a second, and then crashed backward. The kitsune yanked his sword back and dropped to his knees next to his sister, running his hands over her torso, looking for injuries.

"How bad is it?" he murmured, searching the area for any more threats.

Nyx panted, her face creased with pain. "My knee. I felt something tear. I can't walk."

"I'll pull you back." Pyre stood and lifted her into his arms. He ran toward the nearby trees and set her down behind a fallen log. "I'll send someone for you."

His sister waved him off and propped herself up, holding her bow in her hands. "I'll be fine here. Leave me."

He hesitated and scanned the battle. No enemies were close to this area. She was as safe as she could be. "Keep your attention sharp—" His eyes narrowed, and he stilled, spotting his prey in the middle of the battle.

Destin.

A warrior lunged at the king, and Destin stabbed the man with a smile. The king threw his head back and laughed before engaging his next opponent. His bodyguards formed a loose circle around him. Pyre grinned as he recognized each of the Hounds. Destin had no idea that his protection was the enemy.

Taking a deep, shuddering breath, Pyre re-sheathed his dagger and palmed the pommel of his sword before striding back into the chaos, his attention zeroed in on the king. Destin wielded a deadly two-handed broadsword. It would be impossible to battle him within close range until Pyre dealt with the sword. He would not be able to get in a close-range attack until the weapon had been knocked to the side.

A soldier rushed him, and Pyre met him with a quick slash of his sword. Blood sprayed across the kitsune's face as he jerked the blade back. Blood ran down his forearm, and the soldier gurgled before all life fled from his eyes.

Pyre lifted his head and locked eyes with the king.

Destin smiled. "I knew you'd find yourself here. Come here, so I can get a closer look at my long-lost bastard son."

"Gladly," Pyre bit back.

The king waved away his Hounds, and Pyre hid his mirth. Even if Destin hadn't done so, they would have moved aside.

The kitsune studied his sire for a long second. The man was taller and had broader shoulders. It was clear he was powerful. That was where his advantages ended.

Pyre was quicker. Much, much quicker. Thanks to his shifter abilities, he was stronger as well.

"It's been a long time," Pyre said lowly, circling the king.

"Not long enough," Destin responded, matching each of Pyre's movements. "Rumor was you were dead."

"The rumor was greatly exaggerated, I'm afraid."

The king lunged, his sword chopping through the air. Pyre leaped back and danced around the man. Destin feinted several times, but he could see that the king never intended to strike. He was trying to draw Pyre into an attack. It wasn't going to work. He'd waited years for this. He could hold out.

"I heard your betrothed has gone missing," Pyre said conversationally.

A flicker of anger rippled across Destin's face. "So, you're going to play it that way?" The king shook his head. "Do you really think she meant anything to me?"

Pyre shrugged and feinted before continuing to circle. "No, but you've never liked it when anyone takes your things. Does it rankle that she's been mine this entire time?"

Destin's face contorted and then smoothed. "Does it rankle you that I've had my hands and mouth all over her? You should have heard the sweet sounds she made."

It was a close thing, but Pyre barely kept it together. The king couldn't know that he actually cared for Tempest. Pyre forced out a chuckle. "Just another piece to our game, but it's interesting that she never gave herself to you. She made you look like a fool."

Destin snapped.

He attacked, and Pyre blocked his swing and dodged to the side, smiling as he used the snow to slide. The king pursued the attack in a series of blows. The kitsune dodged and blocked, sweat dampening the back of his neck. Destin's sword slammed into his, and it reverberated throughout his entire body, his teeth clacking together.

Pyre leaned closer and bared his teeth at the king. "Even if you win today, you will always look weak because of a woman."

His sire disengaged, his chest rising up and down with his harsh breaths. "Women are tricky creatures. Take your mother, for example."

Pyre stiffened and tried not to let his emotions run free.

Destin smiled. "Such a lowborn pretty thing. So pretty that I could look over her Talagan heritage. She begged me to take her as my mistress, but in the end blamed me for her own mistakes."

Pyre tried not to focus on the sneered words and studied the king's movements, starting to find a pattern. Pyre needed to bide his time. He tensed his back when his sword took the brunt of the king's next swing. Damn, the man could hit hard.

That's right. Use all your stamina.

Destin saw his grimace, eyes glinting and bloodthirsty at what he had clearly decided was an impending victory. "'Tis a shame your mother was a shifter, Jester," he said, wiping sweat from his brow. "You could have been something."

Pyre whipped his dagger out and slashed the king's right arm. His sire cursed and jerked away with a wild swing.

"No, *'tis a shame* my father was you," he countered.

Destin dropped his left arm, presenting a hole in his

defense. Pyre jabbed his sword forward. His blade hit steel, and the king wrapped his hand around the blade and wrenched it out of Pyre's hand, tossing it into the mud. He had not expected that. His sire took a step toward him, and Pyre was forced to take one back, both of his daggers already in his hands. He kept his expression schooled, even as he tasted victory. This was exactly where he wanted the king. He wanted the monster to believe he'd won.

"You know, you would have made a great heir," the king drawled, arrogance seeping from his tone. "My first son—first *legitimate* son—was a useless drunk. It was a relief when he finally died." He chuckled. "At least he had the decency to die in battle. A martyr is always good for the cause. Now, my second son is more promising. He has the makings to be a true ruler. His shortsightedness and lack of vision is concerning, though, as is his charisma. The boy scares people more than he draws them. But you..." He waved an arm toward the destruction around them. "Look at what you've achieved, little fox. You truly are my son, through and through."

Disgust rolled through Pyre. "I'm nothing like you."

"We're more alike than you know." He laughed. "It's not too late. Think of what we could do with the Dark Court and my power. Nothing would be out of our grasp. We could control the kingdoms around us. Be gods among men."

"An interesting proposal, but what will I gain?"

Pyre darted in and slashed at the juncture of the king's

elbow. Destin grunted as Pyre cut through muscle before Destin jerked back and examined his bleeding left arm that now hung uselessly by his side.

"Power, freedom, women," the king offered.

"It sounds intriguing, but I will pass."

"Always difficult." Destin shook his head and then surged forward.

Pyre rolled through the muck and snow, kicking Destin's left knee inward. The king yelled as he fell, landing in the mud hard. The kitsune rolled to his feet and stepped onto the king's right hand, forcing him to release the broad sword.

"So overconfident," the king tsked. "So, you've dealt with me. Now, how do you plan to deal with my Hounds?"

Pyre smirked and ground his boot against his sire's wrist. He leaned down and cocked his head before pointing a dagger over his shoulder at the silent Hounds. "You mean *my* Hounds?"

Chapter Thirty-Six

Tempest

Hack, parry, slash. Hack, slash, block. Hack, jab, parry.

Tempest was running on a wondrous, beautiful autopilot. Her body was a weapon honed to a fine point, and she was wielding it with expert precision. So long as she didn't overthink things—or look at the fallen bodies or breathe in the smell of blood and iron too deeply—she was a whirlwind tearing through the battlefield.

Training every day for thirteen years had its advantages.

Several times, she'd scanned the battle for the kitsune. Pyre was a madman on the battlefield. Tempest couldn't help but feel awe and...possessiveness. Her stomach fluttered, and she squashed her feelings. Now was not the time to think about what he'd said the night prior. If they made it through battle, she'd figure out her feelings once things had calmed down. The fox shifter deserved a true and straight answer from her, with absolutely no uncertainty or pressure coloring her decision.

Today, she would fight. Tomorrow, she would think.

She wiped her bloody fingers over the uniform of one of the king's fallen soldiers. The frigid wind whipped across her face as she stood, and she caught Dima's eye as he signaled her next move; she then sprinted toward Maxim, leaving Dima behind. He'd catch up soon enough.

A soldier spotted her and lunged into her path from the right, swinging a massive battle-axe. Tempest dropped onto one knee and slid in the muddy snow. Time seemed to slow as the blade cut through the space above her head, the slick soft sound of metal slicing the empty air. She twisted in the snow, then swung her sword backward, catching her enemy above his ankle, severing his Achilles tendon. The man bellowed and crashed to his knees, betrayal and hatred burning in his eyes as he clutched his leg.

He may hate her but at least he still had his life. Tempest knew he was just following orders. If possible, she only wounded and moved on.

Tempest pushed to her feet and continued to run, the mud and snow beneath her boots threatening her balance. She wobbled for a moment, then steeled herself, before she crashed into the chaos surrounding Maxim. Her burly uncle bellowed and swung his battle-axe with a crazed smile on his face. Her fingers squeezed the hilt of her sword, and she gracefully avoided a soldier as he clumsily hacked at her. She spun to face him when the man staggered and fell to the ground.

She blinked as Aleks sheepishly smiled at her, a handful of pink powder in his hand.

"Thanks," she muttered. Tempest had never seen him spar once in her life. It was jarring to see him on the battlefield.

"Move it, girlie!" Maxim yelled.

Wind blew her hair, and she rolled out of the way as a scaly tail slammed into the ground three feet from her spot and swept the earth. She grinned at the dragon whose emerald eyes twinkled as soldiers ran screaming from him.

"Lovely, you're always in the thick of it," he rasped in his deep dragon-like voice.

Brine came loping into view, his black cloak wet.

"I can't help it." She nodded toward the regrouping soldiers. "Move on three. One, two three!"

Tempest sprinted forward with Brine at her side. A soldier approached from their left. The wolf leaped onto him, taking the man down. She kept running, jumping over the body of a soldier, and twirled around to knock down an approaching attacker from her right.

"Keep it up, lass!" Dima yelled out, appearing on her left.

She grinned. "Learned from the best, didn't I? Might be even better than you now, uncle!"

"Ha! Only because I am getting old."

"If you're getting old, then I'm already middle-aged."

Their wild, inappropriate-for-the-occasion

conversation was abruptly cut off when Maxim roared past them both, distracting three of the king's men long enough to allow an injured shifter to retreat into the forest.

"Stop yapping and get to work!" Maxim admonished both of them, though he was laughing. "No rest for the wicked, as they say."

With that, Tempest followed the ebb and flow of the battle, her uncles and friends always at her back. She spied Levka holding his own against two opponents but not the third that snuck up from behind. Her jaw clenched, and she narrowed her eyes on the guard about to covertly cut Levka down. Breaking away from Brine and Dima, she dodged attacks and full-out ran toward her friend. The rush of her footsteps must have given her away, but not soon enough to change the outcome she had in mind for the soldier. The man spun toward her, as she leapt over the remains of a huge fallen tree and launched through the air. By the time she hit the ground, the man fell beside her dead. There wasn't remorse or shame or rage—just determination and an animalistic need to save her family.

Levka dispatched the enemy and wiped at the sweat pouring down his face. He nodded to her and stormed forward. She glanced at the felled men and guilt cracked through her shield of numbness. How many would take their final breath today?

A whisper of sound.

Her face snapped to the right, toward the woods and the tension between her shoulders lessened. It was only wounded shifters retreating. She breathed a sigh of relief. Not an enemy.

"Ah, here you are," an ugly, twisted voice drawled behind her. "I thought I'd never find you, *Mother*."

Tempest stiffened and spun to face Maven.

She eyed the prince, noting the sheen of excitement in his gaze and the blood that painted his body. It was as if he'd rolled in it. Her stomach heaved, and she barely kept from retching.

"Nothing to say?" he crooned.

"Not your mother."

He laughed, the sound sending chills down her spine. What was it about him that unnerved her so?

"I've been looking for you. You've been missed."

"And I you." It was partly true. Number one on her list had been Destin; number two was the prince. "In truth, I thought you'd be back at the palace trying to murder your sister since no one would be around to stop you," she remarked casually, circling to his right.

Keep him talking. Distracted.

"You are such a delight." The prince huffed out a laugh, shaking his head. "While my father was blinded by what's between your legs and the idea of expanding his legacy, I was watching. I knew you were more than you appeared to be. You always knew too much and were in the wrong place at the wrong time whenever I looked for you." A malicious smile played about his mouth. "Tell me: how long were you going to let my father bed you for the sake of the *people*? Or had you planned to cut his throat open on your wedding night?"

"Seems like we'll never know," Tempest whispered as he rotated to keep her in his sights.

With his back to the log, she attacked. The prince was quick to parry, his movements agile and liquid. Where he lacked the sheer size of his father, he made up for it in lithe grace. He was good. Better than many of the trainee Hounds if she was being honest.

She needed to be incredibly careful.

"After you disappeared, Father told me what you'd done and how he'd dealt with you," the prince called between blows. "He said you'd be dead before you reached the forest, after you fled Dotae. But I knew you'd still be alive. Gutter rats like you never die when you're supposed to."

"What can I say, I'm resilient."

Disgust crossed his face as he lunged, slicing at her side. She skittered out of the way. "You commoners are all cockroaches. Impossible to kill. Well, not *impossible*."

The prince kicked a fallen body toward Tempest, forcing her to move to her left to avoid it, and he closed the gap between them. They locked blades, and he snapped his teeth at her. Her arms trembled as he pressed her backward. She needed to disengage now.

Tempest caught the flash of a blade a moment before searing pain bloomed in her side. She gasped and dropped to her knees, rolling away. Maven slashed at her, gouging the ground. Climbing to her feet, she touched the throbbing wound at her side, her fingers coming away wet with blood. He'd stabbed her.

"I will cut you down here," he purred. "But you won't die. I'll drag you back to Dotae, and, when I'm through with you, you'll beg for death, but I won't grant your wish. In the end, you'll acknowledge that I'm your master."

"Like hell," she hissed.

Her response seemed to inflame him.

He likes to be in control. Let him have it and then end him.

A dangerous plan, but one that might work.

Tempest screamed and lunged. The prince met her strike for strike. The mud and snow sucked at her boots and she pretended to lose her balance, stumbling into his chest. Maven grabbed a fistful of her braid and yanked her head back. She hissed and kept her eyes pinned to his face as she released the hidden blade in her sleeve. He dropped his sword and wrapped his fingers around her throat and lifted her. Tempest gripped his wrist with her left hand and gasped.

Just a little longer.

"Beg for your life," he whispered as he pulled her closer.

That was his mistake.

She drove her knife into the space between his waistband and chest plate.

Maven's mouth gaped open as he choked on a soundless cry, his hand releasing her.

Tempest stumbled away from him, coughing as the prince stared down at the blade sticking out from his belly. It wasn't deep enough to kill him, but painful enough to stop him from fighting.

Maven lifted his head and glared at her. "You wench!"

He took one wooden step in her direction when movement caught her eye from the left. A giant man appeared at the edge of the forest. His gait was brisk as he approached them. Tempest swallowed hard and kept her sword raised. It was the Kopalian from the palace. He was even bigger up close. The man had to be nearly eight feet tall.

"Don't just stand there! Take care of her!" Maven commanded.

The giant glanced between the prince and herself. She kept her chin up as she contemplated fighting the giant. If he came for her, she had to run. There was no other choice.

"I shall be taking this one off your hands," the giant said, gesturing to Maven.

She blinked. That was not what she expected. "I cannot allow that."

The Kopalian chuckled, the sound like two rocks being rubbed together. "I don't need your permission, my lady. He has committed crimes against my people that must be answered for."

Maven paled and took an unsteady step back. "We had a deal!"

The giant glared at the prince as if he were an ant beneath his boot. "Which was severed when we discovered your treachery and depravity."

Tempest shut her mouth as the giant strode forward and overpowered the prince. He began dragging him by his armor toward the woods, the young man screeching and clawing at his captor.

The giant paused and glanced over his shoulder at Tempest. "We are no friends of Destin. Should you have need of us, we will answer your battle call." He turned around and disappeared into the dense forest. Maven's wailing faded into the distance.

Tempest stared after them in stunned silence.

What were the odds?

Pain cramped her side, and she pressed her palm against the wound with a hiss. There was no time to ponder the prince's future. Maven had made his bed, now he had to lie in it.

She ripped the sleeves of her shirt off and tied them together, then wrapped it around her waist to staunch the blood flow. It wasn't terribly serious, but it hurt something awful.

Tempest waded back into the fray, scouring the fight for Pyre. No doubt the kitsune was on his way to Destin. Hopefully, he hadn't killed the king yet. Destin deserved death but not on the battlefield. He didn't merit that honor. He needed to face up to his crimes publicly. He needed to hang in front of the people he betrayed.

Fighting through the battlefield, it didn't take long for her to spot the circle of Hounds and Pyre kneeling over Destin, a dagger at the man's throat.

"Stop!" Tempest yelled, barreling through the wall of Hounds. "Pyre, stop!"

Both Pyre and his father stared at her with wide eyes.

"You are alive," Destin said, almost in wonder. He

grinned, causing the wound she'd given him to crease. "You always surprise me."

Bile burned the back of her throat, but she ignored the king, her sole focus on the fox.

"Why should I stop?" Pyre bit out, his expression empty of emotion. "He deserves to die."

"I don't disagree," Tempest said softly. "But he needs to pay for his crimes *publicly*."

"But you—Tempest, you of all people should understand. I need to do this."

She shook her head. "What you said to me the other day. When you helped me through…" Tempest glanced at King Destin, who was watching her with confusion that was slowly turning into realization. "Well, with everything," she continued. "You told me to let it go. All of it. It would have eaten me up, otherwise."

His jaw clenched, and he pushed his dagger further against his father's neck. "This is different."

"It's the same," she insisted, taking a step toward them. Around them, the last of Destin's soldiers were beginning to surrender. "He will never be your father, but he is blood. If you do this, it will haunt you for the rest of your life."

"Or I'll sleep better than I ever have."

"His death doesn't belong just to you," she stated firmly. "You're not the only person he's harmed. The people of Heimserya and Talaga deserve their justice."

His ears flattened against his skull.

"Ah, I see," Destin cut in, his tone lazy as if he didn't have a knife to his throat. He grinned. "It seems you have a very particular taste in men, my lady. I never took you for a filthy, animal—"

"One more word, and I'll slit your throat," Pyre said, his voice as sharp as steel. He swung back to look at Tempest. "You'd ask me to spare him? Even after everything he has done?"

"I am not sparing him. Let him hang. In public, for everyone to see. He deserves to be shamed before all like the criminal he is." Tempest locked eyes with Destin. "He needs to know what it feels like to be led to the gallows and have the people scream for his blood."

Pyre gave her a hard look and then glared at his father's face. She knew, from the look on his face, that *he* knew she was right. To kill Destin now was wrong for multiple reasons.

"He will pay."

Her words seemed to resonate with him, and Pyre pulled his knife away. His movements were jerky as he rose to his feet. The Hounds around them pointed their swords at Destin to keep the king from rising.

Pyre stared at his sire and then flicked an apathetic look her way. "You win, Lady Hound."

His hollow words chilled her. "It was never about winning. It's about justice for all."

"Justice? What does this world know about justice?"

"Enough to know that what you planned wasn't just defense but murder."

The kitsune stepped to her side but refused to look at her. She reached for his hand, but he pulled away slightly.

Her breath caught, and she swallowed down her hurt. They watched as Destin was yanked to his feet.

The king smiled at her and then Pyre. "You think taking me back to Dotae to answer for my *crimes* will work, boy? I have more people there on my side than you do. The lords of Heimserya will never allow it." He laughed. "Do you think they will let you cut them off from their source of power? Their wealth? I—"

Destin's gloat was cut short by a sword driven right into his heart, between the crack in his breastplate and shoulder plate. Tempest startled, her gaze moving over Destin's shoulder. Madrid stared back at her, rage, hurt, and guilt churning in his eyes. He turned his attention to the king.

"That's for taking my family away," Madrid murmured to the king, removing his sword and kicking the man to the ground with contempt twisting his face. "For touching what's not yours."

Destin gasped and turned onto his back, his eyes wide.

Madrid stared down impassively at the king. "I hope you burn in hell."

The king gasped one last time before stilling. Tempest's heart pounded in her chest and her bottom lip quivered as Madrid lifted his head and looked at her. So much emotion lined his face. The world melted away, and the air seemed thinner.

"I'm sorry," he said.

It took only two little words to answer the question she'd wondered most of her life.

Madrid was her father.

She didn't even know his first name. "What's your name?"

He swallowed. "Garen."

Temp nodded. Garen Madrid. Her father.

He offered her a small smile before he transformed back into the stoic Madrid who had helped raise her.

"Today, we finish what Destin started. Tomorrow, we deal with the fallout. For Heimserya!" Madrid shouted.

"For Heimserya," Tempest echoed. She peeked at Pyre from the corner of her eye, but he was a thousand leagues away. Her heart ached, and she wanted to reach for his hand again but kept her hands to herself.

He'd come to her when he was ready.

Chapter Thirty-Seven

Tempest

Four months later

Spring basked Dotae in warm, promising sunshine that almost felt perverse in its beauty. Four months had passed in a blur since the death of King Destin at the hands of Madrid.

Tempest's *father,* Madrid.

They hadn't spoken in depth about that significant detail of their relationship yet. Everything was still too raw to talk about such a thing. Too painful.

The kingdoms still mourned.

The Hounds mourned.

Her heart squeezed. They'd lost Aleks and Levka in the fight. Aleks had made some poor choices in the end, but it didn't erase the time he spent raising her. Tempest missed him. And as for Levka… She still couldn't believe he was gone. Maxim was a shell of himself. Sure, he still joked, but it was sharper and his laughter was less often.

In the immediate aftermath of King Destin's death and the successful takeover of the Crown, neither Tempest nor Madrid nor Maxim knew of Aleks's and Levka's fate. It wasn't until hours later, when the Hounds came together to count their numbers, celebrate their success, and mourn their losses, that Tempest and her family became aware of their absence.

Now, it was all they could feel.

Even as Tempest spent more and more time with her quiet, biological father, each of their interactions were overshadowed by loss, trauma, and lies. They both were trying to deal with the loss of Aleks. He'd taught Tempest how to read and tucked her into bed every night. Aleks and Madrid had been raised and trained together.

"Are you with me?"

She blinked at Madrid and rubbed the back of her sweaty neck.

"Why was Aleks in that village the night I ran from home as a child?" Tempest asked Madrid, the words spilling from her lips. She inhaled deeply, trying to calm her pounding heart. They'd been sparring every morning. The routine helped center her; after a while, she realized it helped her father do the exact same thing. They weren't so dissimilar. He'd kept to himself most of her life. He was the most distant of her uncles.

Now, she had her explanation for why that had been: to

protect *her.*

Madrid smiled at her, and it was sad. "I'd sent a band of Hounds out that way under the pretense of dealing with some Talagan rebels. In truth, it was because I learned of Destin's plot to get rid of you and your mother. I couldn't go myself, but I wanted to prevent it from happening."

They cleaned their swords in silence as Tempest took in this information. It was the first time they'd talked about the day of her mother's death, though Tempest *had* discussed the subject with Maxim on nights when sleep had evaded her in the weeks following the king's death. After Levka's death, Maxim hadn't wanted to be alone. She and Dima moved into his house immediately. Maxim was warm and approachable in a way Madrid was not. Tempest wondered if the dynamic between them would ever change.

Or, more importantly, if she *wanted* it to change.

Regardless of what she wanted, though, there was one piece of information only Madrid could give her. Tempest chewed her lip and forced back a scratchy gulp of air as she willed herself to ask for it. There had been secrets between them for too long.

"Speak, child," he said after several long moments of silence.

She kept her eyes on her sword, staring at the distorted reflection of her father. Tempest peeked at him from the corner of her eyes, and he looked uneasy. It struck her that perhaps she was not the only one who felt unsure and nervous about the new dynamic between them. She wiped her blade one final time before facing Madrid.

"The shifter," she began, "the one King Destin sent to take care of me and my mother." She couldn't face saying *murder*. "Is he—"

"Gone. Dead. Destin made sure of it. The bastard always did hate loose ends."

Her breath caught, and she swallowed hard. She didn't know if she felt relief or disappointment. "Why didn't you tell me sooner?"

"The risk was too great. Destin wasn't sure which of his Hounds had hid a child from him, but he wanted us all to pay. You were the example. Once you were placed with the Hounds, there was no escape for you. I did what I could to make sure you were safe, that you had the skills to protect yourself." He paused. "I made sure you knew love and had a family, even if I couldn't get any closer to you."

She understood, she really did. "Did you love Mama?"

His face creased with old grief. "Loved her more than anything, and then you came along, and I knew I didn't know anything about love. Children show you what real, unconditional love means. My only regret is not being able to protect the both of you better. If I had done things differently—"

"Don't go down that road. We can't change the past," Tempest cut in. She reached a hand out for her father—a gesture Tempest had never indulged in before—and was surprised when he took her hand in his and squeezed.

"Wise words. You've grown into an extraordinary woman. Your mother would be proud."

"I know."

There was no arrogance in Tempest's answer. For the first time in her life, she was comfortable with who she was and was certain her mother would approve. Even if she only saw her face in her dreams and only heard her voice in the all-too-short moments before Tempest awoke, she knew her mother would be proud of her.

A beat of awkwardness passed. Two. Three. But Tempest did not care. Eventually, she and Madrid would get used to their new dynamic. She was in no rush to push things between them.

"Lady Tempest."

The two of them turned to see who had addressed her. A servant from the palace, clad in an ankle-length white dress.

The woman inclined her head politely. "Her Grace requests an audience with you."

"I've just finished up here," Tempest said, sheathing her sword before running her hands through her hair. It was sweaty and tangled from fighting, but she knew Ansette would not care. *Queen Ansette,* Tempest thought. *That will still take some getting used to.* "Lead the way."

With a final smile from Madrid, she followed the servant through the winding streets toward the palace. Around the Hound barracks, the faces that greeted her from shop windows and doors were content and excited in a way they never had been before. King Destin had never been a friend to the lower classes, even within the capital's walls.

By the time they reached the wealthiest part of the city, however, the looks Tempest received changed drastically. Many of the lords and ladies had supported their king until the end, and why not? He had been good to them. Spoiled them. Took their briberies and swept away their problems. Too many within the aristocratic classes believed the war against the Talagan rebels was justified, and the idea that Destin had been responsible for the mimkia problem still plaguing Heimserya was still spoken about with some skepticism. Destin's hold over parts of the kingdom would be a difficult thing to break.

She arched a haughty brow at a highborn man, and he dropped his gaze.

How many were still running the drug? The threat hadn't been eliminated. At least, the Hounds had put a dent in the number of recreational drugs that were being moved through the capital. The Jester was probably not happy. Tempest kept her expression placid and gentle as she and the servant finally reached the palace.

Pyre.

She tried to push him from her thoughts, but it didn't work.

He always seemed to be on her mind. She hadn't seen him in *four* months. He'd been in contact with Madrid and was using his people to help ferret out anyone who was still trafficking, but it was like looking for a needle in a haystack. He was doing his best, but it would take time, even years to straighten everything out.

Her heart clenched. She thought he'd come around, but

Pyre hadn't. He'd avoided her and gone back to his prior life.

Without her.

It hurt.

"Lady Tempest to see you, Your Grace," the servant announced, startling Tempest out of her own head and back to the present.

"Let her in," Ansette's soft yet assured voice called back.

Tempest pushed open the door to the private study and sat down opposite the young queen's desk. Despite her new position of absolute authority, Ansette had insisted on no formalities between them. It was bizarre to think only five months prior, she had been set to be the one sitting behind the desk. Winter's bite, Tempest was glad it was Ansette and not herself. The girl would make a far better queen than she ever could. Plus, Tempest wanted to fight with swords not with words.

The queen's lips curled over her cup of tea as she eyed Tempest from head to toe. "Sparring hard, I see. Is that all the Queen's Advisor does with her time? Practice?"

"Only until such time as my attention is required elsewhere," she said. Ansette held out a teacup and Temp took it. "I hate being still."

"So I noticed." The girl set her cup down. "I think you will be glad to hear what I am about to tell you."

"Don't keep me on edge," she murmured, adding a spoonful of sugar to the tea. "I hate surprises."

"You know as well as I do that drugs are rampant throughout the country. While mimkia has many amazing properties, it is also extremely dangerous. We need to regulate it, but that's only one of our main concerns. The northern lords aren't happy with me, and there are pockets of fights all over the kingdom. It's a bloody mess."

"What do you want of me?" Tempest asked, curious about what her new mission would be.

"I want you to find out who is still brewing and trafficking," Ansette replied. "I have a strong feeling that the perpetrators were close with my father. I want to know what my enemies are plotting. If we cut off their income, we cut off their power."

"Is that all you want?" She took a slurp of her hot tea, savoring how it warmed the back of her throat. "Sending the Hounds out would be dangerous as I'm sure Madrid has advised you."

Ansette nodded. "He has, which is why I'm speaking to you. The Hounds will stay here but you will spearhead this."

"That a large task for one person," she said slowly, setting her own cup down.

The queen nodded. "Exactly. I know this is too much work for one person to do, so I'm willing to, um, *pay handsomely* for any such persons as you see fit to use to accomplish our goals. My father's coffers are overflowing thanks to his drug trade. I hear a certain fox has recently lost some of his income, so perhaps..."

Tempest laughed in disbelief. "Are you honestly telling me to hire the *Jester* with official Crown money?"

"Oh, no, I could never be seen to be doing that. But if I

granted my official advisor to do whatever she deems necessary to get the job done—well, that's another thing entirely."

"Well, aren't you just all sorts of gray," she muttered.

Ansette arched a brow. "I'm also looking for a spymaster, and I think Pyre would be perfect for the job. I would be obliged if you extended the offer."

Tempest straightened in her chair. "I think it would be better coming from you."

"I doubt it."

"Then you'd be wrong. He's not said one word to me in months."

"Men are stupid."

She snorted. "That's the damn truth."

"Did you know that Brine is in town?"

Her attention snapped to Ansette. "Since when?"

"Since the day my father died." The girl's tone wavered for one second. "Who do you think he's been looking after? Because it hasn't been me."

A squirm of nerves and surprise twisted her stomach. "Why hasn't he come to see me?"

"I couldn't tell you. I'm sure as soon as you leave the city he'll make his presence known." Ansette stood and moved around the desk. She pulled Tempest from her seat and hugged her tightly. "Wish Pyre well, would you?" she whispered. "And should he find a way to attach himself to you in a more *official* capacity, then—"

"That's enough of that," Tempest said gruffly. She pecked the girl on the cheek and headed for the door. "I'll be seeing you soon."

"Not if the Jester has anything to say about it," the girl called.

She shook her head. Flights of fancy were one thing. Reality was another. She'd reach out to Pyre for the queen and for the people, but as for anything between them…

Well, Pyre had some explaining to do.

Chapter Thirty-Eight

Tempest

A sense of belonging settled over Tempest when she reached the Dark Court five days later.

The sun had long since set as she moved through the looping hallways of the upper mountain palace. The place was as shadowy as its namesake, with torches flickering in sconces along the stone walls, barely breaching the blackness, but she held no fear for them. The Dark Court was like a second home for her now, despite the dubious deals the Court itself dealt in.

Her feet slowed as she neared the door to the Jester's study. Brine placed a hand on her shoulder and squeezed before continuing down the hallway and disappearing from view.

Tempest turned back to the door. How would Pyre react to her presence? She'd asked herself that question time and time again over the last five days of her journey. Their relationship had been a rocky one, but she had believed him when he'd revealed that she was his mate, but now Tempest wasn't so sure. When he hadn't come to her or sent word, she'd written to him and he'd never written back. After that, she'd done some digging about Talagan mates, and learned that the male couldn't keep away from his mate for long periods of time. If that was the truth, then she wasn't his mate. His actions proved it. A pang of sorrow had vibrated in her chest, but she'd ignored it. The Jester took whatever he wanted. The fact he hadn't returned was enough of a message. She shouldn't still be holding on.

Tempest took a deep breath and knocked before opening the door and pausing in the entryway.

The kitsune was sitting by the crackling fire, stretched out languorously on a massive leather chair. He didn't look in her direction as he swirled fire whiskey in his glass.

"If it's about the brawl earlier, Briggs, it was necessary to put the pups in their place. They need an elder to teach them some respect."

"I'm sure they did," she remarked casually.

He stilled, and his attention snapped in her direction.

Her traitorous heart thumped painfully, but she gave him a droll look and entered the room like she had every right. Tempest ignored the way his gaze tracked her movements and she sat down in a vacant chair adjacent to his own. She let her focus linger on the flames for a few moments before meeting Pyre's scrutiny headfirst.

Tempest laced her fingers together over her stomach to keep from fidgeting.

The silence lengthened as he stiffly straightened and carefully set his glass of whiskey on the small table between the chairs.

"Tempest," he said, cocking his head to the side as if studying her. "What a pleasant surprise. I was sure you'd forgotten all about your friends in the Dark Court."

His inflectionless words cut, but she didn't react. That's not why she was here.

She ignored his goading. "You missed me, I take it?"

"You know you are always welcome here." A small pinch of emotion leaked into his voice.

"I can see that from your warm welcome," she retorted.

"What is that supposed to mean?"

Tempest rubbed at her brow. This was not the right start to a diplomatic conversation. She turned her face to the fire. Why was it so hard to talk to him now? Her gaze darted to the whiskey, and her stomach tightened. Researching Talagan mating customs had been eye-opening. One such one was sharing food. It was fine between kin, but if you weren't related, then only mates could share food and drink. Her fingers twitched. What if she just reached out and took a sip?

Don't be stupid.

She shook some sense back into herself and steeled her nerves to get down to business. Pyre's statue impression melted, and he gave her a lazy smile, throwing his leg over the arm of his chair like an indolent royal, the leather of his trousers creaking.

"How is my sister?" he asked.

"Well," Tempest replied. "Or, as well as one could expect. The royal court is not making things easy for her. And the upper classes—"

"Are hell. Of course, they are. They're corrupt, each and every one of them. Plus, I'm sure they're not happy with being cut off from their fun."

That was a bit hypocritical coming from the Jester of the Dark Court. Those were fighting words. She didn't want to stir his ire. They had more important things to discuss. She quirked an eyebrow. "Somebody sounds angry."

"That's because *somebody* stopped me getting all kinds of silly, expensive drugs to my best and most foolish clients." He arched an eyebrow back. "Not that *you* had anything to do with that."

"That was your sister, not me," Tempest said with a straight face. His lips turned down, and he glared at her. She sniggered, not able to hold it in. "You're like a child who's been told to stay out of the honey pot."

He smirked and toyed with the laces of his silk shirt. Her gaze was drawn to his chest and the slice of burnished skin it revealed. Pyre winked at her, and she blushed. Damn him.

Get yourself together.

"So..." he drawled. "What else has been going on within the walls of Dotae? Want me to behead a few aristocrats to prevent an uprising? Or—"

"I'm sure you know more about the goings-on of the

city than I do, what with your spies and all," she cut in, still feeling prickly that she'd been ignorant of Brine's presence the whole time.

His eyes gleamed in the light of the fire, and his smile widened, a small peek of his incisors showing. "How many of my spies have you caught, then?"

She kept her expression neutral. "You don't know?"

"I know everything."

Tempest rolled her eyes. "You *think* you know everything. There's a world of difference in the two."

"That's where you are mistaken. How about I tell you what I know?" He dropped his foot to the floor and leaned forward, all languidness gone, just predatory focus left. "I know that you spar every morning with your father. You live with your uncles, not at the barracks. You treat Ansette as you would a sister and that your still mourn your friends." His gaze narrowed. "You also have a weakness for almond pastries and that the baker's son likes you too much. And that you will not go back to that bakery again."

She blinked and processed all the information he'd given her. "So, you've been spying on me?"

"I spy on everyone."

Her mind latched onto the baker's son. "What gives you the right to tell me what I can and cannot do? I will go where I please, when I please, and speak to whomever I want to."

He bared his teeth at her. "Brine says the baker's son is being much too friendly. I forbid it."

"You get no say. You've forfeited that right."

Pyre froze, and his chest rumbled. "I've given up nothing. You are my mate, and he has no right to you."

"Your mate?" she asked quietly. Her hand began to tremble as her emotions rushed to the surface and exploded. "How dare you! You haven't spoken one word to me in four months, and you expect me to believe that I'm your mate?" The back of her eyes began to burn, and she willed herself not to cry. "You're a liar."

"You think this has been easy for me?" he demanded tightly.

She laughed, the sound bitter. "You seem pretty happy to me in your stone palace. Your actions are opposite of your words which has led me to one conclusion. Your words mean *nothing*."

With careful movements he picked up his whiskey and took a long draught before placing it back on the table warily, leveling his full focus on her. Tempest's skin prickled as he drank her in from head to toe.

"You were needed in Dotae. My sister, your father, and your uncles needed you. You lost loved ones and needed time to mourn." A ragged breath. "My duty was here. My people needed me. Heimserya is still a divided place. Things are not easy. I needed time to adjust."

Because she'd taken away his revenge. Her throat tightened at the memory of him pulling away, refusing to look at her. Rejection washed over her. It felt like it had happened just yesterday. "You cut me off."

"You make it seem like it was something I wanted."

"I wrote to you," she accused softly. "You could have given me some inkling of how you were doing, but you left me in the dark."

"If I gave in, even a tiny bit, it wouldn't have worked," he snarled and tossed his hands up. "I've had Briggs drug me every single day to keep myself from crawling back to you."

Tempest stilled, her pulse pounding in her ears. He'd drugged himself. "Why?"

"Because," he growled, "you have been through so much in the last year. Feelings are heightened during a time of action. Emotion can cloud our judgment. I wanted you to have time to really know what you want." His voice trailed into a whisper. "I wanted you to make a choice because you wanted it, not because anyone or anything was pushing you into it. Including myself."

Her breath caught. Actions did speak louder than words. He'd stayed away not because she'd hurt him or because he didn't want her, but because he loved her and wanted her to know her own mind.

That changed everything.

She peered at his glass from the corner of her eye. There was barely a mouthful left. Her stomach flipped. All it would take was a sip from his glass to answer any unspoken questions between them. Tempest stood, and his hand snapped out, wrapping around her wrist. She gazed down into the kitsune's desperate eyes.

"Please don't go."

"I wasn't going anywhere," she said. "I am getting hot,

so I want to remove my cloak."

He reluctantly let her go, and she pulled her cloak off, her movements clumsy. Her nerves fluttered in her belly, and she took a calming breath before perching on the armrest of her chair closest to the whiskey.

"I have a proposal," Tempest said, speaking a little faster than she wanted to. She brushed at her worn trousers and then leaned forward, closing the gap between herself and Pyre by several inches. His molten gaze was locked on her, his expression placid. How did he stay so calm?

He eased to the edge of his chair, an easy smile transforming his handsome face.

"That sounds intriguing," Pyre murmured, sin dripping from his tone. "What sort of proposal?"

She blushed, knowing exactly what kind of proposal he was thinking of. "It seems Ansette needs some kind of...spymaster, if you will."

He blinked slowly as if that was not what he'd expected. "Oh?"

"The mimkia problem throughout Heimserya is far from over," she continued. "I'm sure you're well aware of this." The way Pyre's jaw tightened at the mere mention of the drug confirmed that he did. "Ansette and I both agree that the people responsible for this are men still loyal to Destin."

"A fair assumption."

Tempest nodded. "But we can't know this for sure, and even if we *did*—"

"You might not be able to find them all and take them in," Pyre finished for her. "So, my lovely sister wishes to push off the work of finding those responsible onto a third party, is that it?"

"Not so much a third party." She licked her lips. "You'd be working closely with me."

His smile dimmed. "And this…would this be a formal proposal from the Crown?"

It's now or never.

She slowly reached for the whiskey, her eyes locked on his. Her fingers curled around the glass. "A formal proposal, yes, but perhaps not *technically* court-sanctioned, given that you're a criminal and all."

His gaze heated as she lifted the cup and swirled the spirits. "Do you know what you're doing?" he asked, his voice hoarse with disbelief and barely contained desire.

"I know this custom." She held the glass to her lips and watched him over the rim.

"Once done, you can't take this back. It's forever." He was on edge, barely even breathing. "You have to mean it."

She smiled and then tipped back the contents of the glass into her mouth. The liquid burned her throat—she didn't think she'd ever get used to the stuff—but when she caught the way Pyre was looking at her, she thought the burning was rather fitting.

"Does that answer your—" she began, but before she could finish what she was saying, he yanked the glass from her hand and pulled her into his arms.

Heat and hunger sharpened his features as he reached

out and captured her chin in one hand. "God help you, you're never escaping me again."

He leaned forward and crushed their lips together. She sucked in a sharp breath and grabbed a handful of his hair and pressed against him. Pyre gasped as she swiped her tongue along his bottom lip. His hands grabbed her waist and hauled her against him, every hard muscle pressed intimately against her. Heat spilled through her body, and tears gathered in her eyes. She'd dreamed of her kitsune kissing her like this for months now.

Tempest gasped as he slid his tongue into her mouth with a groan. Her arms wound around his shoulders as she clung to him. His hands tightened at her waist, and he bit at her lower lip. Pyre claimed her mouth roughly.

He wasted no time moving his attention to her chin, sliding his mouth down her neck. She threw her head back and sighed. A sense of belonging settled into her.

"You took your time," he breathed against her sensitive flesh. The frenzy in his touches slowed to something reverent.

She clasped each side of his face and pressed a soft kiss to his lips. "I had to be—"

"Certain?"

The barest of nods set him off.

He leapt to his feet, and she yelled in surprise as he swiftly lifted her into his arms bridal style.

"What are you about?" she asked with a laugh, one hand wrapped around his shoulder, the other resting on his chest.

"If it took you four agonizing months to be *certain,* then like hell am I wasting any more time in making this official, darling." The way Pyre purred out the word *darling* made her mouth run dry.

Her brain pushed past the euphoria... Official? "Wait, are you talking about a—a—mating ceremony?"

He grinned as he jogged toward the door. "Do you object? I'd rather bloody hope you don't after that show with the whiskey. Many shifters would consider us as good as married."

"You wish to marry me?"

"I want to be tied to you in as many ways as possible. You tell me what you want. I'll be your devoted servant." A wicked smile curved his lips. "I'll be happy to be your love slave as well."

She tossed her head backward and laughed, feeling freer than she had in ages. She leaned up and kissed his cheek. "How about a mating ceremony now and a wedding later?"

"Yes to both." Pyre yanked the door open and cursed as he tripped over the rug in his haste. He stumbled into the hall and gave her a silly smile. "You make me clumsy."

"You make me happy," she said, rubbing her nose against Pyre's as he looked down at her.

"You ready?" he asked.

"I've never been more certain of anything in my life."

And, for once, Tempest did not second-guess her decision.

Pyre's heart belonged to her, and hers to him.

Chapter Thirty-Nine

Thorn

Thorn leaned against the wall of a sketchy tavern; her hood low over her face. Traveling to Betraz had been the right move, but it still unnerved her. There were too many soldiers out looking for a fight. The shifters may have won the battle and put a new ruler on the throne, but the war was far from over. The lords of the north may have sworn begrudging fealty to the new queen, but they were no friend to the Crown. Queen Ansette's policies regarding work rights, freedoms, and regulation of mimkia wasn't going over well. If the young queen wasn't careful, there'd be civil war.

Thorn wouldn't be surprised if the girl was assassinated within the month. Not that she wished for that to happen. Heimserya needed to change for the better. Hopefully, it would stick this time. She wouldn't hold her breath. Those with power and riches seldom liked to share that with others.

Her attention honed in on a tall figure who ghosted up the street and swerved in her direction, his face hidden from view. She eyed how his cloak hung over his wide shoulders and pulled her dagger from the sheath at her waist. A precaution. Thorn had learned over the years to trust no one. Especially anyone who solicited her help. Being a treasure hunter was dangerous.

The man slowed to a stop and leaned against the opposite stone wall. "Good evening."

A cultured tone. Highborn no doubt.

"You arranged for this meeting," she drawled, making her voice deeper than it actually was. She took on all sorts of personas while on the job. It kept her family safe from unhappy customers.

"Your reputation proceeds you. I have to admit that I'm impressed with your skills."

So, he thought to flatter her. Thorn's eyes narrowed. She'd bet her best sword that his task was not legal. The sleazy ones always tried to butter her up.

"The job," she said flatly.

The man chuckled. "Right to the point. How refreshing."

Her hackles rose at the haughtiness that saturated his tone. She pushed away from the wall. She didn't need his money. Working with men like him wasn't worth the gold it paid.

"Stop," he said. He tossed a bag of coins at her feet. "That's just the first half. You'll get the second when you complete the job."

She made no move to pick up the velvet bag even though her fingers itched to do so. What he'd tossed away like trash would buy a plot of land and a home for her sister and nephew. Thorn cocked her head and licked her lips. She'd have to tread carefully with this one. She sensed that a predator lurked beneath his cloak. If she showed one shred of interest in his money, he'd hold all the power.

Thorn nudged the bag with the toe of her right boot. "I cannot be bribed."

"I know. That's why I've come to you." He held out a small scroll, black gloves covering his hands. "Here is all the information you need. If you decide to accept the job, we'll set up our next meeting."

She took it, careful not to touch his fingers. "I'll consider it."

"Do so." He nodded toward the bag as he moved passed her toward the street. "The gold is for you when you take the job."

She stared hard at his back. "That's awfully presumptuous, don't you think? I could disappear with this."

"I'll take my chances." The stranger turned his head, and she caught a glimpse of a smirk beneath his hood. "Be seeing you soon."

He disappeared around the corner as she tucked the scroll away and collected the bag of coins from the ground. Unease skittered down her spine. It was heavier than she expected. What sort of man tossed around coin like this?

She was half tempted to leave the money in the alley but that would have been stupid.

Thorn sulked down the alley and moved through the city, making sure to keep away from any of the rowdy soldiers. The men Betraz employed were known to be brutal bastards. The lord ruled with an iron fist, and his men were even more bloodthirsty.

She doubled backed several times to make sure she wasn't being followed before arriving at her inn. Thorn scaled the side of the building and slipped through a window and into her room. Once she'd checked the chamber for danger, secured the window, and closed the curtains, she finally pulled the small scroll from her pocket and the coins from her cloak.

Her suspicion flared as she opened the drawstring and ran her fingers through the gold coins. It had to be close to ten years' worth of wages. What the wicked hell did he want from her? Was she to find a philandering husband or wife? Retrieve an heir from a drug den? Retrieve a bauble of worth?

Breaking the seal, she unrolled the parchment as she sat on her bed. Thorn frowned. It contained a sketch of a flower that she knew her employer desired to possess and details of how to contact him. Her hands dropped to her lap. He wanted her to find a flower? It seemed simple enough, but the simple tasks always were the most dangerous. They were never what they seemed.

What did he want with the flower?

Not your business.

Thorn stood from the bed and tossed the note into the fire. Her instincts said to walk away, but her sensibilities told her not to be hasty. Her sister was ill and couldn't work any longer. How long would it be before the madam would toss her into the streets? The madam wasn't heartless, but she also couldn't care for every widowed woman and orphan. Times were tough.

The man had seen right through her bluff. He knew she would take the job.

Her attention moved back to the gold. No one paid that much unless it was dangerous. He'd kept something from her—they all did.

Thorn just prayed that whatever it was, it wouldn't get her killed.

Continue the adventure in Book Four of the Twisted Kingdoms: THE BEAST

Epilogue

Tempest

"Close your eyes and lift your hands over your head," Nyx commanded.

Tempest did as she was told and smiled as soft, heavy fabric cascaded over her arms and head, falling to her feet. Nyx's hands tugged at the back of her dress, and Tempest heard the sound of the laces being pulled.

"Now you can look."

She opened her eyes and stared at her reflection.

The gown was black.

Tempest lifted her arms and admired the bell sleeves that fell to the floor. The straps rested on the edges of her shoulders, showing off her collarbone and neck. She smiled as her fingers traced the small crystal stars embroidered onto the dress.

It was perfect. Simple but elegant.

"Where did you get this?" she asked as Nyx fussed with

her hair.

Her soon-to-be sister smiled and clipped back a lock of Tempest's hair with a diamond hair pin. "Pyre had it commissioned months ago."

Tempest's stomach flipped. "He had this made for me?"

Nyx paused and met Tempest's gaze in the mirror. "Did you think he'd dress you in a cast-off gown for your mating ceremony?"

"I was ready to marry in my traveling clothes," she admitted, a blush heating her cheeks.

"And they call *us* barbarians." Her friend grinned and hugged her from behind. "Are you ready?"

She smiled, butterflies taking flight in her belly. "Yes."

Nyx took her by the hand and led her out into the hallway. Her pulse picked up as they rounded a corner and six men came into view.

Maxim, Dima, Briggs, Brine, Damien, and her father.

"How?" Tempest choked out, heat pressing at the back of her eyes as they approached the men who'd become her family.

"I'll let Pyre tell you," Nyx said with a smile.

Maxim stepped from the line and pulled her into a huge hug, his burly arms squeezing the air from her lungs. "I'm happy for you, girlie."

He pressed a kiss to the top of her head and passed her to Dima. Her uncle pulled a ring from his vest. Her Hound ring. He placed it on her middle finger and kissed her cheek gently. "Love you, lass."

Her throat clogged as Briggs hugged her next, followed by Brine. The wolf clasped her cheeks between his huge palms, stoic as always. "Welcome to our family, lass," he said gruffly.

Tempest threw her arms around him, and he hugged her fiercely. When she pulled back, Damien caught her eye and grinned. The dragon lord pointed and did a circle with his finger. She rolled her eyes and twirled slowly. He whistled and yanked her in for a hug before giving her a huge, smacking kiss on the cheek.

"You know you could still run away with me, lovely."

She chuckled and shook her head at him. "Not a chance."

Some of her mirth drained away as she finally stepped up to her father.

"You look beautiful, daughter," Madrid said softly. His eyes became shiny, and he swallowed hard. "Your mother would have been so proud."

Immediately, tears flooded her eyes, and her bottom lip quivered. One ran down her cheek, and her father brushed it away before hugging her.

"I love you more than you know."

She sucked in a shuddering breath and clung to him. "Love you, too."

Her father squeezed her and then stepped back, holding his arm out, his cheeks wet. "You ready?"

"Yeah. I am."

Nyx bustled forward to straighten her hair before she opened the door to a room Tempest had never seen before. Her heart started to gallop as Madrid led her inside. It was a small library. Pine garlands and snowbells had been strung across it to create an aisle that ended at the open double doors that led to a huge stone balcony littered with lanterns, winter flowers, and candles.

She blinked back more tears as Juniper stood from one of the chairs and held her hands out as they reached the balcony.

Tempest laughed as Juniper yanked her into a hug and whispered, "You've been holding out on me. Hiding attractive mates from one of your best friends is a sin."

"Sorry."

June grinned, and waved a hand. "No, you're not. I don't blame you. Go and get yourself hitched."

Tempest nodded and took her father's arm again, the other men and Nyx trailing behind them. She focused on the one man she'd not been able to look at yet.

Pyre.

He stood by the railing, his hands clasped together like he was forcibly keeping himself from reaching for her. His amber gaze ran over her from head to toe, and she couldn't help the massive smile that lit up her face when he grinned at her from beneath the brim of his tilted top hat.

Her pulse slowed and calmness settled over her. This was where she belonged. This was right. She struggled to keep pace with Madrid and not run to the makeshift altar. Before she knew it, her father paused.

"Will you protect, love, and cherish our daughter?" Madrid asked Pyre formally.

Pyre's gaze moved to her father, and he bowed low. "She will be my greatest treasure."

Madrid squeezed Tempest's hand and held it out

toward him. Her fingers trembled as Pyre reached for her hand and pulled her forward. She faced him, and he laced their fingers together, stepping closer, the coolness from his rings causing a shiver to run through her.

"You are the most gorgeous creature I've ever beheld."

Tempest quirked a smile. "Always the flatterer."

"It's the truth. I will be nothing but honest with you, my love."

A lump lodged in her throat. She glanced around the decorated balcony. "How did you get all of this done so quick?"

"I have my ways." A wicked grin.

She playfully narrowed her eyes. "And the dress?"

His smile softened. "Wishful thinking."

Someone cleared their throat, and she glanced to her left, startled to find Chesh standing there. How long had he been there? She hadn't even noticed him. He wiggled his brows and then glanced at the small group of people assembled.

"Please take your seats."

Anxiety flooded her as she realized she knew nothing about mating ceremonies. "I don't know what I'm doing."

Pyre leaned closer. "Don't worry. It's simple. All you have to do is drink some of my blood from a cup."

She blanched, and he laughed, a teasing glint in his eyes.

"You rotten fox," she huffed.

"You're too much fun tease. I won't ever be able to stop."

A retort was on the tip of her tongue when Chesh spoke again. "Do you have the ribbon?"

Pyre pulled a silver, satin ribbon from his black velvet vest, the length unraveling and gently waving in the breeze. “I do.”

“What pledge do you have to your mate?”

Time seemed to slow as he leaned closer and pushed the sleeve of her dress up. He tied the ribbon around her wrist.

“I swear to you that I will protect you with my life, that you will never be alone, and that you will always be my family. I promise you can rely on me to be faithful and honest. Everything I am now lives for you.”

His fingers drifted along her wrist, and goosebumps ran up her arms. He held out the other end of the ribbon for her to take.

Chesh turned to her. “What pledge do you have for your mate?”

She swallowed hard and leaned closer, her fingers sure as she began tying the ribbon around Pyre’s thick wrist.

“I promise to be your partner in all things, to put your feelings above my own, and to love you like no one has before. I will always protect you and will be your family until we’re both dust in the ground.” She pulled back and met his gaze, her heart clenching. They both had come from broken families. *Just say the words.* “I will love and cherish any wee ones that come in the future. They will know what it is to be protected and adored.”

He sucked in a sharp breath, and his eyes filled with unshed tears. Pyre clasped their bound hands and kissed her knuckles.

Chesh clapped. “You are bound by your words and

deeds. May your union never be broken as long as you live."

"Is that it?" she whispered.

"Not quite," Pyre whispered back, stepping into her space. She tilted her head back as he cupped her chin and wrapped his other hand around her waist.

"You may kiss your mate and bride," Chesh said.

Your mate.

Tempest popped up onto her toes and kissed him. He tasted like home. Pyre nipped her lips and dipped her back. She threw her hands around his neck as their guests cheered. Her mate retreated and brushed his nose along the tip of hers before straightening and setting Temp on her feet. He kept her pinned to his chest as they faced the small assembly.

Her cheeks ached as she smiled at their friends and family. This was what she'd always imagined for her wedding. A simple dress, her closest loved ones, and... Her attention turned toward Pyre. And the man she loved.

He brushed his thumb across her cheekbone. "Thank you."

"For what?" she asked softly.

"For giving me everything I've ever wanted."

"You can put me down," she commented dryly.

Pyre shook his head and grinned as he pulled her closer to his chest. His footfalls thumped steadily against the long rugs running along the length of the hallway. Lanterns flickered softly, casting shadows on the stone walls that danced and writhed.

Her heart picked up tempo as he nimbly opened the door to his rooms. He stepped over the threshold and kicked the door shut and strode across his study to open a second door that led to his bedroom. To the right, a huge bed dominated the space with ornate side tables covered with tiny candles, and to the left, a fire roared in the hearth, two comfy looking chairs bracketing the fireplace. Shelves lined the western wall filled with books, trinkets, treasures, and art.

Her mate closed the door with his elbow and moved to the fire. He set Tempest on her feet and gave her a quick kiss before gesturing to a small table laden with food. “Have something to eat while I lock the study doors and windows.”

She nodded, and faced the fireplace, not focusing on the table of food. The last time she’d been in this position she’d ended up almost dying.

Don’t think about that.

Tempest wrapped her arms around herself and inched closer to the heat. She faintly caught the soft click of the door locking. Goosebumps pebbled along her arms a moment before Pyre stood behind her, and his chest touched her back with his next breath. She shivered as he pushed her hair from the left side of her neck, his fingers skimming the sensitive area before his lips retraced where he’d touched. The heat of his kisses soaked in, chasing away the chill of her previous thoughts until there was only her and Pyre. Her mate ran his hands down her shoulders and settled on either side of her waist.

"Are you hungry?" he murmured against the crook of her neck.

She smiled at his determination to feed her. "Not particularly." Tempest tilted her head to the side to give him more access, even as her heart began to pound harder, as desire swirled in her belly. "Not for food at least."

He chuckled and skimmed his lips up to her ear. "Minx. I'm only trying to be an attentive mate." She gasped when he bit her earlobe. "One promise I will make you is that you'll be starving by this time tomorrow night."

"The feast, right?" she asked. Her breath caught as he bit her gently at the nape of her neck. Nervousness fluttered in her chest, but she pushed it away. There was nothing to fear with her kitsune. He'd never take like the king. Pyre had already proven that. She inhaled deeply and sighed as she caught a whiff of pine and spice. God, he smelled good. Her mouth watered and she swallowed. "We usually have the feast and celebration the night of."

"Mmhmmm." He licked the delicate skin where he'd nipped, and then ran his nose up the thrumming pulse in her neck to the delicate spot behind her ear. "Humans have it all wrong. All that food tires one before the real feasting even begins. Shifters have their priorities right."

"Priorities, huh?" she teased as she spun to face him, her head tilting back to gaze up at his face. The brim of his hat cast his features in shadows, and Tempest pulled the offending item from his head and tossed it to the floor.

Pyre smirked, the curve of his lips sinful. He leaned close and bumped his nose against hers. "Yeah, like loving our mates until they're completely exhausted."

His breath fanned over her skin, and heat surged in her belly. Her breath quickened, and she skated her hands up his arms to his shoulders, gripping him hard as desire rocked her. "Prove it."

He stilled at her words, his chest heaving and lips parted. He threaded his fingers through her hair, and then tugged, tilting her head back, as he crushed their bodies together. Their mouths met, and she melted into him. Their teeth clashed together and she shivered as his pointed canines grazed her bottom lip. It wasn't the sort of kiss he'd given her before. This... He traced the outline of her bottom lip with his tongue, and she tasted mint. He nipped at her lower lip, a possessive demand, and she gasped, breathing him in, until she couldn't tell where his desire ended and hers began. This was something hotter than she'd ever experienced. Her eyes closed, and her limbs went languid.

"Wicked hell, I love your mouth," he growled before he pushed his tongue inside.

Their tongues tangled and danced, and the heat running through her veins rose with each lush stroke of his tongue. She'd forgotten what it was like to *really* kiss Pyre, to be consumed by him. He kissed as if he wanted to steal her breath—her soul—as if he couldn't survive another moment without the feel of her mouth on his—and, sweet poison, she felt it, too.

She pressed closer, eyes opening, and tugged at his vest as his hands roamed down her velvet clad body to her outer thighs. He fisted the heavy fabric of her dress and hauled it up, and she jerked back as his warm fingers brushed her skin. He slid his palms to the backs of her thighs and, cupping her backside, hauled her forward.

Her nervousness came back with a vengeance, and she pressed her hands flat between them and pushed. Drawing away to catch her breath, Tempest's heart pounded. No one had ever touched her like this before. It was amazing, but what if she didn't please him? Sure, she'd heard bawdy stories over the years, but she'd never done any of those things. *Stop thinking so much, just feel.*

Undaunted, Pyre peppered kisses along her jaw and up her neck to her ear. Then he whispered, "Let's do this properly."

"Properly?" she questioned as he turned her slowly to face the fireplace.

"Yes, before I lose all my sanity and ravish you like a barbarian." He went to work, his fingers tugging at the laces of her wedding dress.

The bodice sagged, and she caught the dress before it fell to the floor. "Maybe I want you to ravish me." Where did that come from?

His wicked laugh puffed against the top of her spine. "Always trying to bait me. This time it won't work. I'm in charge."

Tempest rolled her eyes and chuckled. Her laughter cut off as her mate grabbed the edges of her dress and tugged. A demand, not a question. She released the dress and shuddered as Pyre slowly disrobed her, leaving kisses along her spine. The midnight velvet puddled at her feet, leaving her in only a transparent, knee length shift. She fingered the slits that ran up each side to mid-thigh.

"Turn around," he rasped, his voice filled with lust, heat, desire, need. "Let me look at you."

Never one to be ashamed of her body, she faced her mate, her gaze dipping to him as he knelt on the ground before her, the black velvet of her dress crushed in his fists. His ears were completely perked forward, and his mouth slack as he gazed up at her with worshipful adoration. Heady power infused her as she stared down at her awestruck kitsune.

"Like what you see?" she asked with a smug smile.

"Bloody hell," he choked out. "How will I ever allow you to leave this room again?"

She stepped out of the dress, her toes curling against the stone floor. *Enough talk*. Tempest leaned forward and grabbed the front of his shirt, pulling him to his feet. "Your turn."

Carefully, she unbuttoned his black vest, making sure to tease him through his thin linen shirt with every slow touch. "For someone who loves anything sparkly and gaudy, I'm surprised you wore something so simple."

He grunted as she finished unbuttoning the black velvet vest and then yanked it off along with his white linen shirt. "You're the only jewel I need today."

"You tease," she murmured, running her hands along his burnished, muscular chest. The heat from his skin licked her palms, stoking the fire of desire low in her belly. As if drawn by the thought, Tempest moved her hands down to trace the curves of his hips and over the dips of his abdomen. The man was too attractive for his own good.

She leaned forward to taste the skin right above his heart. Feeling impish, she bit lightly and licked the spot, tasting salt and steel. Temp was rewarded with a gasp and full body shudder from her mate. There was something completely gratifying about pleasing him.

"If anyone is a tease, it's you," he gritted out before tipping her chin up and nipping at her bottom lip. "You're tempting my beast, love. Last chance to flee."

"As if I'd ever run from this. You're not a challenge anymore," she goaded. "You're mine. So don't you dare stop."

That was all the permission he needed to unleash his hunger for her.

He captured her hips and lifted her as she wrapped her legs around him, very aware she had no undergarment on underneath.

"Bare?" he gasped, his fingers flexing against the back of her thighs, his claws gently grazing her skin.

"Nyx advised me against them," she murmured between kisses.

"Bless her," he groaned.

Pyre spun around and sauntered toward the bed. She bit his bottom lip as he neared the mattress. He growled and jostled her, holding her up with one arm. Tempest peeked at him from beneath her lashes as he fumbled with the gauzy curtain. His claws sliced through the delicate fabric and he cursed.

Tempest stifled a giggle and arched a brow at him as he shook off the curtain with a scowl.

"Should I be worried for my safety?" she snickered.

His attention snapped to her, and he shook his head. "I would *never* hurt you. Never."

The intensity of his gaze drove the air from her lungs, and she nodded. "I know," she replied, her voice breathy.

With surprising tenderness, he laid her onto the bed like a prized possession and sank onto his hands and knees, following her onto the mattress. He kissed her throat, biting just hard enough that she gasped.

"Heaven," he whispered. "You taste like heaven."

Pyre leaned back, sitting on his heels, and stared down at her, his chest heaving. She crooked a finger at him and then reached for the bottom of her shift. Never again would she hide anything from him.

He laid his gentle claw-tipped hand over her hand, halting her movement.

"Pyre?" She questioned his sudden halt to their passion. Her body ached with need, so she didn't understand—

"I want to," he murmured and licked his lips.

Tempest nodded, and her gaze darted away from his heavy-lidded look. She traced the edge of his claw. "I've only seen these out when you're angry."

"It happens with extreme emotion." He gave her a languid smile. "Like loving my mate for the first time."

She shifted on the blanket as he picked up her left foot and began to massage the arch of her foot. Her eyes rolled into her head, and all tension fled her body. Tempest practically melted into the bed as he stroked her skin. Cold air rushed over the tops of her thighs as he nudged the edge of her shift up.

Tempest peeked at him from beneath her lashes and grinned. He'd found her daggers. His gaze flicked to her face. "You brought blades to bed?"

She gave a half shrug. "I never go anywhere without them." She nodded at his hands. "Plus, you came to bed with your weapons." She reached for the sheath at her left thigh, but he halted her, his chest rising and falling heavily.

"Leave them," he demanded gutturally. He shot her a hot look before grabbing the bottom of her shift with both hands and yanking it, ripping it completely up the middle.

Tempest blinked. Well, then. She lifted herself up with her hands and shimmied until her destroyed undergarment fell off. Tossing her head, she stared at her mate lazily. "Got that out of your system?"

"Not by half."

His low answer sent shivers of anticipation down her spine as he soaked in the sight of her. Many pale scars rans across her flesh, but she wasn't ashamed. Tempest was proud of all her body had survived.

She lay down and batted her eyes, hoping to rile him further.

"Bloody hell." He ran a hand over his mouth, his eyes wide, and heaved another breath. Then he ran his hand through his hair, his jaw clenching. "So…damn…beautiful."

She could say the same about him. She could say a lot of things. But Tempest was done talking—except for one last plea. She sat up and slid her hand around his neck and hauled him down to her, his muscled body pressing her into the bed. "Come and love me, mate."

It was exactly the right thing to say.

Pyre captured her mouth in a searing kiss. His heated hands traveled her curves, learning every part of her body. She nipped at his chin before he worked his way down her neck, trailing his tongue along her pulse. A shiver worked through her body as his canines scraped against the skin of her shoulder.

Tempest dug her fingers into his hair, pulling him back to her. She brushed the tips of his ears. He growled and bucked before pulling back and stripping the last of his clothing away. This time, when he crawled back, he settled gently beside her. Pyre leaned closer and brushed his nose against hers once again, equal parts love and heat simmering in his eyes.

"You ready, love?" he rasped. "Ready to be mine?"

She rolled to face him and cupped his cheek. With a wicked smirk, she stretched upward to bite the edge of his ear. His hands tightened on her waist, a soft growl escaping him. Tempest draped her arms about his shoulders and when he rolled on top of her, she wrapped her legs around his waist.

She leaned back to meet his hot gaze and spoke the truth. "I've been yours longer than you know."

He shuddered and brushed a butterfly kiss against her lips before he pressed forward. Her spine arched, and tears gathered in her eyes.

"A minute of pain, for a lifetime of pleasure," Pyre promised. He kissed her tears away before lacing their fingers together and pinning her wrists above her head. "This is forever," he gasped against her throat.

"Forever," Tempest agreed. She bared her neck and

smiled as he cursed beneath his breath before he *moved.* Her eyes closed of their own accord and lights danced behind her eyelids.

Damn. This is why women fell into sin.

"Look at me," Pyre growled.

She forced her eyes open and stared up into his chiseled face as their bodies moved as one.

"You're mine now," he bit out. "*Mine.*"

Heat flashed through her body at his claiming.

His.

Yes, she was his. Irrevocably his now and forever.

"Yours," she breathed.

His lips crushed hers, fierce and possessive. She gave up on thinking and sank into the love and passion her mate offered.

About the Author

Thank you for reading THE HEIR. I hope you enjoyed it!

If you'd like to know more about me, my books, or to connect with me online, you can visit my webpage https:// www.frostkay.net/ or join my facebook group FROST FIENDS!

From bookworm to bookworm: reviews are important. Reviews can help readers find books, and I am grateful for all honest reviews. Thank you for taking the time to let others know what you've read, and what you thought. Just remember, they don't have to be long or epic, just honest.

Complete Fantasy Series

Have you read REBEL'S BLADE?

It's an ENEMIES TO LOVERS epic fantasy series perfect for Sarah J. Maas and Holly Black fans.

Check out what readers are saying: "Frost Kay is absolutely one of my favourite new authors. Hands Down. Her stories are impeccably well thought out and her characters are solid. I can't wait for more!" Bestselling Author Tate James.